Through Verdant Mirrors

Ela Bambust

ISBN 979-8-9873099-2-6

This book was edited by Fiammetta Speziale
This book was professionally typeset by Cassidy Marble:
publishing@marble.sh

Dedication

This book is dedicated, first and foremost to my patron,
Without whom this world and everyone in it would not exist.

Further, I want to thank

Megan,
Who loves Clarus more than I do,

My family,
For showing me what family can mean,

Fiammetta,
My little flame,

Veetle and the gang,
For pushing me to publish,

My readers and patrons,
Who got me this far,

And my many friends,
Despite the distractions of which I managed to finish this
book on time,

And finally Cassidy,
Who made this a reality,

I love you all

Contents

Chapter One

Ashes of War

"Cinero?"

"Hmm?"

"I asked if you were with us."

"Oh," Cinero said. "Yeah, sorry." He ran his hand through his hair and sighed. It was getting longer again. "I'll be right there," he added, and looked back at Caledon Keep. Once a gorgeous building, it overlooked the valley like a silent guardian, its white walls a bastion to keep the people of the Southern Shelf safe. Now it was a ruin. What exactly had happened eight years ago was a mystery. A mystery, Cinero knew, they were hoping to solve.

"Were you lost in your own head again?" Caerella asked. She looked down at him as he walked up, if only figuratively. "We'll need you present in the next few hours."

"Let the boy look," another figure said, swallowing a mouthful of dry bread. "The Keep's not what it used to be, but it's still quite the sight. Besides, this is as good a place as any to take stock. We'll be in the thick of it before long."

"Very well, Rubicus," Caerella said, and shot Cinero a glance he would once have thought to be withering, the woman's subtle sense of humour going right over his head. "Looks like you get off easy. *This* time."

Cinero saluted, pushing down a smirk only most of the way. He saw the corner of Caerella's mouth go up a bit. "Yes, ma'am."

"I could start a fire," the last member of their party added. "If we're taking a break."

"Nah, I'd rather not waste daylight," Rubicus said. "But we can still take a moment to eat. I don't want to have to fight on an empty stomach." He chuckled. Rubicus was tall, a mountain of a man who had been in his prime some time ago and had done his best to stay there a bit longer, but his temples had greyed and the grooves around his eyes betrayed a harder life than his easy-going smile would suggest.

"You think there's going to be fighting?" Cinero asked.

"Could be, Stoneface. Could be." Flaveo knelt down on the rock next to him, resting his arms on his knees. "The place has been abandoned for nigh on a decade, anything could be in there."

"Wouldn't the gates have kept the wild animals out?" Cinero looked at the castle again. He'd been out with the group a few times, but this was definitely the most high profile assignment they'd ever taken. That they weren't expected to succeed wasn't exactly doing much to alleviate his anxiety. Well, the anxiety on top of his base-level anxiety.

"Nah," Rubicus said, still chewing. "Gate's gone."

"How can you tell from here?"

Rubicus pointed. Down. At the base of the mountain. "I can see the gatehouse down there." Cinero could see it, only barely. Something had shattered a part of the Keep, and thrown it down the mountainside.

"What happened here? Thank you." Cinero accepted the piece of jerky Flaveo handed him, and he chewed it gingerly.

"The Empire attacked," Caerella said matter-of-factly. Rubicus shot her a glance, and she smirked.

"I think the boy knows that much," the larger man said. "The thing is that we only know bits and pieces. After Caligon was slain, the last of the Imperial forces made a desperate push to get into the Southern Shelf and kill King Lucius. They hit the Keep, but the Prince stopped them. Something happened up there," Rubicus said, pointing at the tower, "and it killed the Cavean and his demons, but Prince Clarus never made it out." Cinero looked out at the devastation. He'd heard a lot of this already, of course, but he had no idea of the devastation that had been wrought on the area, and the castle overlooking the mountain pass. "The few survivors, the ones who were outside the Keep, told us that the plants grew in seconds, sealing everyone inside. We don't know what caused it."

"And we have to get in there and get the Prince back out?" Cinero asked.

"Yeah," Rubicus said. "What's left of him, anyway. I don't think a decade on there's going to be a lot to pick up. Especially if wild animals got in."

"Don't be morbid, Ruben," Flaveo said, grinning. "We've got a noble goal, might as well act like it."

"*You* never do," Caerella said. Flaveo shrugged, his face a mask of innocence. "And it's entirely possible we'll fail." Flaveo looked a little hurt, putting his hands on his hips, but before he could retort, Caerella cut him off. "We're far from the first attempt to enter Caledon Keep, and we'll likely not be the last. And I'm not dying in there just to bring the King back a corpse and what's left of a crown. If it becomes too much to handle, we leave."

"Yes, yes," Flaveo said. "But what if we *didn't*, though? What if we do bring Clarus back? The King will shower us in gold, praise, maybe some landed titles…" He put his hands behind his head and stretched. Flaveo was… extravagant, when he allowed himself to be. Thin, on the lanky side of things, with greyish blonde hair, but Cinero knew not to pick a fight with him. More than one boisterous wrestling match had ended with Flaveo tying his opponent into knots.

"Yes, I'm sure he'll be ecstatic to see his long-dead son's lifeless body," Caerella sneered. "Are we all ready to head out?"

"You're not eating?" Cinero looked up at her, and she shook her head.

"I work better on an empty stomach. Besides, I had a full lunch." She turned on her heel and started to walk towards the small path that led up to the Keep.

"Two whole carrots," Rubicus whispered as he walked past Cinero.

"She's practically bursting at the seams," Flaveo quipped as he put the last of his rations back into his pack. "Honestly, I think she'll have to watch her weight."

"I can hear you both," Caerella said from a ways ahead, and Rubicus grew red in the face. Flaveo didn't even have the decency to pretend. He just kept the clever grin on his face and followed after.

Cinero felt weird about the whole exchange. Caerella and Rubicus had taken him under their wing a few years ago. After the war, he'd been orphaned, and mercenary regiments always needed hands to help with all the things mercenaries didn't want to do themselves. That's how Flaveo had started out. Technically, that's what he still did, although at this point, he was essentially their little party's cook, field medic, archivist, and accountant. Quartermaster general. While Cinero had been essentially under his command for a lot of his early days, Caerella and Rubicus had both been teaching him more martial skills as well.

And he'd resigned himself to it. With some luck, he'd one day be able to retire, or take a posting at a noble's house for guard work. Less interesting and worse pay, but he wouldn't be wearing uncomfortable armour all day, and, much more importantly, wouldn't be risking his life and putting his body through extreme pressure on a regular basis. Life with the mercenaries had made him tough, and he hated it. He was athletic, and hated every second of it. All mercenaries were. Even Caerella. She was beautiful, sure, but in the way a knife could be beautiful, all steel and sharp edges. He hated that he was becoming like that, although he wouldn't even get to be elegant like her.

He'd talked about it to her, once, one night when he'd first started to learn to drink wine, beer and mead, explained to her in a moment of vulnerability that he didn't want to become what a fighter would make him into. That he didn't want to grow up to be a tough man like Rubicus. That if the choice was his, he wouldn't be a man at all.

Caerella hadn't understood. She'd tried. She'd empathised. But she hadn't understood, not really. She'd told him that most people who end up in mercenary work were there against their wishes. That she too had given up on a life she'd wanted. That people like them had to make the best of things. Cinero had cried that night, and that had been the last time. He'd been fourteen. His stoicism had earned him his nickname, too. He didn't cry. He didn't laugh. Cinero, the Stoneface. It made things easier. A little bit. Not very much at all.

"Cinero!" Flaveo waved at him.

"Coming."

The path up to the castle would have been, once upon a time, well-travelled. It snaked up the side of a cliff-face, five paces wide, and an attacking army would have been in view of the Keep the entire time. How the Imperial army had even been able to push up that far was almost beyond belief, but it had, and it had destroyed the Caledon Keep gatehouse in a fight Cinero didn't really want to talk about.

He pulled gently at the collar of his armour, hoping to let some air in. He didn't like wearing armour, especially on long treks like this, but Rubicus had been encouraging him to carry the weight, get used to it in every situation. Not that he thought he ever would be. It made him feel big, bulky, and he hated it. Not everyone had to wear it, which felt even more unfair.

"When you can dodge an arrow," Rubicus had told him, "you can wear soft leather armour like Caerella. Until then, you wear the plate." That had been the end of that whole conversation.

After about an hour of walking, the path became more difficult to traverse, because a lot of it had crumbled away. Cinero frowned. Eight years shouldn't have been enough time to do that kind of damage. The answer to the question that formed in his mind came into view after a twist in the road. The cliff wall had partially crumbled, but the giant bolt was still embedded after all these years. It had clearly been fired from the Keep, and there were several more like it.

The way became more difficult to traverse after that. Rocks littered the ground, and there were marks on the ground that were vaguely shaped like bodies, shapes Cinero didn't like to talk about.

Not that Cinero had never seen a dead body before, of course. He'd been only three when the war had broken out, and eleven when it had ended, more than enough time to see some death. But these blackened shapes were the wrong shape, and the wrong size. He recognised the silhouette of the infernal shapes, even after all this time, and he wished he hadn't. They were all over, scorched into the ground, like they'd burned up where they'd fallen.

"You seen them too?" he heard Flaveo quietly say to Rubicus. His ears perked up, but he kept his distance. He got the feeling the other two would try to keep things light if they knew he was listening. It was a weird balance. On the one hand, he didn't like that they would sometimes still treat him like a child. But then again, he also didn't like that they expected him to already be a real man, which wasn't any better.

"Yeah," Rubicus said. "More than I expected."

"Do you think there's going to be any up there?"

"Doubt it," the older man said, "but I don't want to rule it out. Keep an eye out and some magic ready if you have it."

"I've got something saved up," Flaveo said with a chuckle, "don't worry."

"Don't get cocky," Rubicus added. "I'm not looking to get killed in here today."

"That would be a rather disappointing end to our story, I agree."

They grew quiet again, their boots on the ground a constant rhythm as what was left of the gatehouse and the entrance to Caledon Keep, came ever closer. Even from here, the mass of thorny vines was easy to see and from the looks of things, the climb was likely to be the easiest part of their journey.

Chapter Two

Old Magics

There was not much left of the gatehouse. It was a pile of nothing, a large hole in the side of the mountain, overgrown with vines thicker than a wagon, covered in thorns the size of Cinero's arm. He understood now, why it had been so hard for anyone to make it into the Keep since its destruction, and this was just the entryway. The unnatural growth extended to the entirety of the battlements, snaking through solid stone as if it wasn't even there.

"Bleeding hells," Rubicus said. "This is worse than I thought." He walked up to the vines and carefully observed them, taking care to keep his distance. Caerella was pacing back and forth, looking for a path of entry that was most definitely not there.

"Agreed," she whispered quietly. "I could, *maybe*, climb over." She grabbed one of the thorns and gave it an experimental tug. "But a false move would probably prove… well, if not fatal, then more than a little painful."

"Poisoned, do you think?" Rubicus drew his sword and poked the fleshy tendrils. A few dribbles of sap ran down the length of it, and he studied the thick liquid. Caerella nodded her head from side to side.

"Hard to say," Flaveo mused. "It's magical, so anything could happen."

"Speaking of which," Rubicus said, sheathing his sword. "Do you think it'll work?"

"Of course it'll work!" The quartermaster was downright offended. "Be my guest, if you have any doubts." Caerella sighed and walked back a little, leaning against the cliffside wall. The pass Caledon Keep had been built in was high up, and a dangerous trek even on a sunny day, but the mountains on either side of it went up for another mile or more.

"Cinero," Rubicus said, jutting his jaw forward, "the short sword, I think."

"Are you sure?" Flaveo asked with a grin. "It's getting a bit brittle, that one."

"It'll be fine. The short one." He held out his hand and Cinero took off his pack. Other than some supplies, he also carried a small arsenal of weapons with him. They hadn't wanted to risk riding a horse up the pass, and he was glad to take it off for a moment, even if he wasn't going to actually say something.

Retrieving the small, blackened sword, he drew it for a moment. Flaveo wasn't wrong. The steel was getting to be fragile. He handed it to Rubicus, who nodded a thank you at him, and then positioned himself where the vines were at their thinnest. Without a word, Flaveo retrieved a small spherical phial with a golden liquid inside it, and held it up against the afternoon's light.

"You got the right one?" Caerella asked. "I don't want to have a repeat of last month."

"Nobody got hurt, did they?" Flaveo snarked. "But yes, I do." He tossed it at Rubicus, who snatched it out of the air. "Half should do."

"Like last time? Not taking any chances, Veo," Rubicus chuckled. He pulled the cork off with his teeth and drank the entire liquid in a single gulp. "How long?" he asked, maybe a *bit* too late, as he pulled the short sword free of its scabbard, and held it up, looking down its edge towards what had once probably been a portcullis.

"Ten, fifteen seconds, I think." Flaveo pulled a piece of dried meat out of a pocket and chewed on it thoughtfully, but he was looking intently. "More than that and you'll take your arm off."

Rubicus counted under his breath while Caerella, Flaveo and Cinero moved aside a bit to stand behind him. Magic could be unpredictable at the best of times, and Rubicus had a tendency to take risks where he didn't have to. Cinero had learned that much over the years.

"Ten," Flaveo mumbled, "Nine. Eight." He was staring directly at the large man in front of him, who took a deep breath and exhaled, pointing the sword forward and his entire body tensed up.

It wasn't a sight Cinero had the chance to see very often. Magic was dangerous, something not usually seen outside of battle, and difficult to control. The kind of power it provided took its toll. The edges of Rubicus' armour began to glow, crackling with a static power that made the air smell unnatural, strangely clean and sterile. The glow began to run down the cracks in Rubicus' armour, following hard lines like weightless water, all beginning to converge on his outstretched arm.

"Four. Three. Two." Cinero was following along with Flaveo's breathless counting. As a group, they all trusted the man's ability to cook up potent magic, but every time it was something of a gamble to take. It was wrestling control of the nature of the world itself. Even a desired outcome was liable to be explosive.

The old warrior, to his credit, seemed to hold his own quite well, although sweat started to pearl on his forehead. Cinero saw him tremble slightly with the energies running through him. The converging was going faster now, and the tip of the short sword was starting to glow softly.

"For the love of the Saints," Flaveo muttered, "fire the damned thing."

"Just another second," Rubicus groaned, but his voice was strained. Then, with a roar Cinero wasn't sure had come from Rubicus' throat, the short sword burst with heat and light, and a stream of red-gold light burned straight ahead, crashing loudly and violently into the tangle of vines. They had to look away before the brightness did harm to their eyes. Even Rubicus had to shield his face. After a few seconds, the light began to die down.

"Brother of a bastard!!"

"I *told* you," Flaveo said as Rubicus tossed the shattered remains of the sword aside, clutching his hand. "But you didn't listen. Take that off." Caerella rolled her eyes and went to look at the damage the magefire had done. There was a hole clean through the massive thicket, and its edges were still burning, where the material hadn't outright melted or evaporated. The high whistling and fizzling of boiling sap slowly started to slowly die down. Cinero went over to look through it as well, following Caerella. Beyond the tangle of vines, they could now properly see the central tower of Caledon Keep. It wasn't a very encouraging sight. The vines ran up and through that, too. Although its spire was remarkably untouched, a decade of rough weather had still taken its toll on the structure.

"We'll make it up there," Caerella said quietly. "Don't worry." Cinero wasn't sure she was talking to him, until she turned to look at him with that faintest of smiles playing around her lips, and pointed. "The vines are thinner going up," she added. "We'll be able to carve our way through."

"Best get to work," Cinero said. "Will take time." Caerella nodded, and then looked at him for a moment again.

"Take breaks when you must, Cinero," she said. "I'd rather have you tired and able than exhausted and extra weight."

"Okay," he said.

Caerella looked over her shoulder, where Flaveo was fussing over Rubicus. "I know you want to prove yourself, but you're still just a boy. Barely a child anymore. You push beyond your capabilities and you *will* hurt yourself." Cinero nodded, quietly. He didn't like feeling like she was patronising him, but she was still right. He didn't want to let them down and he didn't like complaining. "I know I'm hardly one to talk," Caerella added, "but speak your mind."

"Hey, Stoneface!" Flaveo shouted, beckoning Cinero over. "This is why I don't trouble myself with using magic," he said, gesturing at Rubicus, who was nursing his hand, still swearing under his breath. "The gauntlet took the brunt of it, you big baby," Flaveo added. "It's barely a sunburn."

"Flaveo," Rubicus said with barely maintained dignity, "If you keep this up, I'll give you barely a sunburn right across the jaw. You'd be hurting too if you were in my stead."

"I wouldn't be," Flaveo said with a humourless smirk. "That's my entire point. How's the salve treating you?"

"It's helping," Rubicus grumbled. "Thanks."

"Good. Now let's get going. Or would you prefer we leave you here and send someone to pick you up? We can only carry one casualty at a time, I'm afraid." Flaveo laughed as he narrowly dodged Rubicus' gauntlet, which was mostly just scrap metal anyway. Cinero headed back to the entrance to the keep as he heard Rubicus chuckle and the two exchanged some more playful insults.

While he obviously didn't like seeing the older man hurt, it was always nice to hear him and Flaveo banter. It made them feel a little like a family, and he didn't doubt the two men saw each other as brothers. Caerella was a bit more distant, but she definitely fit in, somewhere. But he wasn't quite sure where that left him. He wasn't old enough to be "one of the brothers," and he didn't think he wanted to be, either. The connection, certainly, but the thought of being one of three roughhousing brothers was almost an affront to him.

So his alternative was solemn silence. He'd rather barely be present than be seen as one of the men he had taught himself not to resent for the comfort they'd found in themselves. Stoneface it would have to be, enjoying the connection others shared from a distance. It was going to have to be enough.

"Cinero," Caerella said, "hatchets, yes?" He nodded and retrieved three from his pack, making it markedly lighter. There were still two more swords in there, but they weren't nearly as heavy as they looked.

"You got this, Ruben?" Flaveo asked. The smile was still on his face, but the concern in his voice was real. He glanced at the large man's hand.

"Aye," Rubicus said, retrieving the larger battle-axe from his own pack. Adding that one to Cinero's would have been overkill. They walked across the courtyard. Rain and wind had weathered away most of the devastation the fighting had wrought, painted on the inside of Caledon Keep. The gruesome tableau was left mostly to the imagination. A rusted sword half-buried in the few shreds of what had likely once been a gambeson. Clean-picked bones here and there, although most of those had probably been carried off by the few animals that made the high mountains their home. And there were the shades, of course.

Black silhouettes, burned into the ground and stonework. Grotesque shapes, monstrous in size and shape. Memories engraved into the foundations and Cinero's own recollections. If he closed his eyes, he could hear their roars, like boulders crashing together. He could see their black eyes, reflecting the burning of homes. So he didn't close his eyes, and looked straight ahead, not letting his imagination get the better of him. Besides, they had work to do.

The tower itself had once been barred with massive doors, which had been thrown off their hinges. By magic or by the force of infernal siege engines, Cinero couldn't tell, they were rotten and blackened all the same. Inside, they could see partway up. It had been a beautiful building, once. Fit for a prince.

But the thick plant growth sprouted out of the ground here too, snaking up the spiralling staircase on the inner walls of the tower and barred any easy path upwards.

"How does magic do this?" Cinero wondered quietly to himself. He had only ever known the power to cause devastation.

"I expect we have the Cavean to thank for that," Flaveo said, his hands on his hips again as if he was posing. "I don't know of any man, woman or anything in between that can sustain that kind of power."

"Old magics," Caerella said. "I don't like what it represents, but I can not deny its beauty."

"I can," Rubicus said, and buried his axe into the roots with a wet *thwack.*

Chapter Three

Old Ghosts

"I hear something," Caerella said, halting on the stairs. After two floors of hacking and slashing through a wall of roots and vines, the climb had become slightly easier. Most of the difficulty came from the uneven footing. The plant-growth had crept up the stairs, making a mis-step dangerous, if not lethal. Part of the stairs were suspended over the tower's central chamber, and a fall from that height could easily kill someone.

"You — *hff* — always hear something," Rubicus said, slightly out of breath. They were getting close to the top, and he was decked out in full armour after all. Any implication that he was getting out of shape due to his age was liable to be met with an angry, if slightly winded, glare. He took pride in his ability to take on younger men in contests of strength.

"I'm always right." Caerella's expression was an invitation to challenge her.

"She's got you there," Flaveo said, halting behind the large man, and he already started to rummage through his pack. "I'll get you something," he mumbled. "I'm sure I had another one of these packed." Producing a small vial with a black liquid, he nodded at Caerella, then at the door at the top of the stairs. "Any idea of what's in there?"

Caerella shook her head, then put her hand on the door. "No, I heard a shuffling, nothing more. I wish I had more than that. It could be something as simple as a lost animal."

"Could be wolves,' Rubicus said. "Haven't fought wolves in a while.

"My money's on a bear," Flaveo said, handing Rubicus the little vial. "There's no way a wolfpack would make it up those stairs, Ruben."

"And a bear would? Can bears even climb?" Rubicus crossed his arms and raised a sceptical eyebrow. Cinero had seen them get into arguments like this before. It was just a matter of time before the two of them would start betting on what was behind the door, and then there would be a small wager about who would open the door, or a double-or-nothing.

"Bears can absolutely climb," Flaveo argued. "Remember, there was that one in Va—"

"If there's a lost animal in there," Cinero said, thinking out loud, "why is the door closed?" That shut both of them up.

"Damn, Stoneface," Flaveo said, and gave Cinero an impressed look. Caerella just smiled at him.

"I'm glad someone's got their head on straight," she said, retrieving her own weapon. Caerella was easy to misjudge. She was fairly tall, slightly above six feet and comparatively slender. People expected her to use a bow or daggers. Watching her brandish a battle-axe had a tendency to put people on the back foot, which had come in handy on more than one occasion. "Now, are you boys all argued out and ready for whatever is behind this door?"

Flaveo nodded. He wasn't expected to do the brunt of the fighting, but he could hold his own. There were more knives strapped to him, under his yellow cloak, than even Caerella knew about. Rubicus held up his greatsword in one hand with an affirmative grunt, the vial of magic in his other.

The man was proficient in many kinds of combat, but most of the time, a big, sharp hunk of metal was more than reliable enough. Cinero held up a short sword, making quick eye contact with Caerella.

"Try to stop at ten this time," Flaveo mumbled.

"Eat me," Rubicus chuckled. Caerella looked behind the two of them to shut them up, sighed and pushed the door open. Everyone held their breath. The only sound was the creaking of leather and the very soft rattle of mail as they all tensed up, ready for anything.

The top floor of the tower had clearly been, a decade prior, a strategy room of some kind. The remains of a giant wooden table were strewn across the room, splintered into pieces. Claw marks had defaced every surface. Decayed maps littered the floor, and several large chairs had been tossed to the floor. The only chair still upright was a large and ornate oaken throne. Obviously, the prince sat in it.

Cinero had expected a corpse, recognizable only by his clothes, or a crown, or something like that. But Prince Clarus, Lucius' only son, seemed to be very much… if not alive, then intact. He sat, slumped over, in the throne, the remains of what appeared to have been a sword in his hand. There wasn't a lot left of it.

More striking was the Prince himself. He looked at peace, his eyes closed, serene. Cinero found it hard not to stare. Even after a decade of being here, seemingly asleep, his facial hair hadn't grown that much, outlining his jawline with a thin beard. His blonde hair perfectly framed his face to give him an intense but distinguished look. More immediately important, however, was the creature in the room with him. It was, to Cinero's worry, neither a dog nor a bear. He froze.

The shade had clearly once been a demon. Why it had lingered for so long after the death of the Cavean was a secret the faceless thing couldn't tell anyone. Its bulking grey-ish torso, held together by decaying infernal magic, lumbered slowly across the floor, dragging itself forward by its claws. Its body faded to nothing where its lower half was supposed to be. It had begun to fade, clearly, and without a master to command it, it had, apparently, lived atop the tower since the Cavean's demise. Which was probably why nobody had brought the Prince home in all that time. Cinero was struck by how quickly, how rationally he was taking everything in, considering the fact his limbs were completely ignoring every one of his commands.

"Well," Flaveo whispered, "the good news is that we found the prince." As soon as he spoke, the creature turned its head, two hollow grey voids where eyes ought to be. "Oh, hells." Without much more of a word, the four of them rushed into the room. The last thing they wanted to do was fight a demon on the stairs. Caerella started to strafe around the creature while Rubicus positioned himself in front of the others.

This wasn't the first time Cinero had seen a demon, before or after joining Rubicus' band. The image of them, their colourless skin reflecting the fires of his childhood, had been burned into his memory. He'd never seen one this far gone before, however. Demons often snarled, roared, devoured. They laughed uproariously and uttered guttural, horrible noises. But this one was quiet, too diminished to retain much of its old personality. It was quiet violence, wordless, soundless rage, and it was terrifying in its own right. Pushing itself upright, revealing its faded, barely visible form, a grotesque mockery of humanity, the shade began to lumber forward.

Rubicus uncorked the vial with his thumb and quickly downed its contents. Just at that moment, the shade charged, closing the distance far quicker than Rubicus would be able to unleash the barrage of power that was building within him.

"I need a second!" Rubicus said, raising his sword. If he was forced to defend himself from the creature's attacks, the magic might build until it was too powerful for him to discharge safely, which would spell doom for everyone. Cinero took a breath. Standing there wasn't going to help anyone, and while he believed fully that the others were capable of taking care of themselves, he was going to do what he could to help, even if... well, it killing him was a possibility either way.

He jumped forward, past Rubicus' elbow. Neither he nor Flaveo tried to stop him. He was expected to contribute regardless, and the team trusted each other to... trust each other. He knew that if he rushed forward and didn't get in the way for too long, it would give the man the opening and the time he needed. He also knew that if he *didn't* get it right, if he misjudged it, that Caerella or Flaveo would probably step in to save him in time. Probably. And that was a less-than-ideal outcome. He just had to hope that the demon was too weak to react properly to new information. That it was beyond simple instinct, essentially just reliving an old, barely-remembered battle.

It barely reacted to his rush, raising one of its massive arms to swing at him, a sluggish movement that would be easy to dodge. Cinero sidestepped the swing and struck hard at where the creature's knee was supposed to be. Maybe it simply wasn't visible. He was caught off-balance when he encountered no resistance, and turned his fall into an awkward roll, doing his best not to impale himself on his own sword. What a way to go out that would've been. Getting up, he noticed the creature was turning around, trying to get him with the backswing. Rather than simply blocking the attack, which was likely to fail anyway, he quickly swung forward.

The sword struck the creature's forearm, meeting it halfway. The blow reverberated through his arm, the weapon thrown out of his hand. His wrist, his whole arm hurt, up to the shoulder, but it had stopped the attack and, maybe more importantly, it had bought them some time. He looked past the creature, which was now between him and the others. Caerella was off to the side where he couldn't see her.

Rubicus nodded at him and he threw himself off to the ground and to the side, covering his head, trusting his leader not to charbroil him. There was a moment of absolute silence, like the ringing of a hollow bell, and then a torrent of fire and smoke bellowed overhead. The roaring battered Cinero's eardrums, and he could feel the heat seep into his bones. He'd feel like a lobster for a few days, but that was fine. It was better than being disembowelled.

After just a few seconds, the stream stopped. Cinero rolled over, quickly scrambling to his feet. He'd judged correctly. The creature was still upright, if only barely. As much as it had faded from the world, it wasn't as impacted by magic as it otherwise might have been, but that didn't mean Flaveo's concoction had been without effect. Its grey surface — Cinero hesitated to think of it as skin — was glowing in places where it still burned and it seemed to have been briefly stunned, stuck in place. But it was still facing him, still advancing, and Rubicus was recovering from the attack.

Flaveo darted forward, his wiry body difficult to read through his cloak, but every once in a while, he tossed hard steel, small daggers digging into the monster's arm. It wasn't doing much to slow the creature down. Without a weapon, Cinero wouldn't be able to do much to defend himself if it swung at him. With the pain in his arm, dodging was going to be a crapshoot.

It raised up an arm and Cinero quickly leapt backwards to avoid the blow, but the tips of its talons still grazed his shoulder, slicing through his mail armour like it was made of nothing more than paper. Rubicus rushed forward, but the creature had already raised another hand. Its blow was going to land before the man was going to be able to help.

Then Cinero saw something behind the giant creature. Behind and above. Standing on its shoulders, Caerella had her battle-axe raised above her head. Her face was one of serene, calculated effort. She brought the heavy weapon down, splitting the thing's head bloodlessly in two, immediately halting its movements. With a sigh of relief, the creature crashed to the ground. Cinero wasn't sure if the sigh had come from himself or the creature.

"You okay?" Caerella asked. Cinero touched his shoulder. Where the creature had struck his skin burned, but the wound wasn't deep. He nodded.

"This is going to need bandaging, Stoneface," Flaveo fussed, but Rubicus was already on him, slapping him on the back.

"Hah! It'll make a nice scar. Good job, boy."

"You did well," Caerella said with a nod. "Mistake on the first swing, but otherwise, nicely done on buying us time." She looked over at the prince. "Now, let's get our dear Prince on a stretcher, before we find any others like this one around." Cinero nodded, and looked at the slumped figure of Prince Clarus. He looked almost... sad.

Chapter Four

Cold Stones

"It doesn't look like much."

"Flaveo, it has more floors than your house has *windows*," Rubicus laughed. They walked down the Queen's Way, the wide road connecting the nation's northern border to the midlands.

"Well, I still don't think it looks like it deserves to be called a 'Palace'." The point of contention, in this case, was the Ice Palace. Colloquially known as the Winter Palace, it was close enough to the Northern Mountains to earn itself the frosty part of its name, and contrary to the opinions of some, large enough to be a Palace. The royalty of its inhabitants was the proverbial cherry on top.

"What you think, Flaveo," Caerella said, "matters not one whit to the aristocracy, I believe." She looked up at the building with no more reverence than he did. None of them felt a particularly great deal of respect for the Crown. Becoming a mercenary was work for people who hadn't been dealt an exceptionally good hand in life, and their party had always been more than a little sceptical of the dealer.

Sure, the war had lain waste and all that, but in the aftermath, the King had done his best to bring things back to 'how they were supposed to be', which had been appreciated by many, but not all. Peace and Prosperity were nice, but not distributed evenly, after all. A job like this would, at least, spread a little bit of that prosperity around, if not the peace.

The Prince, breathing gently, would probably fetch them more than a pretty penny. They'd expected to have been paid a generous wage for retrieving a corpse. To bring the lost son of a king home would fetch them, well, a king's ransom, at the very least. Cinero looked down at him. Now that he was out in the daylight, he looked serene. The line of his jaw looked hewn, his whole face a sculpture of lines traced by the soft rays of the sun.

"Not wrong," Rubicus said. "It's a hell of a lot bigger than anything we'll ever live in. What do you think, Stoneface?" He looked at Cinero, who was shaken out of his reverie by the use of his nickname. Rubicus smirked. "Do we need to tell King Lucius we couldn't find anything, so you can keep him?"

"I—" Cinero said, and then clamped his mouth shut. "No."

"Don't tease the boy, Rubicus," Caerella said, and left it at that. They'd had conversations not unlike this before. Rubicus would tease, never overtly hostile. Caerella would step in. And if anyone outside the four of them had a bad word to say about Cinero, Rubicus and Caerella were liable to put them through a wall. Cinero trusted them. It was just a little hard to remember that sometimes. Like when Rubicus made fun of him for a glance or an out-of-place mannerism.

"Ignore him, Cin," Flaveo said, matching pace with Cinero and walking next to him. "Ruben is just jealous nobody is ever going to look at him like that." Cinero felt his jaws heat up, and he was glad for the cold high air, hoping it would look like exertion more than anything. "His old and weathered face, the best he can hope for is Caera's evil eye."

"Shut it, Flaveo," Rubicus said. Despite the smirk still resting on his face, it seemed Flaveo had struck a nerve. That was the only explanation Cinero had for the edge that had crept into the large man's voice. Caerella looked straight ahead, leading the group and ignoring them all pointedly.

Flaveo held up his hands defensively. "Fine, fine." He gave Cinero a pat between the shoulder blades, opened his mouth as if to say more, and then seemed to change his mind, joining Caerella at the front.

They'd been on horseback for a few days now. After they'd come down the mountain and had retrieved the horses, they had sent a message asking for instructions. King Lucius himself was to meet them halfway to verify their claim, which had turned their task into a Quest, with some serious repercussions if they failed on the last leg of the journey.

They almost had, too. For security, they'd been travelling light and incognito, avoiding towns lest people ask questions like "Who are you?", "Where are you going?" and "Why are you dragging what looks like the living, breathing body of the Crown Prince, who was supposed to have died a decade ago, on a cart behind you, while travelling in the direction of the heart of the country?" The normal kind of questions one might ask.

But they had been forced to make a stop at one of the larger northern towns to wait for an answer, where exactly they'd be meeting, that kind of thing, and they had almost been exposed when a particularly curious goat had started to nibble at the cloak they'd tossed over the Prince. Only Flaveo's quick spinning of a tale, of a man who had been born to the far north, who *claimed* to be the prince, now apprehended and to be brought before the king, had satisfied their curiosity, and only barely.

"Why's he asleep?" a particularly nosey villager had asked.

"Hit him in the head," Rubicus had responded, with an unspoken but absolutely implied and promised threat for similar treatment for anyone with the curiosity or lack of common sense to ask more questions.

"Should'a woken up by now," the villager said, who made up for a lack of common sense with curiosity.

"Hit him *hard*," Rubicus had said, and he'd put a giant hand on the villager's shoulder with the kind of weight that transcended the physical, and looked him in the eyes with so much vitriol the clueless man had turned tail and fled.

Beyond that little encounter, they'd been able to travel pretty much unimpeded. Bounty hunters didn't make themselves very popular, and if they hadn't been bringing home a prince, Cinero wagered that they probably would have taken a hit to their reputation for being second-hand lawmen.

And now they were approaching the Ice Palace. And Flaveo wasn't *wrong.* Not really. Compared to the Palace in Coalis, the capital, this one wasn't all that impressive. Compared to any other house Cinero had ever been within spitting distance of, it was an unbelievable marvel of human engineering. The rocky northern landscape meant the Ice Palace had been built on terraced hills, layer upon layer of its many structures overlooking the ones below it. At its foot, a village had become a town had become a city.

"I think it's beautiful," Cinero said quietly to the Prince. "You'll be home soon enough." Not that there was any guarantee that Prince Clarus would wake up right away, of course. Cinero hadn't even touched him and he could taste the strangely sterile air that hung around him. Magic had been at work to put him in that state. Rubicus hadn't even been able to pry the Prince's hand free of his sword, and had given up after a few seconds of trying, saying touching the Prince had made his skin crawl. Cinero bent forward to cover Prince Clarus up a bit more. It was probably his eyes playing tricks on him, but the Prince's handsome face seemed ever so slightly more relaxed. "Do you get cold?" he wondered, keeping his voice down to avoid further mockery. "I don't think you do, do you? You've been up there so long, I don't suppose so." He sighed. This was probably the fullest extent of any conversations he would ever have with the Prince. Maybe for the best.

The town was quiet when they arrived in the late evening. The autumn air, cold with that after-summer crispness, had driven people inside when the warmth of the setting sun had left them. That's not to say nobody was around anymore. Some had come back from the harvest, old and young alike driving their animals to their pens. Others would be talking in doorways, making plans for the next day.

Rubicus and Caerella drew some eyes. Due to his size, the ageing mercenary turned heads quite often. He looked like what people wanted out of a mercenary, the scars on his face and forearms a visible sign of the many battles he'd fought, and his presence living proof that, even if he hadn't won them, he'd survived. That the giant scar that bisected his face and ran across his lips had been caused by a stumble and a fall onto an ornery rooster was something all of them had sworn — under duress — to take to their grave.

Caerella was a different case. Many often thought she was nobility in disguise. Her high cheekbones, her complexion, and her posture all gave some the feeling that she was of noble birth. This often went away when the realisation hit that she not only wore no fineries or adornments, but, much more importantly, didn't have the *eyes* of a noble. That, and the fact that she could swear and drink like a sailor.

That suited Cinero just fine. He and Flaveo didn't draw nearly the same kind of attention. For Flaveo, that meant he could ask around about the best places to stay the night, no, not the one that travellers paid through the nose to sleep in, the place locals used to spend a night of privacy. He had a comfortable, unobtrusive presence around people that made them want to tell him secrets.

Cinero just liked it when people didn't pay him attention. People who spent too much time with him took Notice. Of how quiet he was for his age, how emotionless he seemed. A few times, girls had taken notice, taking his silence for an act of detached coolness, but he had never been able to reciprocate their affections. The more he slipped into the background, the better.

As they got closer to the Winter Palace, there was more talk whenever they passed. Rumours, it seemed, had spread from the King's entourage, to the staff, and from there to the surrounding city. And four travellers with a covered stretcher making their way up to the Winter Palace... well, that was an obvious and easy connection to make, wasn't it? The palace's front gate, a beautiful square building decorated in blues and purples, had a full detachment of guards in front and on top of it.

If there had been any doubt about the King's presence, this would've been the confirmation they'd need. Rubicus stepped down from his horse. He didn't like talking down to working men like himself if he could help it. Well, not any more than was already the result of his height. He nodded to the one who seemed to be the most doffed up.

"We're expected, lieutenant," he said, holding up the message with the King's seal. Cinero didn't really have enough experience with military or guard types to be able to tell their rank from a cursory glance. Presumably, there was something about the armour or outfit that denoted it. If there was, he couldn't see it. The lieutenant took the letter. He barely had to move his lips. He clicked his tongue, and looked at Rubicus sceptically. The old mercenary put his hands on his hips with a sigh. "You must've gotten word about us arriving."

"I was expecting someone more…" The man frowned, looked over at Caerella, blinked, and stopped. "Ah. Apologies." He nodded at the carried stretcher. "Is that how you've been transporting him?" There seemed to be little judgement in the man's voice. Whether he didn't believe it really was Prince Clarus, or he just didn't care how the Prince was treated, Cinero couldn't tell.

"Only way to get here in time," Rubicus shrugged. "Can we go?" The guard handed him the letter back.

"The King's waiting," the lieutenant said. "I hope what you're carrying is the real thing. I haven't seen him like this in five years."

"What happened five years ago?" Flaveo asked as they walked past.

"I don't know. That's when I got the job." He'd already turned away. "Good luck."

"Thanks," Cinero said quietly. Nobody heard him.

Chapter Five

Light and Dark

The Palace's courtyard was beautiful. From the outside, the complex had seemed a bit monolithic and ostentatious, its high walls both a deterrent and a necessary part of its construction on the rocky terrain. But once inside, the architects had gone out of their way to create an atmosphere that was both regal and cosy.

Compared to the southern Palace, it was, indeed, not that big. But everywhere he looked, Cinero saw signs of wealth and comfort that were beyond his admittedly low expectations for living standards. It didn't take much to impress someone who had grown up first in a farming community and then in mercenary barracks, after all.

The largest building, at the far end, was a layered structure, combining the light wood of the hardy northern trees with its basalt stone, and dominated the scene, but Cinero's attention was drawn to the ornate fountain between the buildings. He watched the water gently cascade from the central, spiral pillar, into the little pond, with no idea how they got the water up there. He caught Caerella looking at it too, and they exchanged a brief nod. He didn't want to look like a country fool for being mesmerised by running water of all things but, well, it was new to them nonetheless.

After having passed through the gates, they'd been given an escort, an entire patrol of over a dozen guards, to walk them up the steps to the Palace proper. It was clear some of them had not anticipated carrying a stretcher up those steps, but if they had complaints, they didn't voice them.

Stopping just short of the fountain, the steward ran up to them, with the awkward gait of someone with a king waiting for them while simultaneously trying to look dignified, and not really succeeding very well at either. Flaveo chuckled.

"Shut it," Caerella whispered, but the corners of her mouth had curled up slightly.

"Make me," Flaveo said under his breath, but as the man approached them, he bowed at the waist with the rest of them, quickly standing back up. Cinero wasn't very familiar with decorum, but doing as the others did had always served him right.

"Gentlemen, milady," the mousy man said, "I fear the normal introductions and regulations will have to wait, as His Highness King Lucius is… pressed." He took a deep breath. "Do not look His Majesty in the eye unless he addresses you directly. Do not speak unless spoken to. Keep your answers brief and to the point. If what you claim is true — which His Majesty will verify himself — you will be handsomely rewarded, but impolite or improper behaviour will not be tolerated."

"Righty-ho," Flaveo said with an indecipherable expression that could rival Cinero's own. One of the guards made a noise that *could* be read as someone masking a snort with a cough.

"Excuse me?" the steward said. It was clear he had *heard* what Flaveo had said. His brain was now furiously discussing the matter with his ears, who must have surely made a mistake at some point.

"We understand, and will abstain from impropriety," Caerella said with a voice sweet as poisoned honey.

Somehow, while looking straight at the steward, she managed to give Flaveo a withering glare through her peripheral vision. With a curt nod, the steward spun on his heels. It was clear they were expected to follow. When the man's back was turned and they followed, Caerella walked next to Flaveo. "I'm going to kill you."

"Worth it," Flaveo said. "I'll behave. Promise."

They hadn't met the King when they'd received their assignment. Royalty wasn't expected to interact with the common people like themselves for something like that, obviously. But the news that Prince Clarus might be alive, well, that was a different matter, wasn't it? They were led not, as Cinero had expected, to the largest building, but to one off to the side. It was ringed by beautifully decorated columns and banners, a beautiful, if slightly weathered carpet leading up the steps. Behind him, Cinero heard the guards lift the large stretcher again, and he could've sworn he heard someone mutter a curse under their breath as they made their way up the steps.

The large doors were pulled open, revealing a small antechamber. He did his best not to stare too much at everything, but it was hard to ignore the beauty, from the architecture to the furniture, all masterpieces of craftsmanship and artistry.

"Don't worry, lad," Rubicus said, walking next to him, "nobody's going to get on to you for looking. That's what it's for." The man grunted. "And I doubt we'll ever see the like again, so it might be worth getting an eyeful." Cinero nodded, and let himself stare, his head on a swivel. He felt a little bit like he had the first time Caerella had taken him to a confectionery. He'd been no more than twelve at the time, right after his first outing with Rubicus' party. It had been a reward. The smells coming from every direction had been almost overwhelming. Up until then, he hadn't imagined smells like that even existed.

Similarly, what he saw here defied what he'd thought houses could look like. Windows large enough to fit two horses side by side, with room for riders. Doors inlaid with marble reliefs depicting ancient kings, queens and regents. Everywhere he looked, there was more to see. Even the floor was decorated with coloured tiles, mosaic tableaus depicting events from legends Cinero had never heard of.

And then they were through another set of large doors, and the almost comically exaggerated stare from the steward made it clear that now they would be in the presence of royalty and they had better behave please and thank you *very* much.

The room they'd been led into looked to be some kind of meeting hall. A wooden table had been moved to a far wall, with the centre of the space now occupied by a marble block that Cinero couldn't even imagine having been moved here, let alone on short notice. Behind it, flanked by various men — advisors and different flavours of sycophants, Cinero assumed — stood King Lucius, clad in royal white.

Cinero could see the family resemblance. The one and only time he'd seen the king had been from a mile away, when he'd waved from a balcony at the populace. But now, up close, he saw the carefully kept beard. Where Prince Clarus had blonde hair, the King's hair had long greyed, and the past decade had not been kind to him, but the sharp jawline and high cheekbones he'd clearly passed on to his son. His face was a network of worry lines, giving him a grim visage, and his shoulders carried the weight of a lifetime of service to the people. Even before the war, his kingdom had seen its share of turmoil. Eight years of war and almost a decade without an heir had left their marks on him.

But not his eyes. Even from across the large room, Cinero saw that flicker of terrible hope. It was one he'd seen before. After the war, a lot of people had hoped to see family members again. That flicker of possibility, seeing a familiar face only for it to turn out to be a trick of the light. King Lucius had long given up hope of seeing his son alive again. Next to them, the steward hissed out of the corner of his mouth.

"Bow. *Now.*" Cinero heard a sharp intake of breath from Flaveo, who had been elbowed in the ribs by Caerella, either because she'd seen him about to say something, or as a preventative measure. They bowed before the King as the Prince's body was carried forward and laid on the table, face still covered.

King Lucius was the one to pull the cloak down. None of the others had dared to move. When the Prince's face was revealed, the collective gasp was as dramatic as it was comical. There had probably been the assumption that this had all been a fakery, or that the rumours of Prince Clarus' escape from death had been exaggerated. But the ever-so-gentle rising and lowering of his chest, the almost-imperceptible blush were unmistakable. The only one not to reel back, not to show any shock or surprise, was King Lucius himself. Instead, he only reached forward, putting his hand on his son's motionless cheek. When he spoke, the whole room went quiet. Despite being barely above a whisper, his voice carried across the space.

"My son," he said, and then his voice broke. "My boy." He stepped back, tears staining his beard. Nobody said a word. Cinero wondered what it was like, to be so isolated that nobody even moved to help, so offer a word of consolation. The King looked at the steward, and nodded. The man turned to Caerella.

"We may discuss payment," he said, looking at the door, indicating that such brutish and crude matters should and would not be discussed in front of the King. Caerella bowed to the King, and followed the steward out the door. Cinero briefly wondered if they should follow them, but since Flaveo and Rubicus made no such attempts he decided against it too.

"Cassion," the King said softly.

"Yes, Your Highness?" The man to his immediate right shuffled forward. He had clearly been chewing his attempt at a beard, little flecks of spittle on his lips.

"Don't just stand there," King Lucius said. He was clearly a man of few words. The man he had addressed as Cassion clearly didn't possess that same quality.

"Of course, Your Highness," Cassion said, producing a long, thin vial, no wider than a straw. "I have concocted a tincture of magic that is both safe *and* potent, that would wake even the deepest sleep. It is, in my humble opinion, some of the finest magic—"

"Cassion," the King interrupted, his voice shattering Cassion's rambling like a hammer to a window. The court mage looked taken aback.

"Yes, Your Highness?"

"For every minute you spend snivelling instead of resurrecting my son, I will have you clean every latrine in the kingdom twice over." Cassion's eyes looked like they were going to pop out of his head.

"Yes, Your Highness," he said, and then carefully hurried over to the Prince's side, and carefully held the vial over the young man's mouth, his hand trembling slightly. Then, a single drop of a silvery liquid fell from the glass, and onto the sleeping figure's lips. The whole room held its breath for a few seconds. Nothing seemed to happen for a moment. Then nothing happened for a few moments more. The King started to deflate. Cassion's face went from reddish, to red, to a deep purple.

Prince Clarus gasped. Cassion fainted. The King leapt forward, raising his son by the shoulders. Cinero looked around the room, at everyone intently staring at the scene in front of them, at the men who had no idea what the proper decorum was for a situation like this. The Prince stirred again. Then Cinero heard something. Something that seemed to come not from in front of him, or to his sides, or above or behind him. He heard a voice inside his head.

"Hello?"

His jaw tightened so strongly he thought his teeth would shatter. A feminine voice rang through his head, making it sing like a bell.

"Thank goodness, I thought there'd be only men in this room. Clarus is a wonderful man, but since he doesn't seem to be waking up, I was wondering if I could be in your head for a spell." There were so many things he had no idea what to respond to first, and so he went with the most obvious question first.

"What?" Cinero whispered. Flaveo frowned and looked at him. Cinero quickly shook his head, pretending that hadn't been him. So apparently he was hearing voices now.

"No need to speak out loud, sapling, I can hear your thoughts just fine as is, if you concentrate. I do need your permission, I fear," the voice said.

"For what?" Cinero thought back at it, doing his best not to giggle. This was, he felt, a truly inopportune time for him to go spectacularly insane.

"To ride along. I swear by the stars I will not be obtrusive. I would only like to lay eyes on him, if only once more." Something about the melancholy tone in the voice's, well, voice, shook him out of his oncoming hysteria.

"The Prince?" He looked at the figure in his father's arms. Whoever the voice was, he couldn't blame her.

"Indeed! I can bestow boons upon you in return!" From quiet and sad, to bubbly and happy in a heartbeat, the voice seemed more than a little excited.

"Like what?"

"How does youth and beauty, if not everlasting then at least outlasting any beast, sound to you?" Cinero couldn't argue with that. Women did seem to like beautiful, youthful men. Not that the interest of women was something that occupied his thoughts much.

"Who are you?" he asked.

"My name is Aesling. You can call me Ash, if you like."

"Why are you in my head?" It was hard not to entertain the thought of this voice being real, that this wasn't a stray thought gone too far.

"I am not in your head. I am in the Prince's head. I would like to not be. Would you like green eyes? I could give you those."

Cinero thought for a moment. The thought of being beautiful, what that *meant* to him... Could she really change him, pull him away from the brink of what adult manhood meant? Even if she couldn't, if she was really just a figment of his imagination, would it really matter if it made him happier?

"Okay," he said.

Then, too many things happened. He experienced a fullness in his head, like he was a cup now overflowing, a thousand thoughts and memories that weren't his crashing around in his brain.

At the same time, the Prince's eyes opened, and the sword he'd had clutched in his hand fell to the floor with a loud clatter. His voice was barely audible.

"Father?" Prince Clarus said. "Wait, no!" Then, as a loud cackling began to fill the room and the King was thrown back, everything went white.

Chapter Six

Comes The Hollow

With a flash of light, Cinero was thrown backwards, only barely managing to maintain his footing while he shielded his eyes. All sound was muffled, as if it came from the other side of a closed door. The only thing he heard with crystalline clarity was the voice of Aesling in his head. It was panicked. Terrified. And it was *loud.*

"No!" she yelled. *"His evil was sealed!"* Before Cinero could ask what she meant, who she was talking about, his vision returned to him. All of the colour in the room seemed to be draining away, like paint in the rain, coalescing into a shape next to the table on which the Prince had been laid down. Slowly, the shape gained form. The colour streaming into it did not, as Cinero had expected, give it colour, but instead seemed to disappear into an infinite nothingness, taller than any man. Only its skin shimmered, like he had once seen some of Flaveo's concoctions do when he'd spilled some of his reagents, colours flashing and disappearing into that slick blackness.

It reached down, a gauntlet forming out of the mass, towards the Prince, still prone on the table. Then it spoke, with a voice like cracking marble, like knives on grindstone, sharp noises that hurt not just the ears but the soul. "Look what you've wrought, Princeling," it said. Its hand just above Prince Clarus' chest, its voice dripping with malice. "All of your strife, and it was undone... just like that." It waved another arm that formed out of nothing at the King's lifeless body. "All for *nothing*." Everyone in the room slowly came to their senses, but all were stunned by the tableau before them. "Was it worth it?" Slowly, the Cavean's face began to form, but there was nothing there. Hollow sockets in a colourless mask scanned the room with malice, a rictus grin fixed on its visage.

Prince Clarus rolled off the table. It was clear the years he had spent seated had not been kind to his physique, and he landed roughly on his knees. Nonetheless, he immediately reached for the broken sword he had dropped, and raised it defiantly. "I stopped you before, you ugly bastard, I'll do it again."

"I am certain you will try," the creature said. Cinero was starting to realise that this *thing* was, in all likelihood, the Cavean. The monstrous entity that had almost broken through to the Southern Shelf and the Kingdom's heartlands. The Empire's last general. Cinero looked around. Rubicus had raised himself to his feet, and he had already drawn his short sword. Flaveo was still scrambling to get up, though judging by his sluggish movements, he had been dazed by the fall. Caerella was nowhere to be seen. "Now then, Princeling," the Cavean said, "face oblivion." It grabbed the edge of the giant marble table and tossed it aside like it was nothing. It crashed through the far wall, shattering in a cloud of dust and splinters. The Cavean stepped forward. And then stopped. It turned around.

Behind it stood one of the King's advisors. He held a dagger in his shaking hands. Despite his fear, he had still stepped forward and attempted to halt this *thing* in its tracks. Cinero wasn't sure he'd have had the wherewithal to do the same. The Cavean's hollow eyes fixed themselves on the man.

"Heh," the Cavean said, and struck the man so hard Cinero could hear the snapping of his bones across the room. He was dead before he hit the ground. "Now," the creature said, turning around again, "I believe we were in the middle of something." Prince Clarus had already lunged at it, but it was faster than its size might indicate, catching the Prince by the throat in a single gloved hand and holding him up.

"Clarus! You have to do something!" Aesling yelled in Cinero's head, and her frantic cry shook him out of his stupor. Almost automatically, he took a step forward. The Prince needed help. He was clearly going to die if nobody came to his rescue. Then Cinero felt a hand on his arm. Rubicus charged, the mountain of a man closing the distance with heavy, thudding footsteps. In his off-hand, Cinero saw a vial of magic. Flaveo was on his knees next to his pack, quickly mixing ingredients. Cinero knew he had to do something. Quickly throwing off his own pack, he retrieved one of the smaller swords he knew how to wield with a degree of proficiency, a solid steel blade. He turned to Rubicus in time to see him strike at the Cavean.

Rubicus, despite his size, was still easily a foot shorter than the creature, but that didn't stop him throwing his full strength into the swing. The Cavean dropped the Prince and struck at Rubicus with the back of its hand. Rubicus dodged it, feinting left, then right, the vial of magic to his lips. While he wouldn't have the time to let it build up, a directed blast of magic was enough to kill anyone at that distance. Rubicus extended his already-glowing sword to the Cavean. It grabbed the sword. Cinero thought it would pull the sword aside, direct the blow to someone else. It didn't. With a burst of light, colour returned to the room for a moment. A stream of fire and heat obliterated the Cavean's head. There was a moment of deafening silence. Then, the Cavean's laughter rolled through the room once again.

"So *brutish*." It yanked the sword out of Rubicus' hand, struck out, and the large man went sailing through the air, landing near Cinero with a thud, the wind audibly knocked out of him. A smaller man would have been knocked out, but Rubicus, Cinero knew, was made of sterner stuff, despite his age. That, and his armour likely lessened the blow somewhat. Cinero rushed over and helped him to his feet and, wordlessly, handed him the large two-hander. Rubicus took it with a grateful nod, and prepared himself for a second charge.

The Cavean had now turned his attention to them fully, but didn't approach. He seemed to be ignoring Prince Clarus, who was having trouble even getting to his feet. That was something, at least. Cinero wanted to yell at the Prince, to get out of here, but he couldn't find his voice.

"Please! Help him!"

"How?" Cinero pleaded. At least he could still communicate with Aesling internally. It was a strange relief, even if it did mean acknowledging the fact that he had just accepted the voice inside himself.

"Keep him busy! The Prince contained him once, he can do it again!" Just as Cinero was starting to resign himself to the possibility of dying to give someone else a chance to stop this evil, he felt a warmth in his chest. *"I... I will help where I can, young one!"* It spread to his arms and legs, and he felt... strong. Powerful, even. Terrified, he realised he couldn't direct it to a limb, or expend it in any way. And then it just... stopped. But that wasn't possible, was it? Magic was a destructive force. It couldn't just... stay in you. *"You can worry about that later, child! Please!!"* Aesling's pleading made Cinero's heart bleed, and he nodded to Rubicus. If one assault was not enough, two

might suffice to keep the Cavean distracted long enough for the Prince to do… whatever it was.

The two of them charged, Rubicus catching another phial of Flaveo's magic as it was tossed at him. The Cavean seemed to grow larger the closer he got to it, and the more detail he saw, the more Cinero wished to turn and flee. The roiling skin, soaking up the light and colour from the world around it, seemed to live a life of its own, sometimes like armour, sometimes cloth, sometimes bone.

"Princeling!" the Cavean said, with… triumph? It sounded almost excited. "I will rend your nation's flesh from its bones! And you will walk through its carcass and know *you* did this." It raised its hand and, like from shadow, it seemed to pluck a sword out of the air. "Live, Princeling! Face an oblivion of your own making!" It spun around at the remaining advisors, huddled, cowering against the wall. The Cavean's sword swung through the air, like the shadow of a bird in flight, and cut through all of them. They fell where they stood, but… not all of them did. Cinero stopped, and Rubicus did too, both of them raising their weapons. Where each of the men had died, a shade stood. A shade with hands ending in talons. With a face contorted into mindless hate. The Cavean turned back to the Prince, and then almost casually glanced at Rubicus and Cinero. "Kill them," it said with such disdain, such *disinterest*, it made Cinero feel like an insect, about to be squashed. "Seize the magecraft, he may be of use."

The demons, over half a dozen, swarmed around the Cavean like water around rock, and charged at Rubicus and Cinero. The guards by the door seemed to have finally come to their senses. Some rushed forward, to protect their Prince. Others ran out the door. They were no match for the blind rage and ferocity of the shades. Their bodies hit the floor around Rubicus and Cinero while they fought, the large man keeping the shades at bay with wide swings, Cinero diving under his arms to swipe and stab. He was fast, faster than he'd ever been, and he felt strength in his arms he could have never imagined.

It wasn't enough. They would not be able to keep them back. The Cavean seemed only to observe with mild disinterest as Flaveo was grabbed and dragged away, and the bodies of the fallen soldiers, the ones that were somewhat intact still, were brought by the shades to their master. More demons rose.

Then, with an unmistakable yawp, a shadow detached itself from the far wall. Cinero didn't even know when she had snuck into the room, but Caerella had clearly been lying in wait, and now she had leapt forward, the head of her axe cleaving the air towards the Cavean. Its edge gleamed silver in the dim light of the room, and a sound, like a clear bell, rang through the room as it connected with the Cavean. There was a ripping, tearing noise, and then the axe struck the cold floor. The Cavean turned around.

"That hurt, you know," it said. "I think I'll keep you." It thrust its free hand forward and grabbed at her, but Caerella danced backwards. It wasn't enough. The shadows in the air around her danced and seemed to flow in on her. She tried to pull away, but even from a distance Cinero saw her movements slow down quickly. Darkness flowed around her, into her, until she was obscured from view. When she finally moved again, she was not herself. Caerella was gone. Something that looked like her and yet distinctly alien, faceless, elongated limbs moving as if underwater, had taken her place. "Much better," the Cavean said. It turned to Cinero. "Finish this," it said, and began to stride out of the room. Behind him, the Prince made a final lunge at him, pushing himself off the floor, his broken sword thrust forward. It struck the Cavean's back and… Nothing. Only silence. Even the shades ceased their assault.

"Why doesn't it… why can I not…" Prince Clarus said quietly, his face falling from determination to despair. The Cavean turned around, a horrifying chuckle in its throat.

"Your magic is not real, Princeling. It was a fluke. Now die. Or don't. I care not. I've a kingdom to burn." It turned, the shade of Caerella behind it. The Prince fell to his knees, and the shades once again attacked Rubicus and Cinero. Even with the power coursing through him, the many swipes, the claws swiping at his face, he couldn't deflect them all.

He heard a yell, and saw claws as long as his forearm pierce through Rubicus' midriff, right below his heart. In that moment of distraction, he felt his back suddenly run white hot, as if hot water was being poured over him. Then everything rapidly started to get cold. The strength in him ran out of him in rivulets and pooled around his feet.

It was getting harder to stand. His sword fell from his grip. He sank to his knees. He looked at Prince Clarus, and saw the Prince look back at him. In that brief moment, Cinero was glad to have connected with the man, if even for a brief moment. If he was going to die, there were far worse faces to gaze upon. Then, everything went black, and he was only tangentially aware of hitting the cold floor.

There was nothing, no sound, no smell, no touch, no colour, as Cinero died.

"Oh, no you don't!"

Chapter Seven

Emerald Cove

Cinero was standing. He was sure of it. There was the ground, almost six feet below him. But all of the hallmarks of standing — the weightiness of it, the pressure on the soles of his feet, the sense of "down" being a direction — were missing. He looked around. He appeared to be standing in… a space. It was hard to make out exactly what, or where. There was a sense of forest-ness. The ground was covered in moss. Patterns of light, like sun through leaves, painted bright greens around him. He saw trees, twisted in shapes he'd never seen, thick trunks with reds and yellows on top. A blue sky somewhere overhead. Like a glade on a warm autumn afternoon.

"Where am I?" he asked, and then realised no sound had come out of his mouth. He reached up to touch his lips, his throat, and found that he had none of the above. No hand. No face. He simply *was*. The words he had spoken had appeared as a concept in the air, but it was voiceless, like a whisper on the wind. "Am I dead?"

"I certainly hope not," Aesling said, from a direction that could have been 'behind him' if something like that had any real meaning when he didn't have a corporeal form to speak of. "I'm working hard to make sure you don't. But while that's going on, I wanted to talk."

Cinero turned his attention to her. Aesling was beautiful. Ethereally so. Her face was sharp, with high cheekbones and a hard-lined jaw. Dark lips. A skin that seemed to almost have a glow to it. And bright, vibrant green eyes. She was wearing flowing robes, in various bright colours, that seemed to ripple and flow like an unfelt breeze was slowly stirring them. Her auburn hair, woven in a messy braid, hung lazily over her shoulder.

"What's your name, child?" she asked. Cinero floated forward and back a little bit.

"Cinero," he said. Aesling nodded, and pursed her lips. Even though he didn't really seem to exist in this place, wherever it was, she was looking right at him.

"Well then, child," she said, "to answer your earlier question: You aren't anywhere. This is the inside of your own mind. Though I did make myself at home in this little corner somewhat."

"What is this place?" Cinero asked, looking around. "I've never seen trees like this."

"It's home," Aesling said as she walked through the glade, running her fingers over the barks of the trees. "Or rather, it used to be. Before the Emperor had them all burned down." Her voice was sharp, but not regretful. "I carry it with me."

"That's... sad," Cinero said, and immediately felt like a fool. Of course it was said. The woman's home had been burned down, and 'sad' was the best thing he could come up with?

"It is," Aesling said, "but for now, it's a refuge. It's a place where we can talk while I keep you from dying. I take it you have questions, but I'm afraid those will have to wait until I've had the time to get some answers out of you first."

"Oh?" Cinero was a little surprised. "I don't know what you'd ask of me," he said. "I'm afraid I am not that interesting. But I'm happy to answer, if you'll hear my questions."

"You are most definitely interesting, child," Aesling said, "even if you don't believe so yourself. But yes, of course I'll hear and answer what questions you might have. A gift for a gift, a boon for a boon." Aesling sat down on a large root that stuck out of the ground. "I used to have a place, much like this one, when I travelled with Prince Clarus," she said. "There was a major difference, though."

"What's that?" Cinero asked, trying not to linger on the image her words conjured.

"He visited me, here. He was so tall, so handsome, the way his hair lit up in the sunlight," she said. Well, now Cinero *couldn't* avoid the image. Prince Clarus, golden hair in golden light, leaning against a tree, relaxed and happy. "Do you see how that is different?"

"I am not him," Cinero said. "I'm sorry."

"That's not what I mean, child. And not something to apologise for. Much as he and I... grew closer, I'd rather be able to see him with my own two eyes." She sighed. "But that's not it. Prince Clarus was here. He stood, right where you are." She raised an eyebrow. "In the flesh, as it were." Cinero looked down. There was just the ground. No flesh to speak of.

"Why don't I have a body, Aesling?" he asked. "You say I'm not dead, but..."

"I know," Aesling said. "Quite the conundrum, yes?" She stood up and walked over to him. "But I can sense you. You are *here*. While all of this is... well, I've not had a lot of experience. But in here, you are as you believe yourself to be. Would you believe Prince Clarus imagines himself to be several inches taller than he actually is?" She sighed wistfully. "I did not mind." Cinero would have frowned, if he'd had a face.

"How can I not have a body, then? I exist. I believe I do. So why then?"

"That's the question," Aesling said, "though I believe I have an answer for you. While we speak, you are on the floor, still bleeding, I fear, quite profusely. Thought not as badly as before. I am doing what I can."

"How?" Cinero asked.

"Magic," Aesling said. "Old, *deep* magic. None of that... noisiness you people are fond of. Magic from before the first clay was made into brick, before the first wheel turned. Before words." That was almost impossible to believe. And it would mean Aesling was...

"Not human," Cinero said. Aesling just nodded.

"Not human," she confirmed. "Something like but unlike. A bit older, I think." She smiled softly. "And as I am mending that broken body of yours, I find that, perhaps it need not be the way it was. And then I am in here, and there's nothing here for me. No frame of reference. I have a canvas and no model."

"What do you mean? It's not possible to simply *change*, is it?"

"It's magic, child. It can do whatever the *fuck* I want it to." She cocked her head. "Within reason."

"Then... what?"

"Well, that is up to you, isn't it?" Aesling said. "Why do you not have a body in here, do you think, child?" Cinero thought about it. He existed, right? Certainly, there wasn't much to him. He'd never really considered himself worth exploring. No hidden depths. Barely a person. Because he didn't want to be, not really. No ambitions to be a great man, a great lord. No desire to be anything. Just a slow forward momentum.

"Do I not exist, Aesling?" he asked. The phrase had come to him derisively, almost as a sneer, but when they'd left his mind, he realised he genuinely didn't seem to know.

"Perhaps not the way you think," Aesling said. "Do you know why, in a roomful of powerful men, mages, warriors, I asked to be in your head?"

"You said something…" Cinero said, the sentence, the memory, fresh in his mind and yet refusing to come forward. Not for a lack of ability, but for a lack of trying. He didn't want to really acknowledge it. At the time, it had been drowned in the noise and the confusion, and it had stuck out to him regardless.

"I did," Aesling said. "In a roomful of men, I found you."

"But I am…"

"Are you?" Aesling cut him off. "From where I am standing, you aren't *anything*." She crossed her arms and paced back and forth. "You are shapeless. Consider me… a shaper of clay, if you will. I'm currently sculpting your body, your real one, back together. But perhaps there is work to be done within as well as without, hmm?"

"What kind of work?" Cinero asked. He knew the answer, but the only steps he felt he could take were incremental ones. "What do you mean?"

"Child, I will not spell all of this out for you," Aesling said. "I am doing what I can, but some leaps of faith you have to make for yourself. Why did I reach for you?"

In a room full of men, a woman chose Cinero to exist within. The answer was obvious, wasn't it? And it's not like it hadn't been a recurring thought, for a long time. The conversation with Caerella came to mind. "I'm no man," Cinero said. Aesling smiled and clasped her hands together.

"There we are." She seemed so satisfied. Proud, even.

"How could you tell?"

"A feeling," Aesling said. "So you are no man, child. What are you? Who are you?"

"I've known. I have always known."

"How?" Aesling asked.

"I've felt it. I did not know it was possible, something that could be."

"It can," Aesling said. "I suspect it is not uncommon. I've seen and met a great many people, before meeting Prince Clarus, although few with your… certainty."

"But I'm not certain," Cinero said. "I don't know who I am, who I am supposed to be."

"But you're no man," Aesling said. "It *radiates* off you. Your desire not to be one shines like a beacon for those who know where to look. So if not a man, who are you, child?"

It was there. A word, a thought, there for the taking. Out loud, it would be spoken into reality. Could it just be said, like that? "A woman?" Cinero hazarded.

"If you wish," Aesling said.

"It can not just be that easy, can it?" Caeralla had said as much, back then. But then… Caerella didn't know everything, and the possibility that it *was* that easy, that they could just *not* be Cinero, not be who they'd always been told they were, the possible impossibility of it, was so tantalising it could be felt in the air.

"It can," Aesling said, and with those two words, a tempting world of possibility began to bloom into existence. "Who you are is decided by none but you."

"Could I be?"

"You could," Aesling confirmed again. They didn't want to believe it. If that was true, there'd be no going back. Knowing oneself would be a curse to carry with them forever.

"Aesling?"

"Yes?"

"I think I might be a woman," she said, with all the terrifying certainty that came with knowing herself.

"Congratulations," Aesling said. "Is that woman named Cinero?" That name felt so strange now. It felt wrong, now that it was clear that that person did not even really exist.

"I don't think so?" Words still formed in the air, without a throat for them to come from, but the voice was different now. Lighter, more feminine. "But what name, then?"

"There's a name that I think could fit you," Aesling said. "It means many things to many different people, but I think it could mean the truth, for you."

"What is it?"

"Vera," Aesling said.

"Yes," Vera said. It was like someone had gently tapped a crystal, a silver ringing sound that reverberated through her soul. It sounded *right*. "I think that's my name."

"You don't have to be certain," Aesling said, holding up a hand. "You have time. A lot of it, I think. I plan to grow very old."

"How is that possible?" Vera asked.

"This glade is my home," Aesling said, waving her hand at the surrounding landscape. "But it is only a reflection. Once, I was keeper of the woods. I was once the life in an acorn, the apples on the branches. I was the forest and it was me."

"You are a forest spirit?"

"If that word fits your understanding."

"So what now?" Vera asked, and she realised her voice had rung out clearly through the glade. Spoken from her mouth. She reached up and touched her own face. Soft fingers touched sharp cheekbones. She looked at her hands.

"Now," Aesling said, "I have something to work towards, little sapling. Is this you?" Aesling looked her in the eye with a burning intensity. Vera didn't have to look down to know her body felt like *hers*, possibly for the first time in her life. She didn't have to, but she did anyway, because she *knew* she'd like what she'd see, and she did.

"Oh my," she said, and realised that she hadn't imagined herself wearing clothes. She felt her cheeks blush. It was good to have those again.

"Very modest," Aesling quipped, and turned away, looking up at the sky. "Now, Vera," she said, and turned to look at her, "you are about to wake up in the world as yourself for the first time. Are you ready?"

"No," Vera said with a smile.

"Good. I'd be very suspicious if you were. Now, open your eyes, child."

Vera opened them, for the first time, and smiled. Then she coughed up a little blood, and pushed herself to her feet.

Chapter Eight

The Prince

Vera looked around the room and sank to one knee. The triumph of finding herself was somewhat overshadowed by how unsteady her legs felt and, more strongly, the death and destruction around her. It wasn't helped by the fact that everything was so much more intense than it had been. For most of her life, everything had been muted, like she'd been living from under an opaque blanket, sounds and colours as dim and lifeless as she felt. Now, she felt... well, a lot of pain, while the hole in her chest healed. But she also felt *alive.*

There were bodies all over the room, but she didn't see any of her friends. Where Rubicus had been, there was only blood, a trail that led outside the room. The only one person she recognised that was moving was Prince Clarus, and he seemed to be unharmed. He also seemed to be moving toward her, with an expression on his face she couldn't quite read. She'd never seen an expression like that before.

"*Um,*" Vera thought at Ash, "*what's happening? What do I do?*" Before Aesling could respond, the prince had broken out into a sprint toward her, his eyes wild! Was he going to attack her? Was he angry? Upset? Did he blame her for what happened? She slowly started to raise her arms, momentarily stunned by how soft her skin looked, even if it had an ever so subtle greenish hue. The palms of her hands were a soft pink, and the colour-contrast drew her eyes — and her attention — long enough for the Prince to have closed the distance. Several feet away he'd thrown himself to his knees and came to a sliding halt in front of her, grabbing her by the shoulders. Vera froze.

"H-hello," she said. The Prince's eyes, bright and grey, were *fixed* on hers, and she saw tears forming in their corners. Vera had no idea what to say or do. She saw him mouth something, but even this close, she didn't hear it. Then he wrapped his arms around her. "A," Vera said. Prince Clarus moved back, took her face in his hands and pressed his mouth to hers.

"AAA, Vera thought, loudly. This was not how she had expected or wanted her first kiss to go. She had wanted to close her eyes, to melt into it, instead of sitting, frozen on the spot, with her eyes wide open. Not that she would have been *opposed* to the Prince's affection, but, well, not like this. When he finally pulled away, all she could do was stare. "Wh—" she managed.

"My Aesling," he said, and stroked her cheek. "Finally, in the flesh before me."

"Vera," Aesling echoed inside Vera's head, *"would you mind terribly if I spoke to him for a moment? That will require me taking over, so I understand if you aren't comfortable w—"*

"Yes, please!" Vera practically shouted. She reached out to Aesling in her head. Vaguely, there was a sense of her being in Aesling's glade, and taking her hand, and the two of them suddenly trading places. She was comfortable. Mentally, it felt like lying down in the grass on a warm summer day and looking at the clouds. The clouds just happened to be the Prince's face, which she was not opposed to, despite his... impromptu affection. Now that the shock of it had worn off, she realised he'd *kissed* her! She still felt it, a soft pressure on her lips, a persistent tingling sensation that made her want to giggle.

"Clarus," Aesling said, and for the first time — there were bound to be many firsts — Vera experienced what it was like to have someone talk through her mouth, move with her body. "Clarus, I'm here."

"I know, Aesling. I have missed you so." Tears flowed freely down his face, despite the happiness in his smile. "How can this be, my love?"

"I *wasn't* here a minute ago, Clarus," Ash said. "I fear that, when they attempted to revive you, the Cavean woke as well."

"Then we shall stop him," Prince Clarus said, like it was as easily said as it was done. "You and I, together, as we always should have been, side by side."

"Somewhat," Aesling said. "I'm afraid this is still no body of my own, although I feel it suits me quite a bit better than yours did."

Clarus frowned. "There was no other woman here earlier, was there? I could have sworn I was in a roomful of men. Regardless, could I speak with her, the way we once traded places? I would very much like to thank her, and apologise."

Aesling looked around the room, at the bodies. Vera, at the same time as her, considered that Prince Clarus had some interesting priorities, but things had calmed down a little and, well, Vera had never talked to a Prince before. She'd kissed one, but hadn't talked to one. "That can be arranged," Aesling said, and she and Vera switched places once more.

"H-hello again," Vera said, now that she was in control of her faculties again. Prince Clarus stood up and offered her his hand. She carefully took it and he lifted her, his other hand on her elbow to help steady her.

"Beautiful maiden," Clarus said, "I apologise so deeply for the impropriety. I had never seen my Aesling in the flesh before, and thought you had to be her, the only woman in the room. How did I not see one as ravishing as you earlier?"

"Before you ask," Aesling said, *"Yes, he's always like that, and no, I do not mind."* There was a little pause as Vera didn't know how to respond. *"Whether you tell him is your prerogative, child. But he will not judge, one way or another."* Vera nodded, and decided to take a chance on the Prince. He seemed honest, and she trusted Aesling's judgement.

"I'm… I'm Vera," she said softly, and immediately she stopped, a little panicked, in the best way possible. *"Is that my voice?!"* All she got was a self-satisfied snicker from Aesling, who seemed to be taking a gleeful pride in work well-done. "Um… when you saw me earlier, I would have gone by the name of Cinero." Saying the name out loud felt like a curse, something profane, like ash on her tongue.

"But Cinero is a… Is that possible?" He seemed genuinely confused, his eyebrows knitting together. Vera's inability to answer was exacerbated by Prince Clarus still staring deeply into her eyes.

"It is," Aesling said. *"Would you like me to take it from here?"* Vera gave another slight nod. She and Ash were switching back and forth pretty quickly, but it didn't bother her. Simply riding along allowed her to feel her feelings without worry about how she came across, where she was safe. "My love," Aesling said. "It's me again."

"I know," Clarus said. "Your eyes are different when she's… in front of you." Vera turned her attention to Aesling. That wasn't something she'd even considered. Going off Aesling's response, that wasn't something she'd expected either.

"That's… certainly new. In either case, Clarus, to answer your question, yes, that is possible. There are certain people, like Vera, whose body isn't truly theirs. I was able to help her."

The horror on Clarus' face was clear as day. Vera had never seen someone so expressive before. For a moment, she was worried it was because he was horrified at the thought of having kissed a man, but that fear was very quickly assuaged. "Trapped in one's own body? After having spent a decade in a half-waking limbo, without your voice or presence? I can only relate, my loving Ash. Can she hear me?"

After getting confirmation from Vera, Aesling gave an affirmative nod. "She can."

Passionately, Clarus took Vera by the shoulders. "Vera, I am *beyond* stricken with grief. What was done to you, by the cruelty of fate or some foul curse, is unspeakable. You, nor anyone else, should have to go have to suffer something as vile as that, and I swear to you that, when we leave this room, I will travel this land until I have found a cure for every single person like yourself, and I will hand it to every one of them personally."

"Love," Aesling said, "the Cavean, first."

"Right," Clarus said. "But *after* that."

"*Thank you,*" Vera squeaked. Even with Ash in front, she was squirming and blushing. She could still feel his hands on their shoulders, and found herself, if not drowning, then at least wading into those large, grey pools. "*Is he always this intense?*"

"*Yes,*" Aesling said. "*He is. How could I not fall for this ridiculous man?*" Vera swallowed a little pang of envy. It was okay. She would still get to be there, even if their feelings were for each other. "She says 'Thank you,' love," Aesling said. "And as for you… are you hurt?" Clarus shook his head. "That *is* a relief, at least." Aesling turned her attention inward for a moment. "*You… would you mind if I kissed him? I've never seen him from the outside, and being together in the glade is only a poor facsimile, and—*"

"*I don't mind!*" Vera squeaked. Ash smirked softly at her, and Vera wanted to hide her face. She hadn't intended to sound as enthusiastic as she had. With that consent given, Aesling took the step closer, practically falling into Prince Clarus' arms, who immediately wrapped them around her and pulled her in close.

"I've missed you too, my Prince," Aesling said, and pulled herself into a kiss. Vera found out the hard way that kisses were both better and more intense the second time around. His soft breath against their skin. His hands on their back. His heart, beating quickly and powerfully against their chest. Vera would have been unable to stay upright. Even in a space where she didn't have a real body, she felt her knees weaken. Clarus ran a hand through their hair, and it sent a chill down Aesling's — and by extension, Vera's — body. When their lips finally parted, they were both slightly out of breath.

"Does — does Vera not mind?" Clarus asked. Vera squirmed a little at his mention of her name. Even at a time like this, when the two of them were in each other's arms, he had a thought to spare for her. She felt Aesling's attention on her, without judgement or any kind of jealousy that Vera might have expected.

"I do not think so," Aesling said. "But who am I to speculate?" She took Vera's hand, who tried to protest quickly and loudly, but it was too late, and with a swap of consciousness, she was in front of Clarus, his hand still resting on her back.

"I — Hello!" she said. The Prince withdrew his hands and simply smiled. Vera felt her cheeks glow. "I… I just wanted to say that... I don't mind! You two have clearly been apart for a very long time and I wish you all the happiness in the world."

"That is no justification," Clarus said. "Our desires should not come at the cost of your comfort, Vera. Besides, happiness mustn't be a balancing act. When Aesling lived inside my soul, she and I found ways to make things work." Vera wondered if she was imagining things, or if there really was an ever so gentle blush on his cheeks. When she looked at Ash, she got a similar sense of... oh. "And so it will be with you, beautiful maiden. If I understand correctly, you're only now free of the curse that bound you to your flesh. You deserve to feel true happiness in it."

Happiness. It was strange. Surrounded by death, still, for the first time in her life, happiness felt like an achievable goal. Speaking thereof... "Thank you, Prince Clarus," she said softly. "But I fear the shadow cast over the world, and my part in it, will cause a slight delay."

"Yes," Clarus said, and he turned to the door. "Where do we start?"

"Rubicus," Vera said with determination. "If he is able to stand, he will be moving."

"A man after my own heart! Let us follow the trail!" Clarus said, already moving to the door.

"*Do you mind if I...*" Ash asked, hesitantly.

"*Go right ahead.*"

"Clarus," Aesling said, out loud now. Clarus' head snapped around to look at her. When Aesling spoke, her voice, her inflection, was different from Vera's. He'd probably picked up on it. "Your father." Ash gestured at the motionless figure, barely visible against the far wall.

"Oh," Clarus said, and Vera saw his heart break.

Chapter Nine

Keeping Company

Clarus picked up his father's broken body with remarkable ease. It was clear his strength, lost after a decade of unnatural sleep, was returning to him, faster than should have been possible. Vera didn't say anything. Aesling didn't have much to add, either. Sometimes words aren't there, and *shouldn't* be there. Sometimes grief itself is the only appropriate sound to make. She didn't know where he was going. All she could do was follow him out the door, quietly, softly, trying not to be too self-aware of the fact that her clothing was hanging remarkably loosely around her. She was going to have to have her armour refitted. She was liable to trip over herself at this rate.

Carrying the body down the hill, Clarus was determined in his movements, in his tread. The path was littered with bodies. Guards thrown haphazardly left and right, their bodies strewn about like discarded dolls, the gashes and claw marks of the Cavean's demons marking the terrain, all of it spoke of a battle that had begun and ended in seconds.

The wind stung against Vera's face. Had it always been like this? It was like her skin was more sensitive now, and she wished she had a cloak to pull taut around her. Or was it because of that creature? Had it sapped the warmth out of the sunlight somehow? She couldn't tell.

Running up the hill were several people from the surrounding town. They were careful, frightened, but not fleeing. The Cavean must have moved on, then, Vera figured. Whereto, she didn't want to speculate. She knew she wouldn't like the answer, no matter what it was. But the people of the town were, at the moment, safe. After a fashion, at least. The Kingdom's enemy was within its borders, mustering an army, and the King was dead.

The people running up the hill recognised their late ruler, and some of them his son. Clarus was certainly a striking figure, his blonde hair and chiselled jawline the kind of person who stuck in your head. An older man, a servant, didn't understand and, clearly, didn't question it, stepping back to let the Prince walk past. Clarus paused.

"Does the corpse-witch still live in the city?" he asked. The man seemed stunned into silence by the question. It wasn't hard to see why. Vera hadn't had a lot of experience with those whose business was taking care of the dead. She had always been surrounded by the people who got them there. After life winked out, Vera didn't really deal with it much. Too many memories there. But corpse-witches, she understood, were a necessary part of small communities.

"I — My Lord, the majordomo will—"

"Dead, I'm afraid," Prince Clarus said. Even with his father's body in his hands, white clothes slowly soaking red, his voice was one of gentle kindness. "And there's no time to find another." He looked ahead, not at the horizon directly but more at the idea of one. "There's no time for funerals yet, my good man. The corpse-witch. Please."

"Y— Yes, Lord. By the east village gates, My Lord. Surely you oughtn't—"

"He's my father," Clarus said. "I'll carry him there. Thank you for your help." He continued his walk down the hill. There was an air of authority around him Vera couldn't put her finger on. Sure, the King had come off as authoritative, but, well, he'd been King for decades. That kind of leadership was not unlikely to come with age. But Clarus wore decisiveness like a cloak. He had made a decision, and now that decision was going to be carried out. It was like he didn't move through the world, he just moved his feet and the world moved itself to accommodate him.

"He's always been like that," Aesling. *"An unstoppable force, when he wants to be. Clarus is a man of purpose."* Vera could absolutely see it. It was intimidating. *"You get used to it. At the end of the day, despite his purpose and strength, he is still a man. Don't let the Prince in him distract you of that. Clarus is Clarus first. Prince or no."*

Vera caught up to him, feeling distinctly awkward. People were already shooting her looks, wondering who she was, although most bowed their heads in deference when they saw who Clarus was carrying. "Are you…"

"I'm afraid not," Clarus said, and she heard, ever so subtly, a crack in his voice. It was clear he was keeping a brave face, but he was holding his father's still-warm body. Nobody could be alright under those circumstances. "I feel guilty," he said. Vera was about to reassure him that there was nothing he could've done. She tried telling herself that, but it was hard. After all, she was the only person left alive — that she knew of, anyway — who had brought the Prince back to his father. This was her fault, more so than his. "I feel guilty for being so short with that man. He was only trying to help."

"I… Your father just…" Vera mumbled, but couldn't get out a coherent statement. Clarus just tightened his jaw and kept walking. "I'm sure he'll understand," she finally said.

"I'll have to see about compensating him," Clarus said, more to himself than anything as he walked through the palace gates and onto the street, turning left and right for a moment before picking a direction. Vera had kept an eye on the trail on the ground. The blood, Rubicus' blood, had followed the same path they had. He had been following the Cavean's trail of death. But now it split off from where Clarus was going.

"Prince Clarus," she said softly, "will you find the way yourself?" He looked at her and nodded with a gentle, if forced, smile. "I'll join you soon," she added. "I just need to know where they've headed."

"Of course," he said, straightening up a bit. "We mustn't lose the trail. Clever thinking." There was a trace of his previous enthusiasm there, still. But it was fragile, and fraying.

"I — I know," Vera said. "I must... must make sure—"

"Yes," Clarus said, his smile fragile but nonetheless genuine. "Go. I will see you momentarily." With that, he turned around and strode to the town's eastern gate. Vera stared at his back for a few seconds.

"I wish I could help him," she mumbled.

"He is in pain," Aesling said. *"He'll grieve. And I'll be there for him, as I have been before. He's strong, but no man is an island. Despite all of his..."* Aesling waved her hand noncommittally in Vera's head, *"Clarus-ness, he's a sensitive creature. Sometimes, it isn't just the still waters whose grounds run deep."*

"I don't understand," Vera said quietly as she turned around to find the trail again. Where the Cavean was headed wasn't hard to follow. The marks on the buildings, and the bodies, were enough to infer the creature's general direction. But Rubicus' trail of blood was harder to glean. He'd clearly staunched the flow somehow, but Vera still saw the occasional bloody handprint on a wall or doorframe along the way. And she noticed the direction changing along the way. Not fleeing, not lost. Deliberately, Rubicus had stopped following the Cavean.

She followed the road to a building. She didn't recognise it, but she knew the symbols by the door. Not many mercenaries could read, so buildings like these made themselves universally known by simple markings. A horse, a drawn carriage or a sword, with a half empty circle beside, could indicate a need. A full circle was an offer. She knocked on the door. There was a shuffling on the other side, but no answer.

"Do you mind?" Aesling asked. Vera stepped backwards, and felt the woman slip into her boots effortlessly. She heard Aesling's voice come out of her mouth when she spoke. "If I were demonspawn — or worse — I would not've knocked," she shouted. "We only want to ask some questions!"

After a moment, the door opened with a grumble, and Aesling retreated again, with a little mental bow. "What?!" the woman asked, opening the door only a fraction.

"My friend was here," Vera said. Do you know where he went?"

"There wasn't nobody here," the woman said, and started closing the door. Vera quickly put her foot in the gap and was very glad for the reinforced tips, or she might've lost a toe. It would've been an ignoble way to get maimed, for sure.

"His handprint," she said, pointing, "is literally still on the door." She could tell the woman wanted to argue, but sometimes proof is too obvious to ignore. The woman squinted her eyes shut and groaned.

"Ol' Rube just needed some supplies and a horse," she said. "He paid his dues."

"I know," Vera said. Rubicus had always been extremely particular about paying dues to the various supply houses around the country. Clearly, it had paid off. "Where did he go?"

The woman glared at Vera suspiciously. "What's it to you? He doesn't need some trollop to badger him with nothing right now."

"He's got a hole in his chest the size of an orange," Vera said. "He'll not stop, because he's a stubborn bastard, but maybe he'll let a friend bandage him before he kills himself." The woman's expression softened as she looked Vera up and down.

"Fair enough," she said, chewing her tongue. "He said he's headed south, he said. Told me to send any of his company that-a-way too."

"Why didn't you say that to me first, then?" Vera tightened her jaw. She wanted to take a stand in defiance, but, well, she was used to not being taken all that seriously.

"A girl like you? You ain't company material," the woman scoffed. "But maybe you ain't all bad, yeah? Maybe he needs a young leaf to take care of him." And with that, the woman shut the door. Vera scowled.

"Well that was unpleasant," Aesling said.

"Rubicus is like a father to me," Vera said as she retraced her steps, moving to the eastern gates. "That's…"

"Yuck," Ash said with understanding. *"I understand. How did you come to be in his company?"*

"Him and his company took me in after the death of my family. I had nobody else, and they treated me with kindness and gave me a purpose," Vera said. "They *are* my family." She slowed down. "And now they're gone." She tried not to think about how that made her responsible for them. For what happened.

"Not gone," Aesling said. *"Not yet. Not if we hurry. Who are the other two?"* It was clear Ash was trying to

distract her. Vera let her. *"I noticed you paying particular attention to the man and woman they took."*

"Flaveo is… well, if Rubicus is like a father, Flaveo is as his brother. He taught me how to cook, and he's a gifted speaker and magecraft. Caerella is… I've always looked up to her."

"I'm not surprised," Aesling said. *"She was certainly imposing."*

"What did that creature do to her?"

"I don't know," Ash said, *"but we will find a way to save her. Save them."*

"I hope you're right," Vera said. She slowed down as she approached the door to the corpse-witch's cabin. If it wasn't for the small crowd outside, she wouldn't have known this was the building. She shoved past people and opened the door without waiting or knocking. The room inside was dark. The windows were covered, and every possible surface, even the walls, were filled with objects. Vases and urns. Wards and symbols. A lot of books. Immediately, Vera saw Clarus, his bright eyes like a beacon. He stood by his father's body, which had been laid to rest on a table. A woman, no older than thirty at the most, was bent over the King. She looked up in annoyance, but Clarus held up a hand.

"She is with me," he said, then turned to Vera. "Thank you for coming back. Have you found your friend?" Vera shook her head.

"No, but I know his heading." She didn't want to say more yet. This wasn't the time for making plans. Despite the Prince's intentions to mourn later, grief still hung thick in the air, sickeningly sweet, like the incense the witch had lit.

"He'll keep for two weeks," the witch said. "After that, the rot will set in, and the funeral will be an unpleasant affair." She stood up. "I can also speed it up. Have him embalmed and done by week's end. It'll not be pretty before then, but it'll be fast, it'll be clean, and it won't smell as much." Clarus seemed conflicted. He looked at Vera for guidance. Aesling asked. Vera answered.

"My love," Aesling said out loud, "you will need time to grieve, by his bedside. That body may not be your father anymore, but that is still his face. It will help you mourn him."

"But then we'll only have two weeks," he said.

"So," Ash said resolutely, "you'll have to save the world before then."

Chapter Ten

Trialogue

When they stepped out of the witch's cabin, the atmosphere was strange. On the one hand, of course, they had just trusted a stranger with King Lucius' body, and his death still hung over them like a shadow. But there was also the sense that a weight had been lifted, like a warrior taking off a heavy cloak before the fight. Sure, later the cloak would have to be picked up, but for now, there was a freedom of movement, emotionally and mentally if not physically, that had not been there before.

The two — technically three — of them headed back to the palace in determined silence. Well, that wasn't quite accurate. Clarus, head high and eyes focused, headed back in determined silence. Vera followed him, and had a lively and heated conversation with Aesling in her head. She had more questions than she could count, and the more time went on, the harder it became to just ignore them.

So Vera had just been allowed to exist, and that had been good. Well, it had been *great*, actually. She hadn't exactly been able to enjoy it, because of the Cavean, but that didn't mean things didn't suddenly feel right. But that also meant that there was now... *extra*, under her chest plate, and it was a little uncomfortable, and that discomfort was comforting in its own way, too. Her legs and hips moved a little differently from before. If she walked like she used to, it sent a weird jolt up her spine, but armour didn't exactly allow for a lot of freedom either. Speaking of which, she'd need new armour, too. Ideally before they left, because she dreaded to know what riding a horse would be like now. Her thighs were… wider than they had been. She knew in her heart of hearts that there would be chafing.

She also couldn't stop from occasionally touching her wrists and the inside of her arms. Her skin was so *soft* now. She couldn't, of course, look at her own face up close, but she could tell it was different. The damage done by adolescence had been reversed, and at times, that overwhelming feeling of rightness made her balance precariously between laughing and crying hysterically. It was almost too much, but there was no *time* for that yet.

"*And speaking of which,*" she said to Aesling, "*if we find them, will my old comrades recognise me? How can I prove to them that I am myself?*"

"*When* we find them, dear. Where there is hope, there is life," Aesling said, her singsong voice bouncing around Vera's skull. She'd worried that having someone else live in her head would prove to be troublesome, but it had turned out that Aesling was a very pleasant tenant. At times, it reminded her of times when mercenaries from another company had resided in Rubicus' barracks. There was a sense of respect for shared resources. Ash took up no more space than she had to, seemingly content to exist within her grove, observing the world through Vera's eyes.

"*I don't think that's how that—*"

"*Regardless,*" Aesling interrupted her, "*I believe you know your old companions well enough to be able to convince them of your identity. You have spent most of your life, adult or otherwise, with these people. They've seen impossible things; they will be able to accept the changes within and without.*"

"But what," Vera asked as they rounded a corner, *"will I tell them if they believe my changes — and my willingness to accept them — is some form of corruption? The Cavean did something to Caerella. It could have done the same to me."*

Aesling was quiet for a moment while she considered this. *"Would the Cavean not have made you a more formidable threat, then?"*

"Not if I'm to be an infiltrator of some kind, I don't think," Vera said, thinking.

"But if you were to be an infiltrator, you would not have changed at all, would you?" Aesling said. That did make a degree of sense. *"Besides, you knew for a long time something was wrong, something that needed mending. You must've mentioned it to somebody, at the very least? Could you not use that as proof that you are who you are?"*

"Only Caerella," Vera grumbled. *"I did not know how to broach such a subject with the others. I do not think they would've understood. Caerella did not, either, but at least I did, indeed have that conversation with her. But she is..."*

"Indisposed," Aesling said diplomatically. *"I understand. Now, eyes forward, I believe our beloved prince will wish to speak with you in a moment."*

"How can you tell?" Vera asked, ignoring the weird little knot she got in her stomach when Aesling said 'our prince.' They had just reached the palace gates, the ruination all around them. It seemed community spirit had kicked in now that the danger had passed, and people had started to move the rubble and bodies.

"He squares his shoulders when he is about to say something he does not want to."

Just as predicted, Prince Clarus paused and Vera did indeed see him move his shoulders just before. He turned around to her. "Vera," he said, his eyes piercing hers. She felt Aesling giggle a bit. Well, at least Vera wasn't the only one affected by the prince.

"Yes, Prince Clarus."

"The road ahead will be long and treacherous," he said, putting his hands on her shoulders. "If needs be, I can recognise and find your old compatriots. And to Aesling, my dearest, I can only say that I love you. If I confessed my love once for each star in the sky, it would not equal a fraction of the adoration in my heart for you."

Vera nearly fainted as he said all of this looking directly at her. Sure, it wasn't at *her* specifically, but the distinction was lost on her in that exact moment. It was almost too much. Thankfully, Aesling stepped in. "I hope, my love," she said, "that you're not proposing Vera and myself *stay behind*."

"That is, it pains me to admit, exactly what I'm saying," the prince said, lowering his head. "If harm were to come to you, or one as innocent and beautiful as Vera, I would not be able to forgive myself in this or any lifetime."

"Vera," Aesling said internally, *"I'm going to kiss some sense into this fool, with your permission."* Her politeness made Vera almost accept automatically, but she hesitated for a moment. She wasn't sure how she'd handle kissing him again. The first time had been in shock, she'd barely been *aware* of the experience, but now she was ready for it, and she worried it might overwhelm her. *"If you must, you can close yourself off from outside experiences within my grove. Would that help?"*

"Yes," Vera said. Strangely, the thought of Aesling 'using' her body for this didn't bother her. Sure, it was Vera's body, her mouth, all that, but this was Aesling's too, now. *"If I asked you not to,"* she asked quietly, *"would you not?"*

"No," Aesling reassured her. *"I'll do nothing with, or to, your body without your permission, Vera. I'm here because*

you've allowed me here. My memory is long, and my gratitude quite boundless."

"Thank you," Vera said. *"Uh, you can kiss him now, if you want."*

"You're not… retreating to the grove?" Aesling asked. Vera knew she'd be blushing if she was fronting at that moment.

"Do — do you want me to?" she asked. It wasn't that she wanted to watch Aesling or anything like that, but, well, she'd never had a *proper* kiss before, and the first time didn't really count because she hadn't been ready for it and it hadn't been meant for her, and sure, this one wasn't really meant for her either, but maybe it would be good practice, and, well, it had felt pretty nice the first time and she was okay just kinda being there again this time and—

"Oh, you don't have to. I just don't wish to make you uncomfortable…"

"I'll be fine," Vera squeaked. Aesling gave her a look, which was a strange feeling when neither of you had a body inside your own head, but a look was given and a look was received nonetheless. Only a few moments had passed. Talking between them seemed to take almost no time at all. Aesling hooked one hand behind Prince Clarus' head and yanked his head forward into a kiss. Almost reflexively, his hand rested on her lower back, pulling her in close. His heart hammered against hers, his breathing slow and steady, his presence everywhere around her. Vera felt safe in a way she had never felt before. Sheltered. And, to a lesser extent, desired, even though this desire was obviously not for her. Was this what it was like, would be like every time? Was this just what kissing was like? Or was that Clarus?

"Are you remaining behind, then?" he asked. Aesling slapped him softly across the jaw, despite still being in his arms. He gave her the same look a dog might give if someone stepped on its foot.

"Of course we aren't, you beautiful fool," Aesling said. "I am coming with you, because you are far too likely to stumble into danger and adventure on your own. And if I wasn't, Vera would still wish to travel with you. Her companions, her *family* is in danger, and she will not stay behind while someone else rescues them." Aesling looked within. "*I said that correctly?*"

"*You did,*" Vera said, nodding happily. "*Perhaps you might add that I know more about the country as it's changed in the past decade, things he and you might not.*"

"*Good point!*" Aesling said, and relayed the information. "In short, my beloved, we are coming with you, and you'll not get rid of the womenfolk as easily as that." Prince Clarus blushed, and it was the most precious thing Vera had ever seen. She had to resist kissing him herself.

"I... That was not my intention in the least, Aesling, my dearest! I only wished—"

"If you'll say that you wished to keep me safe, my Clarus, I'll slap you again," she said with a little smirk. "I need no protection, my love. You know I can keep myself, and Vera, alive. No matter what. Not to mention the fact that Vera is a valued member of the company that saved your life. She is, despite her age, a weathered mercenary."

"*Um,*" Vera said, "*I'm not sure that that's—*"

"*Just roll with it,*" Aesling said. "*You want to go with him, don't you?*"

"*Well, yes, of course. Ah, I see. Carry on.*"

"*Thank you,*" Aesling said, and then continued out loud. "So please, don't patronise us, my love. We will be coming with you." The prince opened and closed his mouth a few times as if he was going to offer a rebuttal, and then snapped his mouth closed.

"Of course, dearest Aesling. I... I apologise," he said, seeming a little uncomfortable. "I know what you're saying is correct. The task ahead is so monumentous, it is hard to resist the temptation of taking it on alone."

"I know, love." Aesling said, putting a hand on his chest. "But do not. You are no island, my beautiful prince. Do not weather the storm like one."

"Very well," he said, then took her hand in his and very softly pressed his lips to it. "Then we shall ride. The Cavean has gone south, so we shall head south, too. He is fast, he goes on dead winds, but we will catch him nonetheless." He straightened his shoulders. "Are you ready to ride, my love?" Aesling nodded. "And Vera..."

Aesling stepped aside, and Vera moved forward. "Yes, Prince Clarus?"

"Thank you. I know this must all be overwhelming. If you need comfort, I'll be at hand at a moment's notice," he said. Vera noted he had not actually let go of her hand just yet. "You and my Aesling are bound together, and that means you are important to me in ways I can scarcely put to words. Should you need me for anything, say but the word and you'll have it." This time, Vera *was* fronting, and she *was* blushing so fiercely she could hear Ash losing her composure.

"I have nothing," Aesling said, laughing, *"to add to that. Best of luck, Vera."*

"Thank you," Vera said, and her voice almost failed her. What does one say to something like that?

"You seem upset," Clarus said, and then he wrapped his arms around her and pulled her against himself. It was only because her face was pressed up against his chest that Vera managed to avoid screaming.

Chapter Eleven

Southward Bound

After they'd retrieved horses from the royal stables and Clarus had found himself a sword — nobody was going to stop the two of them — Vera, Aesling and Clarus rode south. Vera let Clarus ride ahead, partially because he seemed to be a capable tracker, and partly because she wanted to adjust her armour. Aesling was a great help, since she seemed to have a greater awareness of their body, and between the two of them, they at least managed to reduce the discomfort to a minimum.

It wasn't all that difficult to follow the trail, really. While the southbound road was well trod, the inhuman demonic tracks left by the Cavean's creatures were visible even to the untrained eye. Horses didn't have claws that left deep grooves in the mud. Still, Clarus was being thorough, not wanting to waste time following the wrong trail. They probably didn't have a lot of time left, and neither did Rubicus.

Vera pulled her cloak a bit tighter. Had the temperature dropped? A chill went down her spine, making her wonder if the Cavean's influence on this world was so great it would blanket even the nation's south in frost. Was its grasp really that terrible and terrifying? She squeezed her eyes shut, imagining windswept tears freezing on her cheeks.

"Don't be dramatic," Aesling said. *"No, it isn't any colder. It's not the Cavean, it's you. No frostbitten tears on your face, Vera. Your body is just not as good as withstanding heat as it was before."* Vera blinked a few times

and reached up to her face. Yeah, sure, it was cold, but Aesling was right. The air wasn't all that much colder than it had been before, just her perception of it. *"I think I might be able to do something about it, if you like, but my reckoning is that you'll be hungrier if I do."*

"I can live with that," Vera replied with a little smile. It was strange. She'd heard women speak of being cold while, back then, she'd been fine wearing only a loose-fitting shirt, and had chalked it up to a lower tolerance. Now, being as cold as she was, she understood. In a strange way, the discomfort was validating. It made her feel like things made more sense now. On the other hand, she really didn't like shivering in a cold that made her teeth chatter.

Inside her, Aesling did whatever magic she did, and slowly, Vera felt herself warm up a bit. Her fingers got some of their feeling back, and she stopped shivering. *"Is that better?"*

"Much," she said quietly. "Thank you."

"My pleasure," Aesling said. *"I enjoy the cold as little as you do. Winter is the season of death before rebirth, and it's a natural part of the cycle of life and so on and so forth, but it's also really rotten cold, and if I could do the entire thing without it, I would."*

Vera chuckled at Aesling's little tirade, causing Clarus to turn around and raise an eyebrow as he slowed his horse down a bit. "It's nothing, Prince Clarus," Vera said with a smile. He returned it brightly. "Aesling does not like the cold."

"She never has," Clarus said. He exhaled softly, his breath a little cloud on the wind. "I personally have never minded. You aren't cold now, are you?" There was some visible concern in his eyes, even if he made *some* attempt at hiding it.

She shook her head. "I'm not. Not anymore." She smiled reassuringly. "Ash saw to that." There was a pause as Vera bit her lip. "Can I be frank, Prince Clarus?"

"Always," Clarus said. "It's my deepest wish that you always speak your mind." Inside her head, Aesling smirked at Clarus' always ridiculous, always delightful superlatives.

"Initially, I was worried about sharing a body with another being," Vera said. Aesling perked up, but said nothing. Clarus just nodded. "To have my body not be my own anymore. Not entirely. But it is also not unfair to say that it never felt like mine, and that perhaps it is easier to consider sharing a house that isn't yours to begin with." Clarus looked ahead to the road, but he nodded.

"I can relate to your trepidation, at least," he said, "though I never experienced this disconnect between myself and my body. No body is perfect, of course. Milk does not agree with me, and I have a knot in my shoulder that will not go away no matter what. But it's always been mine, and I've been quite proud of it." He looked at his hand. "The thought of sharing it with another was... scary, at first. When I first met Aesling."

Inside her, Vera felt Ash flickering up a bit more, and a sensation of warmth washed over her. It must have been a happy memory, then. Aesling smiled, and Vera felt herself responding in kind. *"It was,"* Aesling said to Vera. *"You could ask him about it."*

"Where did you two meet?" Vera posited. Clarus looked at her. "She told me to ask you," she added sheepishly. Clarus grinned.

"I had been travelling. The seas, the mountains, the plains of the world. This was before the war, of course. When the Empire declared its intent, began its campaign of conquest, I hurried home as fast as I could, and I decided to take a shortcut through what had been described as a haunted forest."

Aesling chuckled. *"And haunted it was,"* she said.

"And haunted it was," Clarus said. "I stopped to rest in a glade, where I bathed in a river. An angry voice told me to cover myself, so I did, quickly, for I thought I had been alone and I did not wish to cause impropriety." Vera felt herself blushing at the thought of Clarus stripping down to wash himself off in a forest stream.

"It was... more difficult than you imagine," Aesling said. *"He's a, uh, beautiful man."* The blush got worse. *Way* worse.

"When I was somewhat presentable, Aesling showed herself. She was beautiful beyond compare, a wisp on the wind, barely a whisper, barely visible. I was sure I had met the haunting spirit, and despite my fear, we spoke. She had not, she told me, met with a living, talking being in some time, and she told me she wished to see the world. I told her of the war, and of the Empire's advance." The Prince's face fell a bit. "I promised her I would do what was in my power to save her forest, her glade, but one man cannot do much to stop an army."

After only the shortest of exchanges with Vera, Aesling now rode next to him, and she reached over to take his hand. "You've done nothing wrong, love," Aesling said. "Had you stayed, had *I* stayed, we would have burned with it. Trees burn. Ash falls. Life begins anew, in a new place, as it always does." That seemed to bring Clarus some comfort at least, and he continued his tale.

"Thank you, my Aesling," he said. "When you... when she learned of the war, and of the Empire, she asked if she could come with. It was strange to share a body with her, but we had a space, within our souls, where we could speak, and be together. In time, we fell in love, quite deeply so."

"We did," Aesling said as she retreated to the back of Vera's mind again. *"Those were beautiful days."*

"What fascinates me," Clarus said, "is how often she seems to exist without as well as within. When we shared a body, she only asked to speak through me once, maybe twice. She said she found it uncomfortable."

"As it turns out, I too did not enjoy being in control of a masculine body. You and I have that in common, Vera," Aesling said.

"I think that's because being a woman in a man's body is difficult, Prince Clarus," Vera said. "Or even one a lot like one."

"I… Of course," Clarus said, his jaw clenching and unclenching like he was chewing on the idea. "Knowing people like yourself exist, that makes sense." He turned back to her, and his glittering smile dazzled her again. "Then I am happy for both of you, *and* myself, that Aesling, and yourself, now have a body in which you feel more at home. And it allows me to look into her eyes with my own."

"You're an incorrigible romantic, my love," Aesling said. Switching back and forth, for Vera and Aesling both, was getting easier and easier. Every time, there was a request for permission, from both ends, but it was getting faster each time, less spoken and more… simply understood.

"I know," Clarus said. "And I'll stop the day you ask me to."

"Not until the last day of the last year in all of time," Aesling said with a candid smile, and then slipped back. Vera took the reins and looked ahead. She wanted to ask more, but there was movement ahead. She pointed. Clarus followed her gaze.

"I see it," he said. "Frantic, too. A fight, I believe!" Without saying another word, he whipped the reins and with a shout, his horse shot forward. It took Vera a moment to do the same; his charge had been so sudden and abrupt, she hadn't had the time to react.

It didn't take her too long to catch up to him, though. She was quite a bit lighter than he was, she realised, and it was actually harder to control the horse in full gallop than she was used to. Her weight shifted differently.

As the skirmish came into view, Vera's heart began to thunder in her throat. She recognised the hulking figures as Demons immediately. Four of them, circling a lone figure, struggling to stand. A figure in rust-coloured armour. This, Vera realised, must have been where Rubicus had caught up with the Cavean. This was where he was going to die, unless someone did something.

Something stupid, possibly, she realised, as she saw Prince Clarus throw himself off his horse with abandon at the demon closest to them, having turned itself around to face the new attackers. Vera had seen people fight like that. Almost always the sons of nobles, in small border skirmishes between duchies and baronies. They never lived long, usually hitting their head on a rock on the way down.

"He's not just a noble's son," Aesling said. *"He's Clarus."*

Unsheathing his sword mid-jump, Clarus came down blade-first, and it pierced the creature's mask of rage and hatred, splitting it in two. The creature screamed and raged, swinging its claws wildly at Clarus who twisted and pulled his blade back and, in the same movement, deflected the raised claws of the dying creature.

"There," he said, panting slightly at Rubicus. "Three against three. I'd take those odds, wouldn't you?"

Rubicus had obviously turned to see who had joined the fray, but the look in his eyes was hazy. It was clear he was not doing well. Despite that, his face lit up in a grin. "I may consider it, your highness," he said. "If your handmaiden can fight, we may escape with our lives just yet."

It took Vera a moment to realise that he'd meant her. Well, she'd show him. He'd trained her, after all. She dismounted quickly, pulling her own short sword out of the sheath, and immediately dodged sideways as one of the remaining demons threw itself at her, infernal profanities dripping from between its jaws like toxic bile. Her reflexes had saved her, but when she was back upright on her feet, she found it impossible to move. Memories, old and new, buried their ways forward.

She was a child again, her parents dying before her. She felt their blood on her face.

She was facing an unstoppable horde of claws. She felt them pierce her heart.

She was here and now, and the creature barrelled down on her.

"Vera," Aesling said. *"Move!"*

She did. Dodging again, faster than she used to be able to, she swiped at the monster's arm with her short sword. It didn't cut through the limb entirely, but the creature's roar of rage and pain was confirmation that she'd struck true. She rolled under its retaliatory swipe and came to a stop next to Clarus and Rubicus.

"Good of you to join us," Clarus said. "Now I feel our large friend is losing some strength, so I'd like to finish this quick."

Vera blinked. There were still three demons. Even one old, fading one had been almost too much for four experienced mercenaries (well, three experienced mercenaries and Vera. She wasn't exactly battle-hardened), and now Rubicus was swaying on his feet. "Prince C—" she said, but Clarus was already gone, lunging forward with a battle cry as heroic as it was ridiculous in its zeal and conviction. "He's mad," she said.

"He is," Aesling said. *"Now, go help him before the fool kills himself."*

Vera shook her head. She couldn't believe she was about to do this. She charged.

Chapter Twelve

Reunion of Strangers

With a final wet gurgle, the last demon's head fell to the ground with a flat thud. It had been accompanied by a shout of exertion and victory from Clarus, who had delivered the death blow with a lot less pomp and flourish than he had entered the fight with. His flashing smile had been reduced somewhat, but it was still there. His normally annoyingly-perfect hair clung to his forehead, and streaks of mud and grime covered his clothes and face. But when he turned around to look at any other possible attackers and found none, he was once again that vision of royal calm Vera had grown to... admire. From a distance.

"*I know,*" Aesling said, "*I think he's beautiful too.*"

Vera grew red in the face, which would have been more of a problem if she hadn't already been out of breath and flushed. She mumbled something incomprehensible even to herself, and then straightened up when they found no more foes around them. The fight itself had been over in just a few minutes. Fights with demons had to be, apparently. Either you killed them quickly or they killed you quicker. She turned to look at Rubicus, who had slumped down to one knee. She'd never seen the old warrior brought so low, and she hurried over.

"Hold still. We need to... stifle the bleeding," she said, trying to remember the first aid they'd taught her. She hadn't had a lot of chances — or need — to do so. Not only did Rubicus not get seriously wounded very often, but if and when he or someone else in their band had, it had always been Flaveo who had dressed their wounds.

"Stem," Rubicus grunted. "You 'stem' the bleeding." He sat down with a grunt, holding his armour. He looked like he'd fall apart if he let go for even a second. Blood had seeped into his clothes from his midriff down.

Clarus kneeled down next to him, helping the large man lie down in the grass. "I'm surprised you are still breathing, friend. A lesser man would have died on the road ten miles back, let alone fought the Cavean's fiends with such vigour." He looked around at the bodies. They were already starting to dissolve. They'd become silhouettes in the dirt where they'd fallen, and nothing would grow there. Not for a long time.

"You do me a kindness, Prince Clarus," Rubicus said quietly. Now that the danger had passed, he seemed to be a lot less lively. Colour had drained from his face, and he looked tired, more than anything. "I am afraid that I will not be staying by your side for much longer to thank you for my rescue," he grunted, "I think I'm not long for this world."

"Hey, no," Vera said as she began to unclasp his breastplate, "you aren't dead yet, Rubicus. We just need to make sure—"

"Prince Clarus, please tell your handmaiden to… give it a rest," Rubicus said. It was obvious he was already too weak to really protest. "I'd like to die with dignity and my armour on. I'll not be found naked by the side of the road if it's all the same to you."

"You're not going to die, you big oaf," Vera mumbled, more to herself than anything. Rubicus wasn't going to die because she needed him not to. He had to help her get Flaveo and Caerella back, and to stop the Cavean, and then he had to lead them, because that's what Rubicus *did*. Rubicus didn't die, and certainly not in a ditch by the side of the road. She was grateful Clarus didn't try to stop her, at least.

"I may be able to help," Aesling said softly. Immediately, Vera's own wounds came to mind. She'd been thoroughly perforated when Aesling had saved her. Even if it meant letting go of Aesling, she was willing to do what she had to give Rubicus a chance to survive. Aesling, hearing her thoughts, protested slightly. *"Oh, I'm not leaving you behind any time soon, child,"* she said. *"I may be able to heal him through you. And I would rather not be stuck in the body of a man again if I can help it."*

"I can relate," Vera said. *"What do I do?"*

"Who is she talking to?" Rubicus mumbled, but Vera shut him out as Aesling instructed her to put her hands on the wounded flesh. Now that the armour was out of the way, she was able to reach and put her hands on his skin. It was slick with sweat and blood, and she tried desperately not to think too strongly about the sensation. If he lived through this, Rubicus would have a scar that would last him a lifetime.

"Now," Aesling said, *"hold still, and allow my magic to flow through you. It'll hurt him somewhat, so maybe get Clarus to hold him down while I do it."* Vera nodded, trying to remember what else Flaveo had taught her. If it had really been that painful…

"Prince Clarus?" she asked. The Prince looked up at her. "Might you… uh… take off your belt?" He looked at her nonplussed for a moment. She realised how that'd sounded. "I need him to bite down on something.

"Oh! Yes, of course, very well." He quickly did as was asked, and then sat by Rubicus' head to hold him down as

Vera instructed. "I see what you're about to do, Ash," he said. "You'll have to hurry; the man isn't long for this world."

"She's doing what she can," Vera said. She felt Aesling help her steady her breathing, and then the strange sensation of magic running through her was suddenly there. It reminded her of a day, a year ago, when she'd taken a wrong step onto a thin patch of ice and had fallen through up to her shoulders. The shock had knocked the wind out of her, and it had taken her a few seconds to even realise what had happened. This was like that, but in reverse. Warmth blew through her, knocking the air out of her as she became more aware of her body, and her limbs, than she ever used to.

And it all seemed to be flowing, like rivers, from her hands into Rubicus, who inhaled sharply. Vera couldn't tell exactly what was happening, but she had a very distinct feeling. The longer it went on, the more strongly Rubicus began to struggle, his breathing more laborious and agitated by the second. He'd been seconds away from drifting off before, but now he stirred like a man in a fever dream, and Clarus seemed to be having trouble keeping him down. It was all Vera could do to keep her hands in place.

Finally, with a sudden growl, Rubicus shoved them both away and practically jumped up to his feet, backing away from both of them. He blinked several times, as if to clear his eyes. "What — what are you *doing* to me, woman?" he half-grunted, half-shouted. Vera thought for a moment he'd fall to his knees again, but he managed to keep his balance. He reached up to touch the wound in his torso and then frowned, looking down. "What..." he mumbled, and then looked back up. "What kind of... sorcery is this? What kind of witch are you? This isn't possible. Who are you? Aesling, was it? What did you do to me?"

"I'm not Aesling," Vera said quietly, "I'm Vera."

"This'll take some explaining," Aesling said. *"Good luck, child."* Vera grimaced.

"I've only done what I could to heal your wounds, Rubicus. I've been told... As I understand it, you should still try not to move too much. You are still wounded, even if not as much as before. As for who I am..." She tried to smile, hoping there was enough of her still in there for him to recognise her. "I'm surprised that you didn't recognise my bladework, even if my appearance has changed." She hoped that mention of battle would help jog his memory. It was a language he understood well, at least. Rubicus scanned her face carefully.

"I would have remembered fighting alongside a waif like yourself, girl. Who is she, Prince Clarus?" He turned to the other man. "I am sorry, Your Highness, but if this child knows forbidden magic, I feel that, if a man such as yourself—"

"—listens to her, then you should too?" Clarus cut him off with a smile. "She means you no harm, mercenary. Heed her words, if only at my request." With that, Clarus looked at Vera and gave her an encouraging nod.

Vera stepped closer to Rubicus, who immediately regarded with suspicion again. "Rubicus, it's me," she said. "I travelled with you since I was yea high. Only days ago, we went up the mountain to collect the Prince. You, Flaveo and Caerella saved my hide when we went up against the shade still in the tower."

Rubicus frowned, which was to say that the frown that had already creased his forehead brought his eyebrows even closer together. "The only one that was with us was Cinero, and you do not look like Cinero to me."

"Well, you aren't wrong," Vera said, "but not in the way you think." She tried to very quickly explain that, when the king's mages had tried to rouse the Prince with a potion, it had stirred not only the Cavean, sealed inside the Prince's body, but another spirit as well, who had given Vera that unspoken thing she'd always longed for. It took a moment, because it was such a strange series of impossible events, and even she had trouble believing what she was saying. "And it is that spirit, living inside me, that allowed me to heal you," she concluded.

"I've heard more plausible lies in my lifetime," Rubicus growled. "Ancient healing spirits are one thing, but to have those spirits turn a friend, a *deceased* friend, into a woman who can heal one with but a touch, that stretches the limits of belief. Prince, if you trust this woman, I will of course trust your judgement. But that trust does not extend to her madness, Your Highness."

Vera opened and closed her mouth a few times, trying to think of ways to prove that she really was who she said she was. "You taught me how to hold a sword, Rubicus," she said quickly. "You taught me where the weakest points of a man's armour are, and you taught me how to maintain the weapons you had me carry up and down the countryside behind you."

Rubicus looked her in the eyes for a few seconds. "It's all just words, girl," he said eventually. "If you really are Cinero, you'd know actions mean more to me." Vera glared back at him.

"Fine," she said. "But call me Vera." Rubicus shrugged, and then went to pick up his dented, punctured armour.

"Very well, Vera." He turned to face the road. "Prince Clarus. As I gave chase to the Cavean, I saw they took my companion Flaveo off westward to a nearby hamlet. Not only is he a trusted friend, he is also an accomplished magecraft. While I wish to give chase to the Cavean as much as you must, I would ask that we help release my friend." He paused, apparently realising who he was talking to, and dropped to one knee with a barely audible grunt. "If it would please Your Highness, more people may serve you better than one old warrior and a young girl." Vera tried not to be insulted, and focused instead on the fact that Flaveo was not only alive but nearby.

Clarus looked at her for confirmation, and she gave a quick and enthusiastic nod. "Very well, Rubicus. We'll go and collect your comrade, though we must hurry. We can not let the Cavean get too far ahead." Rubicus nodded and stood up with determination, then went to go fetch the horse that had run off a little bit. Vera saw him touch his chest where the wound had been. Sure, he didn't trust her, or even recognise her for that matter. But he was alive, and that's all that mattered for now.

Her train of thought was interrupted when she felt Clarus' hand on her shoulder and she almost screamed. She turned to face him. "Are you okay?" he asked. "That mustn't've been easy."

"I'm fine," she said softly. "I'll have time to prove myself to him, to prove who I am. And that's thanks to you. If you hadn't—"

"You're the one who saved his life," Clarus said with a reassuring smile.

Vera shook her head. "That was all Aesling," she said. "I didn't... really do anything."

"It was your decision to save him, Vera. You," Ash denied.

"Oh," she said, and smiled a little bit. "Thank you."

"You are very welcome, lovely Vera. Now!" he turned around, "let us go save your other comrades!"

Chapter Thirteen

Strategy And Tactics

"Did you serve in the war, Master Rubicus?"

It was clear to Vera that Rubicus was more than a little uncomfortable. Not that she was any more at ease around Clarus — if for reasons that made Aesling smirk internally at her. He seemed not to know how to treat the Prince, who seemed intent on friendly, casual conversation. Rubicus didn't know where to put himself.

"Aye, Your Highness," he said. "Second Draft Company." He looked over at the Prince. Clarus was wearing his 'calmly paying attention'-smile, which was one of several smiles Vera had categorised in her head. Clarus had a lot of smiles, and they were all maddening in different ways. This one was hard to deal with because it made you feel like you ought to keep talking even when you thought you were done.

"*It'll be what makes him a good King,*" Aesling pondered. "*People have a tendency to say just a little too much around him.*" It was true. Clarus had a disarming smile. The thing about disarming smiles, of course, is that they leave you distinctly vulnerable.

"I was a mercenary 'forehand," Rubicus continued. "Your Highness' father saw fit to pay my Company fair wages in the draft." Clarus nodded. "Had the honour of riding with t—" He hesitated for a moment. "—with the King.

But our Company never saw much battle. Ours were skirmishes in burned-out villages." Vera remembered. Rubicus' Company had been the one to fish her out of her own village, after all.

"Important work, nonetheless," Clarus said. "I have to wonder if you and I ever stood on the same field, facing Caligon's hordes." He shrugged. "Not that it matters. The old fiend is dead, and soon, the Cavean will be as well."

"As you say, Your Highness." Rubicus said, bowing his head.

"Oh, don't say that," Clarus said with a hearty little chuckle. "That's what people say when they think I'm wrong but they're scared to say something because of my lineage." Rubicus looked distinctly guilty, but completely unsure of what to actually say in response. "Master Rubicus, as long as we travel the road together, I urge you to think of me as Clarus. I may be the only person who has successfully stopped the Cavean once before, and treating me like some frail thing to be tiptoed around will only make that feat harder to achieve a second time. Are we understanding one another?"

Rubicus looked at him for a few seconds. The only thing breaking the silence was the whispering of the wind and the gentle thudding of hooves on the road. Then he seemed to come to a decision and his face split into a wide grin. His hand landed on Clarus' back with the sound of a shovel hitting sheet metal, nearly throwing the Prince out of the saddle. "Aye then, Clarus. If you say so."

For a brief moment, Clarus had been shaken out of his usually unflappable demeanour, his eyes watering a little bit, and then he let out a coughing laugh. "E-exactly, Master Rubicus. If we're to fight side by side, all of us need to see each other as equals."

For the first time in their conversation, Rubicus shot a glance at Vera, who had been trailing slightly behind them the entire time. "Aye," Rubicus said darkly. "We ought to." He jutted his jaw forward and looked back at the road. "We'll be coming up on the town Flaveo's liable to be held in, Y— Clarus." He nodded ahead. The terrain was slightly hilly, and the winter snow had turned the surrounding fields into a murky painting of fog and wet dreck. The hamlet sat on the top of a slight slope, barely more than a few dozen houses and an old windmill. "Thoughts?"

"I'm afraid I'm not much of a tactical mind, Master Rubicus." He looked behind him at Vera with an expectant smile. Another one of his, perfect for getting people to speak. She knew what he was doing, of course, and she was grateful for it. He was offering her a way to prove herself to be who she said she was to her old mentor.

"I reckon," Vera said, pointing ahead, "someone'll be stationed at the windmill. They'll see us coming." She looked at Rubicus. "And I think they'll have been expecting us, so they won't be keeping Flaveo there."

"Hrm," Rubicus said, chewing his tongue in silence. She knew if he'd disagreed, he'd have interrupted her. Instead, it was more likely he was annoyed at the fact that he didn't. Vera decided to push on.

"But they'll want their lookout to be within range of their captive, so likely to be close to the centre of town." Vera pointed at the tallest building, close to the top of the hill, next to the windmill. "The Prefect's house," she said.

"How'd you know all that?" Rubicus growled.

"That's what I'd do," Vera said with a shrug. "Like you taught me."

"Hrm," Rubicus grumped again, but he didn't contradict her any further.

"I think young Vera is likely right," Clarus said. "So what we need next is a plan of attack." His hand rested on the hilt of his sword. "Rubicus, you've seen what took him to the village, what can we expect?"

Now that practical matters were at the fore again, it was clearly easier for Rubicus to focus on the task at hand, instead of on Vera. He nodded. "I saw at least two of the Demons that-a-way," he said, "but I've heard tales of what the Cavean's forces can do. The creatures they'll bring forth." Vera shivered. She'd heard those tales too, and if she strained — which she very deliberately didn't do — she could remember some of them more vividly as well. "And I dread to think why they'd take Flaveo."

"He's a magecraft, correct?" Clarus asked. Rubicus nodded.

"Among other things," he said. "Flaveo's a man of... many talents." That was an understatement. All through Vera's upbringing, there had been many rumours about Flaveo's life before he'd joined Rubicus' company, and Flaveo had done nothing to stop the speculation and he had, in fact, happily fanned the flames. Sometimes he had been a young orphan, raised in a circus. Other times, he'd been a nobleman's son, escaping after a tryst with the heir of a rival house. Then there were the rumours he'd actually been raised as an assassin in a faraway land. Flaveo only ever giggled and tapped his nose.

"He'll be alive for a while longer, then," Clarus said with a certain nod. "The Cavean's magic is powerful, but it has its limits." They slowed their horses down as the village got closer. There wasn't a soul in sight. Not that Vera had expected any, but it was nonetheless unsettling. There were no bodies. She hoped that meant the townsfolk had managed to run away. "It can create its demons, but they're monstrous, brutish creatures. In order for it to create its shadowy lieutenants, it requires a magecraft like your friend. Flaveo will be alive as long as he is useful to them."

"That's something, at least," Vera said. "Though... does that mean we'll be seeing one of those lieutenants?" She felt Aesling shiver inside her.

"Hope for the best," Clarus said, "but prepare for the worst." With that, he got off his horse. They'd reached the first of the houses, and the three of them hitched their horses. Against something like the Demons, they didn't want to be on horseback. It was too difficult of a position to defend themselves against the Demons' savagery.

"The Cavean's sorcerers," Ash said quietly, *"are malice incarnate. I hope we don't see them, Vera. The Cavean is a void in the world. It is a horror, to be sure. But its lieutenants are the parasites that fester in the wound their master leaves behind."* Vera shivered at that description. She imagined in her head something like the demons, but eyes glowing with malicious glee, tearing her apart in her sleep. *"I will protect you best I can, Vera,"* Aesling added, sensing her growing unease, *"but I must admit... I'm afraid."*

"Well," Vera whispered to herself, "let's save Flaveo and get out of this town as fast as we can, then."

"Aye to that," Clarus said as he stood next to her, putting his hand on her shoulder. Then, more quietly, "Are you all right?"

"Yes," Vera said, and it was true. His presence next to her, the comforting weight of his hand on her shoulder really was a relief. "I am. Do you see anything yet, Prince Clarus?" He looked around and shook his head.

"I've only ever fought the Cavean's sorcerers once before," he said, raising his voice slightly so Rubicus could hear them. The thickening fog was muffling their voices slightly, and they all made sure to stay close together so as not to lose sight of each other. "In direct combat, they're not all that formidable. Their bodies burn themselves up with magic. It takes little to cause them to dissolve themselves."

"I sense," Rubicus said, "that you're leaving out a very critical 'but' there, Clarus." The two men shared a slightly performative grin, as if trying to reassure, if not each other, then at least themselves.

"I am," Clarus said. "The Cavean can't create, only corrupt. With magecraft at its disposal..." Vera couldn't tell if the shiver running down her spine was Aesling's or her own. "Its sorcerers drain the life from around them, releasing it when they see fit."

"Like we do magic," Rubicus said, understanding. "That's... worrying."

"Aye. And it doesn't build up in them like it might with us, so we can not just wait them out." The hand that usually rested on the hilt of his sword now gripped it tightly. "When we see them, we must move and act quickly, or we'll be dead afore we hit the ground."

"Let us move and act quickly, then," Rubicus said, and he turned to look down the street. The hamlet was quite small, but a little denser than Vera had originally given it credit for. From a distance, it had seemed to be a crossroads-town, buildings on either side of the two streets that met atop the hill, but it had clearly grown since its humble beginnings. There were a few smaller side-streets, and more than enough shadows for something to hide in. Her imagination had a grand time of summoning up images of red-eyed monstrosities, grinning unnaturally in the dark, and it took sincere effort to look for real threats, rather than to lose herself in the imagined ones.

"Up there," Rubicus nodded. He slowly drew his sword as he advanced, keeping a wall close to his left flank. The Prefect's house loomed out of the mist, followed closely by the stairs leading up to the town's one windmill. Even through the thick fog, Vera heard it creaking softly. She squinted, trying to see anything up ahead. She thought she saw movement, but it could have just as easily been the coiling mists. She drew her own sword, and briefly caught a glint of herself in the blade.

She hadn't had a lot of time to really reflect on the changes to herself. She was... not all that unrecognisable, all told. She saw a lot of herself in this person. Sure, it was undeniably a woman looking back at her, but then again... it always had been. Now she was just more slender. The biggest difference was how vibrant and green her eyes were.

Although... it seemed they were losing their colour. She looked ahead at Rubicus tunic, the deep red of its fabric slowly draining of life.

Get down! Aesling said. There was no time to think, only to act. She put her boot against the small of Rubicus' back, and shoved as hard as she could, pushing herself back in the process. Just a second later, a jet of inky blackness exploded where they'd stood only a moment earlier, crashing a hole through the wall house in horrifying silence. A second later, sound returned to the world, and all Vera could hear was malevolent cackling.

Chapter Fourteen

Teeth In The Mist

It took Vera a few seconds to get her bearings. She couldn't tell if the ringing in her head was because of the blast of energy that had just barely missed her a second ago, or if it was her blood rushing in her ears. Rubicus had pushed himself upwards and forwards, going from prone to sprint with surprising deftness, considering his age and size. Vera had no idea what it was he was charging at, considering the fog still obscured everything around them, and she had the feeling he probably didn't either. After a second, it was almost impossible to see him anymore.

Behind her, she heard the Prince shouting, and the sound of his blade hitting… something. She scrambled for her sword, and just barely made out the glint in the thick mist. She grabbed the handle and pushed herself to her feet, and turned around. Clarus was gone too. Looking left and right, she heard the spiteful giggle ringing through the air again, and just barely caught a glint of Prince Clarus running down a path between two buildings.

Not wanting to do *nothing,* she broke into a sprint after him, her heart hammering in her chest. The attack had been so sudden. She'd been in fights before, of course, but usually a fight breaking out involved seeing the other party, everyone drawing swords, and then charging. This ambush was something else. Her pulse thudded loudly in her ears, and she could feel it in her fingers as she gripped the sword tightly.

At the end of the alley, she saw the Prince's figure round the corner without slowing down, and a creeping suspicion made itself real in her head. Aesling was thinking it too. She could tell. As she got to the end of the road, she skidded to a halt in the cold mud. Clarus was nowhere to be seen.

"That wasn't Clarus," Aesling said. *"One of their sorceries."*

"Aye," Vera said, clutching her sword more tightly, and quickly scanned her surroundings. *"They wanted to separate us."* And they'd succeeded, though she didn't say that part out loud. The question now, of course, was what they'd do now that they'd achieved that goal. *"Do you think there will be Demons?"* she asked, just as she heard a rustling from just ahead of her. Something moved in the mist.

"You're about to find out, I think. I'll do what I can to help," Aesling said. Just as Vera was about to ask her what she meant, something changed. Drastically. All of sudden, the world was pulled into extremely sharp focus. She felt she could see everything much more clearly, hear everything slightly more loudly. Her sword's hilt suddenly felt coarser than ever, every crack in the leather scraping against her skin.

And the thing in the mist, skittering towards her, was a lot easier to make out. It was the size of a rat, or a small cat, and it was moving towards her quickly. At Aesling's urging, she didn't lower her guard. *"The Cavean's devilries?"* she asked. *"Or another foul sorcery?"*

"I don't believe it matters," Aesling said as the thing came out of the fog. It had... too many legs, and skittered left and right, like a centipede. Instead of a head, however,

it seemed to just have several concentric rings of teeth with what she assumed to be a mouth in the middle. Its long, spindly legs were moving it forward and toward her with unsettling speed, until it was some six feet away, where it stopped. Vera readied her sword.

The thing pushed itself up on several of its hind legs, and hissed, a spine-chilling screeching sound that reminded her of a time a pebble had been stuck under the door. In that moment, where she shivered and dropped her guard for only a fraction of a second, it launched itself at her face.

Vera felt a nudge in her back, not from anyone else but from Aesling, and she swung her sword up to meet the creature just in time to catch it only inches from her face, where she bisected it cleanly. She was splattered in a black liquid she was keeping her mouth closed to keep from tasting. The last thing she wanted was that on her tongue.

"Thank you," she mumbled as she wiped her face. The thing curled up into a ball, like a coiled rope, and Vera looked around again to see if there were more coming.

"Don't mention it. You should move. I'm sure there's more where that came from," Aesling urged. Vera nodded and began running again. She'd been turned around in the brief fight, and all the buildings here looked identical in the fog. Maybe that was another Sorcerer's trick. Aesling seemed to be confused. *"Where are you going, Vera? I don't hear fighting, and you don't know where you are."*

"I don't have to know," Vera said. She tilted her head upwards so Aesling could see it too. There, sticking out in the fog, barely visible but nonetheless casting a shadow over the town, was the windmill. *"If I get there, I can find Flaveo."* Her boots thudded on the wet ground as she made her way through the alleys, keeping one eye on the windmill so as not to get lost.

It didn't take long for more of the skittering creatures to start approaching her through the fog. She briefly considered stopping to try and hold them off, but she didn't know how many of them there were, and the last thing she wanted was to get overwhelmed. Instead, she tried to keep moving while straining her ears for signs of one of the others. Easier said than done, of course, when noise bounced off the walls of the town, not to mention the fog itself, and while she absolutely did hear the sounds of fighting, she had no idea which direction it was coming from. Behind here, more and more legs joined the chorus of pursuers.

"I have to hope the others had the same idea," she mumbled to herself as she turned a corner. If she had it right, she was only a street or two away from the landmark she'd been aiming for. All she could do was hope, she figured, slowing down for just a second to catch her bearings. Just then, one of the creatures landed in front of her with a wet splat. It seemed the thing had thrown itself down at her from a rooftop. If she hadn't paused, it would have landed on her head, something she didn't want to think about. Quickly she slashed at it with her sword before the thing could get its bearings, beheading it in a swift strike.

"Can you behead something that's essentially a mouth with legs?" Aesling mused. *"Behind you!"* Following Aesling's instincts, Vera spun around, her sword at the ready, and deflected another attack that had launched itself at her from behind. Before she could finish it off, another jumped at her. She caught it, with the brace of her forearm, but instead of bouncing off it seemed to clamp onto her arm with its mouth and clawed legs.

"Get off get off get off getoffgetoff*getoff GET OFF!"* Vera shouted as she broke into a sprint again, hitting the thing with the pommel of her sword. While the idea of the thing being attached to her was incredibly upsetting, it was better than several more. She could already hear the shapes behind her in the fog. Ahead of her, she saw the main road, and she heard the sound of fighting.

Prince Clarus came into view, his face a mask of concentration. Not particularly worried, he seemed to be focused on advancing carefully. There were bodies of the creatures all around him. Not one seemed able to touch him, though, as his blade wove through the air like a silver thread.

"Clarus!" she shouted, and immediately clamped her mouth shut when she grasped the impropriety of just shouting his name like that. Nonetheless, it caught his attention, and he swung the sword at her before he had even turned around to look.

For a second, Vera was worried she was going to be beheaded by the Prince. With the sickeningly slick sound of metal striking flesh, the creature on her arm was cut away, without the blade even coming close to hitting her. Where the creature had been latched to her arm, a circular hole had been chewed almost all the way through her bracer.

"Beautiful Vera!" Prince Clarus said with a roguish grin. "So good to see you! I was worried you'd lost yourself in these accursed mists, but it seems you've held your own, eh?" He talked casually as he cut two more of the creatures in half in mid-air, and the two of them moved forward to the windmill.

"Did — did you see the sorcerers?" Vera asked. She deflected one of the creatures and gave it the *coup de grâce* while it squirmed on the ground.

"I can't say I have," the Prince said. "After their initial attack, it seems they've sicced their pests on us. Not that it will do them any good. I can do this all day!" He poked one out of the air with deft precision, and turned to look at her with a smile that could only be described as dashing.

"I love this fool so much," Aesling sighed. Vera couldn't blame her. People weren't supposed to be… well, like *this.* Not in real life! *"And yet,"* Aesling said.

"And yet…" Vera agreed.

"Hmm?" Clarus asked. Vera quickly mumbled a denial of ever having made a noise, before the conversation was — luckily — quickly interrupted by more of the creatures.

"I think they're being directed," Vera said. She nodded at the windmill. "If they're conjured up by those sorcerers, that would be the best place to see everything from."

"Aye," Clarus said. "We should head up there, then!"

"Well…" Vera hated the idea of splitting up, but they couldn't afford aimlessly fighting through the mists indefinitely. "I think I can see the house where Flaveo most likely is. If you go up to the windmill, that will likely give me the time I need to get into the house and rescue our friend. And another hand in the fight can only be a good thing."

"Good thinking!" Clarus said. He started to turn away, then paused, and reached out to her with his free hand. Carefully he cupped her face and looked into her eyes with the kind of intensity she was sure was burning a hole through the back of her head. "Be careful, Vera, Aesling. I can not stand the thought of losing you." With that, he was gone, slicing creatures away left and right.

"Bwh," Vera said. For a horrifying second, she'd thought he was going to kiss her.

"Girl… I know."

"Fztl," Vera said as she shook her head and tried to dredge up her brain again from where it had just been unceremoniously flung into a gorge of fuzzy feelings. Thankfully, her legs moved before she did, and the creatures seemed to be focusing on Clarus.

The Prefect's house was the largest house in town, easily three floors and an attic, and it had also been the most well kept, until something had torn the door off its hinges. Vera could think of what that had been. She slowed down as she approached the door. Anything could be inside. There were shuffling sounds coming from the entrance hall, but no voices or anything of the like. Sticking her head around the corner, Vera tried to get an idea of what she was up against.

"Get out of here, girl!" Flaveo shouted. He was seated at a table, tied to a chair, and all of his gear had been strewn onto the table. Behind him stood a… thing. Tall, thin, four long arms with thin, almost sticklike fingers. Its face was featureless, with the exception of a mouth, although there was the *idea* of eyes and a nose. Its maw was filled with long, thin teeth, all bared in a horrifying rictus grin.

The creature looked at her, and extended a long, bony finger. That's when she noticed that there were several of the creatures in the room, and with two of its hands, the sorcerer seemed to be spinning another from sheer shadow. More importantly, there also seemed to be a Demon in the room, snarling as it started to approach her.

"ASIDE!"

The bellow came from behind her, and she did as commanded almost before thinking. Just as the Demon reached the doorway, Rubicus' giant frame crashed into it and the two went flying into the room. A second later, she heard Flaveo's voice.

"Oh, hello, Ruben."

"Flaveo."

"Thought you were dead, man."

"That can still happen," Vera heard Rubicus say as she hurried into the room. The older mercenary had made short work of the Demon, taking it by surprise, but was now finding himself surrounded by the smaller creatures, and having trouble turning fast enough to throw them off. Vera sliced them off him before they could burrow into his flesh. She'd seen what one of them had done to her reinforced braces.

The sorcerer seemed to be observing them with what appeared to be curiosity, although it was hard to tell. Its grin only seemed to grow wider as the two of them fought with its creations. But Vera knew how Rubicus fought, and she was able to complement him well. Though it was hard to dodge the attacks as they came one by one, she held her ground. When the last of them fell to the ground with another horrible screech, they turned to the sorcerer, who held out all four of its hands.

"Move!" Flaveo said, just as Vera saw colour drain from the area around them, and she knew what was coming. Throwing herself to one side, Rubicus jumped in the other direction, crashing into the table and knocking it — and Flaveo — to the ground. Behind her, with the sound of something heavy and unnatural hitting brick and wood, magic blew a hole through the wall of the building. The creature looked between her and Rubicus and extended a hand to either of them. Rubicus rolled back onto his feet, but Vera could tell he'd landed badly. She knew she could probably get out of the way a few more times, but it could aim at her a lot faster than she could get closer.

"Hey!" Rubicus shouted at the sorcerer. "Look at me!" It turned its horrible grin towards the man. "Yeah, I'm talking to you, you ugly bastard. Don't look at her." He started circling the creature, swinging his sword left and right. "That's right. Look at me. She's just a girl. I'm the one that's going to tear your head off if you look away for even a second *for the love of all that is holy Flaveo kill it already.*"

The creature having been distracted long enough for him to have pushed off his restraints and to down some of his magic, Flaveo pushed himself to his feet. "Ten," Flaveo said, and golden fire erupted from his outstretched hand, engulfing the sorcerer completely.

Chapter Fifteen

Signs

Quiet descended on the room like snow, settling between the floorboards and allowing all of them to catch their breath. Not only was everything silent for a moment, but there seemed to be no threats, either. Then, slowly and gently, Rubicus walked over to one of the chairs — one that was still intact — put it upright, and sat down.

"How are you doing, Flaveo?" he asked, as casually as if they were at a bar. He took a chair himself and set it down too. He was rubbing his fingers, probably still sore and tingling from blowing raw magic out of it.

"I," Flaveo said as he flopped down onto the chair, "have been better." He looked at the contents of his pack, now strewn about the floor, tools shattered and destroyed, phials broken. "How are you? Last I saw you, you'd been perforated pretty severely, Rubicus." His face grew dark. "You and C—"

"Hi!" Vera said, interrupting the conversation before things could get bogged down. Rubicus glared at her for a moment, but he didn't seem keen to say anything. Flaveo, however, seemed to pick up on it.

"Hello," he said thoughtfully, rubbing his chin with his thumbnail. "You'll have to excuse me. Usually I'm a slight bit more chipper when a young girl excitedly tries to introduce herself, but I have had a *very* long day, and my friend

Rubicus here looks like he's being forced to swallow a peeled lime." He crossed his arms. "Either of you care to tell me who you are and why he's so ticked off?"

"She claims," Rubicus said, "she's Cinero." Flaveo frowned and leaned forward, resting his elbows on his knees and clasping his hands together. "That she's bound to some kind of forest spirit that changed her body."

"But you don't believe her," Flaveo said, chewing his tongue.

"Magic like that don't exist, Flaveo," Rubicus said, leaning back in his chair. "You know that better than anyone. I've seen your magic and I've seen black magic. Not five minutes ago it was putting a hole through this bloody house. None of that can make someone look like..." He waved at Vera, who was getting thoroughly frustrated with being talked about like she wasn't there.

"I know better than anyone, old friend," Flaveo said, "that there's things in this world we have neither knowledge or understanding of. I've heard of spirits, roaming their mountains and forests." He waved his hand. "Most of them likely nonsense, but one or two of them *could* be true. Should be easy enough to verify." He looked at Rubicus. "You *did* verify, didn't you Rubicus?"

The old mercenary, as he always did when he got a chiding from Flaveo, deflated. Or rather, he seemed to be trying to hide inside of his armour, like a turtle in its shell. "Um."

"For the sake of grace, Rubicus," Flaveo said as he shook his head and smiled. He stood up, turned the chair around, and sat down again, resting his arms on the back of the chair. "Then, girl, prove it."

"I'm... well, I'm Ci— I'm him, but I'm not. I'm Vera," she said. "I — I've always had a rough time being myself but it's only when I met..." She stopped.

"Take a deep breath," Aesling said. *"Collect your thoughts. These are your friends, and it seems that Flaveo, at least, seems like the kind of person who'll listen."* Vera nodded, and did as Aesling bade her.

"From the beginning might be easier," she said. "When the Cavean was released, something else was, too. A forest spirit named Aesling. When... When I almost died, it was her power that brought me back. And it helped me look, like, well..." She waved at herself. "I'm happier this way. Much happier. But I'm the same person you raised." Flaveo was clearly still more than a little sceptical.

"An example," Aesling said, eager to help. *"Something only they'd know!"*

"You, Rubicus and Caerella have raised me since I was... too young. Rubicus taught me how to fight and hold a sword. Caerella taught me footwork more appropriate to my frame. You taught me how to maintain my armour and weapons," Vera said, chewing her lip. She was trying to think of more. "We went to find the Prince's body, and Rubicus was too eager with the magic and nearly melted his hand into his gauntlet!" That got an indignant scoff from Rubicus, but Flaveo seemed to smile.

"That's... not bad, girl. But I'm going to need something a little more... Something any old person wouldn't know if they just knew Ruben well enough."

Well. There was one thing. Vera felt Aesling strengthen her on the inside, trying to send her courage. "When... when you found me, Flaveo," she said, "Rubicus pulled me away from what was left of my house. But it was you... you were the one who tried to make me look away from my parents," she said, dredging up a very old, very ugly memory. "You weren't very good at it, but you tried to juggle some rocks so I'd look away as Caerella carried them away."

Flaveo blinked a few times. "Y-Yeah, that'll do it." He shot Rubicus an accusatory glance. "That wasn't so hard, was it, Ruben?" He shot Vera a smile, which she happily returned. "It really is our boy."

Her smile disappeared as quickly as it had formed. It was like she'd been punched in the stomach. "No, I'm... I mean, yes, I'm that person, but I'm Vera. I'm not a boy. I'm not a man. I'm a woman, Flaveo, I—"

"What you are," Flaveo said, "is bound to a forest spirit, probably some kind of nymph." He stood up. "I've been told those are female. So what do you think is more likely, that a benevolent nymph just happened to cross your path and 'fixed' you just when you needed it, or that some sort of parasitic spirit made you *think* that's what you wanted? She's already in your head, isn't she?"

"I — I —" Vera stammered. This wasn't how she'd imagined this conversation going. Internally, Aesling was frantically trying, it seemed, not to panic.

"Vera!" Aesling said, almost begging. *"You have to believe me! I'd never do something like that! L— Look at Clarus! If I wanted to do something like that, I would've done that to him too, right?! Vera?"*

"I believe you," Vera said ever so softly, but there was a fear that was making it hard to think, hard to form words, and Flaveo was right there, putting his hands on her shoulders.

"Look, when we get to Coalis, I'll get my tools. I've seen how these things work." He thumbed over his shoulder at where the remains of the sorcerer were still smouldering. "It's foul magic, but it's hollow. I can make something that'll pull the spirit right out of you. You'll be right as rain in no time, Cin—"

"I'll ask that you don't, Master Flaveo," Prince Clarus said as he walked into the room. He was covered in black ichor. Vera felt guilty for almost having forgotten about him, but right now she could kiss him for interrupting Flaveo. "I caught the last of what you said, my good man, and whether or not you're correct does not, right now, matter."

Flaveo's eyes almost rolled out of his head. Vera realised it was probably a bit of a shock to see a long-thought-dead Prince just walk into the room. "Prince Clarus?" he asked.

"The same," the Prince said casually. Flaveo tried to kneel, but Clarus immediately stopped him, and made the name situation clear as well, when Flaveo tried to resort to overly flowery titles.

"What do you mean, Prince Clarus," he asked, "that it doesn't matter? Our comrade—"

"—is clearly upset by the way you speak about and to her," the Prince said. "*If* what you posit is true, and I am not saying it is, then your antagonising will not help anyone."

Rubicus grunted, but didn't say anything. His brow was knit tightly together, and he'd been quiet since Vera had proven her identity to them. He seemed unsure, to say the least. Flaveo shook his head. "Look, I understand where you're coming from, Prince Clarus, but there were never any signs. If this was true, she would've said something. When all this is over, she'll thank us for—"

"Flaveo," Vera said, her lip trembling and her eyes stinging, "you taught me how to cook. You taught me how to sow. You showed me how to read the stars and how to make a good campfire." She wiped at her eyes to keep from crying more obviously. "I swear to you, on every memory that I have made with you, that if you push this, if you push me, then I will not be around to thank you, when 'this' is all over, and you'll never see me again."

Flaveo raised his hands. "Very well," he said. "As you say, Your Highness." He nodded at Prince Clarus first, and then Vera, but he seemed far from convinced. He turned away to fret over Rubicus, who was covered in small cuts and bites, and led him outside, leaving Vera to stand there. Anxiety washed over her. There should've been relief, over having found Flaveo, but instead, there was just pain and the fear that she'd lose him all over again, but in different ways. Or worse, that he'd try to hurt her while doing what he thought was helping her.

"I won't let him hurt you, Vera," Aesling said.

"He... he's not right, is he?" Vera asked the spirit.

"I would never, Vera," Aesling said. *"But I understand that your trust is shaken. Flaveo is wrong. There were signs."* Vera could feel Aesling sighing, internally. *"Of course, there is no way for me to prove that I can not change your memories."*

"Can you?"

"Hah, no. It took me months to even comprehend the way creatures like you understand the world around you. Humans, I mean. So short and unfocused. But... Look, if you are worried... then I'll subject myself to whatever trials and tests Flaveo wishes to subject you to when you are safe. Just... ask him to try and find a way other than the sorcerer's dark magic? I feel that it will hurt."

"I will," Vera said, and she felt like she was being split down the middle. On the one hand, she felt like she'd been rejected by one of her oldest friends. On the other, the person who had given her what she'd never known she'd always needed had just been questioned, and she didn't know where to place that feeling. She didn't know what, or who to trust.

"I'm sorry," Aesling said quietly as tears started to run down Vera's face and she shook in her boots. Then, two strong arms wrapped themselves around her and she was being pulled into Clarus' arms.

"I am here, Vera," Clarus whispered quietly. "I understand that this hurts. That you hoped… for better. And that's okay. It's okay for this to hurt. It's normal. I'm here." He kept repeating those last two words over and over again as she sobbed into his chest. "Listen… we'll make camp in this village tonight. Tomorrow, we ride South. We'll find the last of your friends — Caerella? — and then we'll stop the Cavean. And then… whatever it is that you want or need, if it is within my power to give, you'll have it." He took a step back and smiled at her. She couldn't help but smile back. She had to look like a wreck, her eyes probably red and puffy, and her nose clogged up. That, and she felt like she was freezing, cold mud and fog having soaked into her clothes, which was probably in no small part contributing to her shivering. And he'd just fought off demonic creatures and infernal sorcerers and he was covered in grime and blood and he looked like a painting. "Come on," he said, "let's get you warmed up." He put an arm over her shoulder and led her out of the building as he wrapped her in his cloak.

Chapter Sixteen

Roadwork Ahead

To Vera, winter mornings had always been different from others. In spring, it came softly and gently, accompanied by birdsong and the starting of the day. In summer, the crickets and grasshoppers played their instruments, the air warm before the first light really hit the ground. And in autumn, it was a reminder of summer, gently reminding her that even on cold, rainy days, the sun was right there, behind the clouds.

But winter mornings were different. The sun took a long time to show if it was there at all, hidden behind the thick fog that didn't seem to want to leave. It was morning in only the most technical sense of the word, a transition from night to not-night, and that was all there was to it.

Night had come and gone. Breakfast was mostly quiet, as winter morning breakfasts often were, except for Flaveo and Rubicus' occasional attempts to have an easy conversation between the two of them, not saying anything of consequence because, when they did, they'd be back on the mission, and Rubicus seemed to need a moment. He'd been more thoughtful than ever since the night before, and his worried expression was put aside only to chew on some dried jerky.

Vera didn't really mind. After the conversation from the night before, she wasn't highly keen on talking to either of her former comrades any more than she had to. And Prince Clarus was… keeping her mind occupied. He sat next to her and kept his cloak over her shoulder, to keep her warm. It was working, in more ways than one. She looked up at him occasionally, but when he turned to ask her if she wanted to say anything, their faces were so close together she worried he'd feel the glow coming off of her. She'd nearly fallen over herself to pull away, pretending to get herself some more coffee, while Aesling quietly giggled away in her head.

"Love, you've got it bad, don't you?" Aesling said, and Vera made sure to keep her head turned away from Clarus so he couldn't see her trying and failing to keep a straight face.

"Quiet, you," Vera said, but a stubborn little smile kept pulling at the corners of her mouth and betraying her. "Like you don't feel the same way."

"Oh, I do. But I've no misgivings about my own feelings, Vera. You, however…" Vera could feel the amused looks Aesling was giving her coming from inside her little grove. For a few seconds, Vera focused on pouring and drinking the coffee, letting the tin cup warm her hands in fog. She could feel Aesling pacing back and forth inside her own head.

"What are you?" she asked. *"I know you're a spirit of some sort, but is there a… name? And don't say A—"*

"Aesling," Aesling said with a snarky grin. *"And yes, there's been many names for beings like me. Personally, I've never been all that bothered with them. A quiet forest has only the trees and the critters that live between them. A bird has no need for words."* She seemed to ponder for a moment. *"I quite like the word your countrymen have for those like me, for what it's worth. Meliae. It rolls off the tongue quite nicely. Or Nymphs."*

"Huh." Vera emptied her cup and quickly dabbed it dry, before stowing it away, still making sure not to make too much eye contact with Clarus.

"Do he and I need to have a conversation?" Aesling asked out of nowhere. Vera nearly choked on her own tongue. She waved Prince Clarus away as he tried to help her with her coughing. At least it gave her a reason for her head to be as red as it was.

"What about?" she asked when she'd caught her breath.

"About you and him, child." When Vera didn't respond, Aesling pushed on. *"You seem quite taken with him, and he certainly has a soft spot for you. Do he and I need to talk?"*

"No," Vera mumbled as they broke up camp and saddled their houses. *"There's no need, Aesling. I promise I won't get between the two of you."* The thought of that conversation was drawing a dark cloud over her thoughts quickly. *"I won't be a pr—"*

"Girl," Aesling interrupted, *"no. That's not what this is. If you and I are going to be coexisting like... well, this, then Clarus and I will likely share some intimacy, and unless we acknowledge the fact that your feelings for him and his beautiful, stupid face are getting strong enough for me to touch, that'll only cause hurt in the future."*

"You're not wrong," Vera said. *"Does it even matter? We might not even make it through this. I... We need to focus on moving forward. On catching up with Caerella."* As she mounted her horse, she saw Rubicus helping Flaveo onto the back of his. "Speaking of which... Flaveo!"

"Hmm?" He turned to look at her, like this was his first time seeing her. She decided not to make a big deal out of it, though not rolling her eyes took some effort.

"Caerella. Which way?"

"South," Flaveo said as they began to ride. Clarus brought his own steed up on her other side and Rubicus kept his eyes straight ahead. "I didn't see much of her, though whatever that thing did to her, it seemed to have her in its grip."

"What *did* it do?" Rubicus said. "She seemed to become… something… worse."

"I've seen it before," the Prince said. "The Cavean will take the strongest warriors he comes across and make them into something other altogether. I don't know if they can be saved, but while they are this way, there is no reasoning with them."

"Why not do that to everyone?" Flaveo thought out loud. "I would think the Cavean might quite like the idea of turning an army against itself, no?"

Clarus shook his head. "Too unpredictable. Easier to kill its foes and use them to create its Demon army. Those it turns are powerful, aye, but I believe it finds them hard to control." Vera frowned and looked over at him.

"Then why do it at all?" she asked. "And why Caerella?"

"Because it makes them powerful," Prince Clarus said. "And because the Cavean, despite all of its power and loyalty to its master, is cruel in the smallest ways. Turning friend against friend is not worth the effort it takes from a tactical viewpoint, but it'll do so anyway. Because it can." They rode in silence for a bit with Clarus' words hanging over them.

"Can anything be done about it?" Rubicus asked. "I'd like to avoid losing ano— a friend if I can help it, Your Highness." Vera pretended not to see the sideways glance he'd shot her.

"I believe so," Clarus said. He looked at Vera quite pointedly. And at who was with her. "Aesling might be able to bring them back to who they are. They've not been drained of life like so many of its victims."

"Yes," Aesling said. *"It wouldn't be the first time I've kept a darkness at bay, and that was the Cavean. Something weaker than that, I might be able to drive out entirely. Might."*

"Aesling's the demon inside C— 'Vera', right?" Flaveo said. "I'm not sure we ought to trust the word of a creature that isn't even human, Prince Clarus."

"While I appreciate your candour, master Flaveo," Clarus said, "I'll not have you question the integrity of my companions in my presence. Question my sanity, if you must, but know that Aesling was with me for quite some time before you and I ever met. And she is no demon."

"If you say so, Your Highness," Flaveo said with a bow. "In that case, I hope you are right." He glared at Vera. "If she comes back, we'll know if what you say is true, 'Aesling'. I've no desire to see my friends hurt, but I'm a vengeful bastard when it comes to them."

"That's *enough*, Flaveo," Rubicus said quietly, but with a viciousness to his tone that was hard to ignore. Even Flaveo seemed stunned for a moment. "Just… focus on the task at hand. Caerella. The Cavean. Then we can worry about spirits and such."

"Right," Flaveo said. "Well, then." He seemed grouchy for a moment, and then perked up. "At the very least, it shouldn't be too long for us to catch up to her." Everyone turned to look at him. "I saw the Cavean giving her — or trying to, leastways — orders. I don't know what they were, but as it left, Caerella didn't go with it. She left an hour or so later, alone."

"What are you thinking?" Rubicus asked. "One woman can't do much damage."

"Not to a nation," Flaveo said, "but to one person? I think it knows you're following it." He nodded at Clarus. "Might be more worried about the Prince than it let on."

"Speaking of which," Clarus said, "why leave you behind?"

"To make Sorcerers," Flaveo said. "It needed a magecraft to make magic as a base. It used what I had in my pack, but I was stalling for time to avoid giving them the ammunition to make more."

"What of the people in the village?" Clarus asked. "It was empty;"

"Dead," Flaveo said, and that was, it was clear, that. The Cavean had an army of Demons at its beck and call by now. Even if it took several people to make a single Demon, they'd be numbering in the dozens by now, and those creatures were not easily beaten.

"So we'll likely see Caerella soon, then," Clarus said. "You've all known her a long time, what am I to expect? What could we do to subdue her?"

"I... hadn't considered that," Rubicus said, and he seemed to deflate in the saddle a bit. Vera couldn't blame him. Flaveo was easily underestimated in a fight, Clarus' bladework was masterful, and Rubicus was a warrior through and through. But Caerella was...

"She's a killer," Flaveo said. "If there's anything of her left in there, there'll be no fancy sword fighting, no battle as you think of it." He looked at Clarus with a grim resoluteness in his eyes. "She'll kill you where you stand if you make a single wrong move. She does not and has never cared about subduing an opponent unless it was an absolute requirement."

"I take it she won't hesitate to attack us, the way she is now?" Rubicus asked. The Prince shook his head.

"Indeed, she won't," Prince Clarus said. "Although she may stay her blade once. I've seen creatures like her hesitate, although never for long."

"Not something I'm willing to gamble on," Flaveo said. "I've never seen that woman hesitate to do anything in her life. I don't see her starting now." He chewed his tongue for a second. "That'll be the only way to subdue her. We have to fight her as if we are fighting to the death. She will be, and if we're not willing to harm her, she'll use that against us."

"I will do what I can to restore her if she does come to harm," Aesling said.

"If she's hurt, she can be healed," Vera passed on, "like I did with Rubicus." The large man rubbed his abdomen where he'd been wounded only the day before. When he looked at her, she couldn't quite read the emotion on his face. Conflicted, to be sure. "I think we need to get her on the ground. From there, I think we might be able to bring her back to her old self."

"Good," Clarus said. "*Very* good. Hah!" He smiled jovially as he brought his horse closer to Vera's. "Thank you again, sweet Vera. And Aesling. Speaking of which…" he lowered his voice. "I would like to speak with Aesling tonight, Vera, if that is alright with you." He caught the stunned expression on her face. "Oh, no, nothing like that! I truly wish to have a conversation with her. It's been some time since we've had some time to really spend time, her and I."

"I understand," Vera said, her heart hammering in her chest as she still tried to stop her brain from coming up with alternatives to what that 'conversation' might have meant. Aesling, struggling not to laugh, stepped forward with her permission.

"We'll speak tonight, love," Aesling said. As always, it was slightly strange to hear her own voice so differently, coming out of her own mouth. The Prince reached over to touch her face, but with a look to the others, seemed to change his mind. As Aesling slipped back into her grove and Vera stepped back, both of them were fighting their respective disappointment.

"And you and I will speak more, too," Aesling said, *"There's a lot w— LOOK OUT!"*

Vera saw the attack out of the corner of her eye, and moved with a speed she wouldn't have been able to before she'd met Aesling. Her hand shot out, and caught the arrow mere inches from Clarus' face. A shadow dropped down from a lone tree down the road.

"Well," he said as he drew his sword, "it seems we've found our quarry. Or she's found us."

Chapter Seventeen

Rule of Three

A second arrow whistled through the air, but Vera saw it coming this time. Time seemed to almost slow down as she saw the projectile's trajectory, and she only had to shift in her seat to let it fly past her.

"Off the horses!" Clarus said. He didn't need to explain more. While three horse-mounted fighters could easily run down an opponent on foot, not all of them would be able to dodge an arrow like Vera had. Especially if fired with that much precision. All four of them jumped off their mounts, Vera drawing her short sword.

Rubicus had been carrying his own weapons, strapping them to his saddlebags. It couldn't be comfortable, for him or Flaveo, but he was still clearly hesitant to trust her with keeping them. For a moment he was just an old man, hesitant to draw his sword, but once he'd brandished the blade and raised the buckler, all that reluctance melted away, and he was a warrior again.

Flaveo just drew a small dagger, but she knew that was far from the only blade he had on him. He'd be hanging back, since he didn't have most of his magic to rely on. "Careful," Rubicus said as he raised the small shield, moving forward.

The figure under the tree was hard to make out, barely silhouetted against the surrounding landscape, but Vera recognised it clearly as Caerella nonetheless. She saw the figure nock an arrow and let it fly. Clarus struck it out of the air with practised precision. Vera knew most people wouldn't be able to pull such a feat off, but even without Aesling's help, the Prince was more capable than his demeanour would let on.

Caerella was clearly testing them, and the next arrow would likely strike at Rubicus or Flaveo. Vera looked at the Prince, and they nodded at each other, putting themselves between Caerella and the two older men, before advancing. Their opponent would find her attacks fruitless if she continued attacking like this, and she seemed to realise it.

Tossing the bow aside with careless disregard, Caerella retrieved a pair of axes — one large battle-axe and one hand-axe — from the foot of the tree and began to approach them. Vera looked around at the others, and they spread out. There were four of them and one of her. The problem, of course, wasn't subduing her. It was doing so without her killing any of them, and the closer the figure came, the clearer it became that the thing that had been Caerella was no longer human, and had not an ounce of pity or mercy to spare. It was her eyes and the inky nothing contained within them that chilled Vera to the bone.

"You can do this," Ash said. Vera just swallowed and nodded. She hoped it would be enough. Caerella was only a few dozen feet away now, and Rubicus began to speak. Clarus interrupted him.

"Remember, we may only be able to surprise her into stumbling once," he said, "attempting to appeal to your history or her humanity now might waste a chance we'll not get twice." Clarus began to circle to the right, while Rubicus and Flaveo started to move left. If they could surround her, it might give them the opening they needed to step in and stop her before she did irreparable damage to anyone.

Caerella let them circle her, and seemed to be remarkably calm about it too. At this distance, Vera got an uncomfortably close look at her. Her limbs were longer than they ever had been, longer than was reasonable. Her whole body looked knotted and twisted, like a gnarled, rotting tree. Other than the two jet-black pools that were her eyes, the face that was once Caerella's was gone. Well… not gone. Not quite. It was like her facial features were still there, but as if merely shadows on a pale canvas, overcast and barely visible. The only real expression Vera could read was the slightest hint of a cruel smile on the creature's visage. Then, just as Rubicus and Clarus both started to move in, it attacked.

The movement was unnaturally fast, her elongated legs making her move with preternatural speed, the long battle-axe swinging at Vera's head, slicing the air in half. It looked like there was enough force behind the attack to bisect a tree.

Vera dodged it by only a hair, and jumped sideways as best she could in the direction the swing had come from, hoping it would give her a second of respite before the monstrous being could turn the weapon around. No such luck. She'd underestimated this Caerella's strength, and out of the corner of her eye, she already saw the weapon come at her again. Clarus was still several feet away, unable to help her.

Vera raised her weapon and deflected the blow as best she could, letting the weapon sail just past her face as she redirected the attack, and followed up with a strike of her own. She missed, of course — Caerella's reach was easily twice hers, between the long arms and the size of her weapon — but the point was to force her opponent to stop her sweeping assault.

It seemed to work. The creature blinked in apparent surprise, and raised both its weapons, before swinging them both at Vera in a shorter arc, following every strong strike with one from the hand-axe. It was harder to react to, but it made deflecting them easier. Vera raised her sword and just barely managed to block the first blow. The second sliced the air in front of her throat uncomfortably close.

She took a step back, and again Caerella attacked. Rubicus and Clarus were almost on her, but Vera could barely focus on them. She had to put in everything just to stay alive, but she was holding on. In fact, she noticed, it was getting easier to stand her ground. Every strike was a little easier to strike aside or dodge, and she was moving faster and faster, a rhythm building in between the blows.

Caerella seemed to notice too, the creature growling at Vera. She'd probably expected the young girl in the party to be the easiest target, which was why she'd attacked Vera to begin with, and had found an opponent who, while not a direct threat, was remarkably difficult to take out of the equation.

And then Clarus and Rubicus were on her, both striking at her simultaneously. She spun around and deflected both. Vera jumped backwards and rubbed her sword-arm. She hadn't realised how sore her muscles had become from the constant impacts, or how damaged her sword. She'd been lost in the moment.

But now Caerella was attacking the other two, and they seemed to be having a rough time. Caerella was playing them out against each other, forcing them to spend as much time avoiding each other as they were avoiding her strikes. Clarus was a gifted swordsman, and Rubicus a great warrior, but neither of them had fought side by side with the other often, especially against an opponent who could use one's bulk and the other's slighter frame against one another.

Behind them, Flaveo was pacing back and forth, still holding his dagger, glaring. Vera had seen him like this only a few times before. He preferred a more supportive role during fights, but without access to his magic, he was reduced to more crude attacks, and waiting for an opening at that.

The demoness dodged left, putting Rubicus between herself and Clarus, and then struck high, followed by a strike from one of her unnaturally long limbs, causing the large man to stumble back into Clarus. While the Prince was able to avoid hurting himself or Rubicus with the sword, the two still fell prone. Vera rushed forward, recovered enough from the assault on her person to save her friends. On the ground, they wouldn't be able to avoid Caerella's attacks for long.

It didn't turn out to be necessary. Flaveo's arm moved like a blur, and suddenly there was a dagger in Caerella's shoulder. Even Vera had barely seen the movement. The shadow creature screeched and turned to him. Flaveo's hands disappeared in his cloak, and his arm flashed once, twice, three times, and more small daggers dug themselves into Caerella's twisted flesh.

Caerella ducked low, dodging another dagger barely, and then jumped. With impossible speed, she landed in front of Flaveo. Vera sprinted as fast as she could trying to close the distance between them. Only Flaveo's clenched jaw betrayed his nervousness, stepping back calmly as he threw dagger after dagger at Caerella. She deflected some, while others struck more or less true. None of them, however, seemed to be enough to stop her. Vera was getting closer, and she dropped her sword. While Caerella was distracted by Flaveo, she might be able to take her to the ground and end this.

Caerella raised her weapons, dodging a few more attacks, and Flaveo's expression shifted to one of grim resolve. He reached for his belt, but Caerella's arm lashed out, and the hand-axe spun out of her hand towards him.

Vera caught it. There was a moment, frozen in time. She'd reacted instinctively, snatching the weapon's handle out of the air. It only dawned on her how vulnerable of a position she'd left herself in when the battle-axe dug into her shoulder.

"Vera!" Aesling screamed, at the same time as somewhere, on the other side of what felt like a waterfall, Clarus did the same. It was nice of him to care about her, at least. She was surprised at how little it hurt.

Maybe it was the shock. She looked down. The weapon's giant blade seemed to have cut down by at least a foot. That was a lot, wasn't it? Her armour had been useless against an attack like that. She looked up at Caerella, whose uncaring eyes bore into her own. Vera reached out and touched the creature on the wrist.

"Can you help her?" she asked Aesling. She was surprisingly clear-headed even as her face and limbs started to feel cold. The Nymph mumbled something to the affirmative, and she felt the magic rush through her limbs and into the creature.

Caerella seemed to realise something was wrong, as she pulled back, pulling the axe loose. *Now* it hurt. It was getting harder to breathe, like she had a bad cough. But she didn't remove her hand from Caerella's.

The demoness' other hand wrapped itself around her throat, elongated fingers squeezing the remaining air from her and lifting her off the ground. But Vera didn't stop. Magic filled them both, and Vera could tell it was working.

Whatever the Cavean had infected Caerella with, it was like a blight on the soul. And it was something Aesling's magic could wash away.

Bit by bit, like peeling parasitic moss off a healthy tree, the infection started to give way. Caerella screamed, the strange reverb in her voice slowly giving way for more human expressions of pain, more every second.

Then the whites of her eyes defined themselves, and the last thing Vera saw before she was dropped to the ground was recognition. Caerella seemed to come to her senses and threw herself next to Vera, pressing her hands on the open wound without a word.

"I'm doing what I can!" Aesling cried. *"I'm sorry! There's so much, I—"* The spirit's voice trailed off. It was hard to stay awake, even with Aesling's comfortably warm magic filling her limbs, the wound in her chest tingling as it healed.

She looked up at Caerella, hoping to reassure her that it was okay, that it was going to be okay, now that her three friends were reunited. She looked up just in time to see Rubicus' sword pierce through the woman's ribcage with a sound like ripping cloth. Caerella frowned in confusion as she slowly toppled over and fell down. Vera tried to scream and reach out, but couldn't catch her breath in time to do so.

Everything went black.

Chapter Eighteen

Roadside Manners

"Vera?"

"Hmm?"

"Oh thank the stars, you're alive."

"Thanks to you, I should think." Vera looked up. Her voice, and Aesling's, had sounded like she was underwater. She was in the grove, seated against a tree. Her eyes were heavy, like she'd just woken up from a nap. It was still a bit hard to focus, and her vision swam. "Aesling?"

"Here," the Melia said as she stepped from behind a tree holding a handful of nuts and berries. She offered some to Vera. "I was worried, Vera."

"I'm sorry," Vera said. "I just… had to. I couldn't let Flaveo get hurt."

Aesling sat down next to her. "Have a berry," she said, then sighed. "Don't put yourself in harm's way like that, Vera. I can heal you, but there are limits to what even I can do." They both sat in silence for a moment, chewing. "Just be more careful. Please?"

"I'll try," Vera said. "But even with how they've been treating me these past few days, they're still family. They took me in. Raised me. Taught me everything, you know? If I hadn't caught that, it would've split Flaveo's skull, and Caerella would have never forgiven herself."

"I know," Aesling said. "I *am* sorry. Truly." She looked up at the trees, blooming gently, all kinds of flowers budding between the bright greens, then gently put an arm around Vera's shoulder. It was a strange gesture, and not one Vera knew how to respond to.

She'd never been on the receiving end of much physical affection. Both Flaveo and Rubicus had been standoffish, expressions of fondness being relegated to words and punctuated only by the occasional slap on the back or nudge on the shoulder. Caerella's touches had only ever been very distant, a tap on the wrist or a nudge of an ankle when teaching her how to fight.

There had been the occasional girl who had wanted to get in close, some days. Back at a barracks or town festival, they'd sidled up next to her. Vera had never known how to respond. What she'd taken for warmth had been a request for more that she had not been able to reciprocate.

This was none of those things. This was only what it was. A hand on her shoulder. A reminder that she wasn't alone. That she was safe here. The presence of someone closer to her than any other person had the capacity to be. She leaned into it gently as they both relaxed back against the tree. Aesling wasn't particularly large, but she was taller than Vera, and that offered a sense of comfort and safety she wasn't familiar with. It was a sensation she hadn't experienced since she was very little.

"Do you think Caerella will be okay?" she asked quietly. The last thing she'd seen of her had not given her much to hope for. A wound like that was likely to be fatal. Her diaphragm, her heart, her lungs or all three had likely been pierced. She'd seen enough fights to know that any of those were not something easily walked away from.

"I do not know," Aesling said. "The woman is full of magic, both mine and the Cavean's. The two could have collided and already weakened her. Or they could have cancelled each other out. But there's a chance." She tossed the last few of the berries in her mouth. "There's always a chance. Magic is wild and unpredictable."

"Explosive, too," Vera said grimly. "Destructive."

"Only yours," Aesling replied. She sounded almost offended. "Humanity has never deigned to afford magic its due respect. They found only the most rudimentary ways to use it and did not examine any further." Vera felt her tense up a little bit. "Magic such as mine does not destroy as freely and readily as yours. But it still does as it wills." She looked at Vera. "But that means there is hope. Because if nothing else, it desires growth."

Vera tried to smile, to let Aesling's reassurance really seep in, but she was having trouble holding onto that hope. "Thank you," she said. "With luck, she'll live."

"You look crestfallen," Aesling said, "and not just out of worry. Speak your mind, Child."

"If... if she recovers," Vera said, "the three of them will be together again." Subconsciously or not, she found herself emphasising 'them'. Aesling caught onto it, and ran a hand over Vera's hair.

"There is hope there too, Child," she said. "You are not as alone as you believe yourself to be, and your friends are not as distant from you, as scared of you, as you think they might be."

"But what if they are?" Vera asked. "What if they never accept me for who I am now?"

"Then that is how these things are," Aesling said. "Some folks come into your life and walk with you as far as they will go. Others are with you until the end. You can't know which is which until you've reached that end." She held Vera a little closer. "Though it'll hurt, of course. But not all will fear you to change." A smirk played on her lips. "Clarus will not. You'll still have him."

"Not really," Vera sighed before she realised what she'd said. She grew a little red in the face. "I — I mean that I won't *have* him. Not — not that I want to—"

"Vera," Aesling interrupted, "I do not know who it is that you're keeping up this deception for, because it certainly isn't for me." She stood up and pulled Vera upright too. "I have no *claim* over Clarus, Child. He is his own man. All life is fleeting, and human lives more so than most. To pretend that these relationships are any different, and should be *possessed...*" She shook her head. "I've no interest in such a thing."

"But it doesn't mean that Clarus thinks this way, Aesling. He's a Prince, he can't—"

"I believe that he's set to be King, actually," the Nymph interrupted. "I doubt there's a lot he can not do. Besides, with you on his arm, nobody would know I'd be right there with him, would they?"

The thought of Clarus walking down some royal hallway with her on his arm, wearing some dress that was more expensive than any she'd ever seen, was barrelling through her mind like a wild steer. Her heart felt like it was trying to escape out through her throat. Though technically she was not in a real, physical space, that was hard to really believe, considering she found her hands shaking and her skin noticeably hot. "But I — He —"

"We'll speak when you wake up, child. But I've seen how he treats you. Not me. Not the body I live in. You." Aesling put a hand on her head. "I'll speak with him, but when it comes to Clarus? I think he's in your future, and mine."

All Vera could do was squeak for a moment. It took her longer than she would later dare to admit to drag herself back together. She liked to imagine that she was realistic about her future, and even tended towards pessimism. That said, she also couldn't stop thinking about it. About Clarus in a few years, by her side. Ten. Twenty. Seeing the world together. Watching sunsets and night stars and the sunrise after. Of her hand in his. His arms around her. His sleeping breath on the back of her neck…

"Vera, we *do* still share a mind while we're in here, and while I do not actually disagree — all of that appears amazing — you may want to… take a deep breath. Before you lose yourself in those daydreams. Besides, I think someone wants your attention."

She could tell. Her chest hurt. Her *everything* hurt. That's how she knew she was waking up. She heard her name, spoken softly, through the haze of pain. His voice. Ugh, she realised she probably looked like a mess. She'd barely survived, after all. She tried to open her eyes, but they wouldn't budge. "Ugh," she groaned, and immediately regretted it. Breathing hurt, let alone speaking.

"Try not to speak, dear Vera," Prince Clarus said. "This may be cold for a moment." Even though she'd prepared herself, she still drew a hissing breath when the cold rag went across her face, and her eyes fluttered open. They were in a darkened tent, and *he* was quite close, his eyebrows knit together in concern. He lowered his voice. "I see Aesling's helped you heal substantially, but still, do not move too much. I do not wish to see you hurt." She could see his jaw tense up.

"I'll be fine," she whispered. "Thank you, Clarus." A blush spread on her cheeks as she addressed him so casually, and she smiled a little at her own daring. The Prince seemed to have noticed too.

"You only called me that once before, Vera," he said, his voice still quiet. "Am I to understand that you no longer see me as royalty? You wound me." His face split into that roguish grin that made her weak in the knees. It was good she was lying down.

"Maybe I simply prefer the sound of your name," she said, then made the mistake of laughing softly. "Ow."

"Much as your honeyed words are a balm, I would ask that you keep silent a mite longer, Vera. You've healing to do." He lifted the bandage on her shoulder. "I suspect you'll be in travelling shape in less than a day, however. Aesling is doing divine work."

"Speaking of which, Clarus," Aesling said after swapping out quickly with Vera, "I believe you and I should speak." His eyebrows went up, and then he smiled when he recognised the eyes of his love.

"Anything, my Aesling. Speak and I'll listen. Talk and I'll answer."

"It's about Vera," Aesling said. Internally, Vera started to panic. While she'd stepped aside after the Nymph had requested to front, she feared more would be said out loud than she was entirely comfortable with. *"Trust me, child,"* Aesling reassured her, then turned her attention back to the Prince. He nodded, waiting for her to proceed. "How do you feel about her?" Then something impossible happened. Something magical. He stammered. He sputtered. He blushed.

"I — I — To be entirely and, and, entirely frank with you, my Aesling, I have to admit that I am quite put on the spot here," he said, and Vera had to suppress a very distinct sense of satisfaction at his bashful response.

"I know," Aesling said. *"I've only seen him like this once before, and... well..."* She left that thought and the implications thereof hanging in the mindspace between them. Vera was glad she was taking a backseat at that moment.

"If I am entirely honest," Clarus said, clearing his throat, "I find Vera to be a strong, capable young woman. She's wittier than she lets on, has a sharp, tactical mind, and cares deeply about her friends. Every action I see her take speaks to her character." Vera, of course, was wishing for death to take her away under the barrage of kindness, exacerbated by Aesling's playful mockery.

"I know all this, my love," Aesling said, "but that's not how you *feel* about her, is it?"

"Please," Vera squeaked, *"no more. I concede defeat!"*

"I… find all of those traits… as attractive as the… rest. Of her." Every word slowly and deliberately chosen fell out of his mouth, and Vera was certain she'd never recover.

"Thought so," Aesling said with a smug grin. "Well, carry on and do as your heart wills, my love."

"I… You are certain, Aesling? Know that the last thing I want is to cause you—"

"I'm certain, love. Now please, excuse me, I must rest if I'm to heal this body properly." Vera slipped back to the foreground, and she knew the Prince had seen it in her eyes. They looked at each other, neither of them saying anything, and both of them red in the face. There was a noise outside, and both were grateful for the rescue.

"What's going on out there?" Vera asked. "Is Caerella okay?" Clarus grimaced, worrying her a moment.

"Yes," he said, "and no. She has been… combative." He pulled the tent flap aside, and Caerella's crystal clear voice rang loudly through the tent.

"—m telling you she *has* spoken to me of it, and I have *no* intention to let you two old bastards ruin this child's life only because you've never meaningfully connected with anything you couldn't eat, drink, fuck or fight!" Vera had never heard her so angry before. Saints, she'd never heard Caerella so *emotive* before.

By comparison, Flaveo's response was positively muted. "Caerella, that isn't fair at all! The boy is just—"

"*One more word from you,*" Caerella hissed, "*and I will snap you like a toothpick, Flaveo. And you!*" There was no response from Rubicus, but Vera knew he was next on the chopping block. "Why didn't you oppose his mindless fantasies? You *know* who Vera is. It took me *one look.*"

"I saw him... *her...* die, Caerella. I did not want to believe." Rubicus sounded tired.

"Do better, Ruben," the woman said. "We've raised her. Even if she *hadn't* told me how she'd felt *years* ago, we knew she wasn't alright. We called her *Stoneface*, for fuck's sake. Now look at her! I recognised her eyes in an instant, and in one moment she showed me more hope, pain and happiness than she ever had in her life. She is *clearly* happier now."

"Caerella—" Flaveo said, and then there was a loud snapping sound, like someone stepping on a twig. "*OW! BY DOSE!*"

"I warned you, Flaveo. I do not need use of both arms to put you in your place. Now sit down, before we wake her up."

Clarus moved the tent flap back in place. "As you've heard," he said, "she's been..." He made a vague hand-gesture. "At least she and I see eye to eye, although I worry she may attempt to flay me if she fears me a threat to your safety, so I should step outside."

Vera nodded. "I understand," she said. Then, at great pain, she reached out and carefully touched his hand with the back of hers. "Thank you."

"No need," he said, then reached over and ever so softly planted a kiss on her forehead. "Get some rest, Vera."

Chapter Nineteen

Coffee, Eggs

They took their time. Caerella and Flaveo had figured out they could afford to. As she'd pointed out, the Cavean was on foot, and the Capital was several days on horseback. Even if, as Clarus warned, it didn't tire or rest, it would still have a long way to go, and the main road south had no major settlements. So it was decided that Caerella and Vera would heal up for two days before they went riding again. That was two days ago.

Vera stepped out of the tent and stretched. Her shoulder and back still ached when she moved, and breathing too deep still stung, but Aesling had reassured her that this would lessen as they travelled. She took slow shallow breaths as she let the cool morning air brush her face and play with her hair.

"Spring is coming," Aesling said with satisfaction. Vera smiled too and wrapped her arms around herself. The three were back together. Everyone was alive. And while Flaveo and Rubicus stumbled over themselves and their words, Caerella was there to raise an eyebrow at them, setting them straight. In the distance was the largest city in the Kingdom, somewhere over the horizon, and it was under threat.

But right now? Things weren't so scary. She *barely* even jumped when she felt something touch her shoulders.

She spun around and almost smacked face-first into Clarus. "Hey," he said, his voice joyful but soft so as not to wake any of the others. "Careful." He adjusted the cloak he'd laid over her shoulders. "I'd hate for you to fall ill."

"Thank you," Vera blushed. She found it hard to look anywhere. If she looked straight ahead, she was face to face with his chest, and the buttons of his shirt came apart slightly and to keep looking there would be, well... But looking *down* was obviously not an option, and turning away might be seen as too rude. She tilted her head up and looked him defiantly in the eyes. "Good morning, Prince Clarus," she said, and realised that she had miscalculated the difference in their height. He wasn't wearing his boots and she *was* and his face was close to hers again and...

"'Morning," Rubicus said as he walked past them. Vera spun around and trotted away from a softly chuckling Clarus, towards the fire. Flaveo had already made coffee. He was a few years older than Rubicus, and didn't sleep all that much. Even less, she suspected, after having been captured by the Cavean, although she'd had some trouble feeling really bad for him. Clarus started doing some exercises with his sword. For the past two days, he'd been running drills every day, and watching his sword flash through the air was a pretty impressive spectacle. Doubly so when she remembered that he was just as quick and cool-headed in a life-or-death situation.

Vera sat down by the fire too, and Flaveo wordlessly handed her a cup of coffee, and she took it with a whispered "Thank you." Small steps. Rubicus walked over to their packs. More specifically, he'd walked over to *her* pack, and started to pull her armour out of it. The chest pieces had been ruined by the axe, and Vera was a little fascinated to think that the dark stains across it were *her* blood. "Rubicus?" she asked, curious as to what he was planning to do with it. She'd planned on mending it herself, on the road if she had to. Flaveo had taught her how to handle a needle and thread, after all.

"It's too big," he said curtly, looking between her and it. He frowned, calculating. "Fixing the gap won't fix that." He took out a toolkit from Flaveo's bag and sat down with his back to the fire — and the rest of them. "I'll get it done before we head on the road." Vera gave him a quiet word of thanks, but he only responded with a grunt. She sighed. The three were together, but the distance was still there.

"He needs time," Flaveo said to her surprise. He took his own cup of coffee and sat down next to her. "I do too." He sipped his cup. "I don't... I don't know how..." He sighed. "How much of the magecraft do you know? What've you picked up from me?" His sideways glance indicated this was as much a genuine question as it was a test. Vera shrugged, making her shoulder twitch.

"Not a great deal. You've kept me in the dark a lot, Flaveo. 'It's too dangerous' and all that." He nodded and chewed his tongue for a moment.

"Aye, that's true. Then know and believe that when I say magic is an unstable and dangerous thing, I know what I'm speaking of." Internally, Vera heard Aesling scoff. "I've never seen human magic do these things." He gestured noncommittally at her. "But I've heard of spirits and demons taking possession of the minds and bodies of innocent folk. How do I *know?* I believe Caerella, and Saints help me, I'll not risk her wrath again, but that's belief. How do I know, C— Vera?"

"*Best of luck*", Aesling said. "*Worst comes to worst, you can always wake her up and have her break something else of his.*" Vera resisted the smirk that image conjured up in her head actually showing up on her face.

"I don't know, Flaveo. Caerella said it well," she said. "I was not happy, before. You know that." She sipped the coffee. It was a little too sweet. Flaveo put some kind of honey in his coffee that made it keep longer, but it wasn't always to her taste. "Not that the mercenary life is a happy one, and I had plenty reason to be a miserable child."

"You're still a child," Flaveo said with a grin, and then lowered his head. "Continue."

"But I was... numb. Numb to the world, numb to myself. And I thought for the longest time that it was a kind of... sickness. That I was broken. From what was done to me. My parents... There was so much." She sipped her cup again, if only to collect her thoughts. Flaveo nodded again. "But then I met Aesling — the spirit — and she asked me straight and forward what I wanted. I already knew the answer to that question, and I told her. She only gave me the tools to make that a reality." She leaned her chin on her hand and looked at the fire. "I do not feel I'm a different person, only that I am more myself than I've ever been. Although I'll grant you that I behave... differently."

"Certainly more talkative," Flaveo said, and he didn't even flinch under Vera's withering glare. "What you say makes sense, Vera. But it is hard to see you and try to... think the right way? A part of me sees your face and tries to see how I remember you being *underneath* that." He scratched his chin. "Although I suppose a better way to think about it is that this —" he waved at Vera again, "— is who you were underneath, isn't it?" He shook his head. "I thought I had a handle on the world, girl, but you're making an old man's head hurt."

"I think Caerella does a well enough job of that already," Vera said with a little smile.

"Yes, she does," Flaveo said, and dramatically rubbed the back of his head, where she'd rapped him on the skull with her knuckles the night before. "Now, have you been taking care of the weapons like Ruben and I showed you?" Happy to be talking normally, Vera went over to retrieve some of the weapons to show that they had been, indeed, well taken care of. Flaveo got onto her for not doing a perfect job, but in the same way he'd always had. Even if he might need some more time, he was getting to trust her, and to trust Aesling, and it was hard not to be optimistic at that.

Caerella took a bit to wake up. Flaveo had decided to let her sleep in. If they were riding out today, she needed the rest. While she'd recovered quite quickly from what should have been a lethal perforation, the shock to her system from the various daggers had taken her some time to heal from. Her right arm, especially, had needed to be in a sling. Aesling had reassured Vera that she was still healing well — and fast — but there wasn't much more she could do without compromising Vera's own recovery process.

This had not, however, limited Caerella in her grace, or her stealth. She appeared so quietly from behind Flaveo, he nearly spilled all of his coffee. "I heard my name," Caerella said as she poured herself a cup. "I hope you've not been gossiping or offending." Her face was calm, as if she was just waking up, but her eyes met Vera's and seemed to wait for a signal. Vera just nodded with a smile.

"Nothing of the sort, Caerella. Just an old man trying to feel relevant by teaching me how to whet a blade like it's my first time." Flaveo's eyes nearly rolled out of his head in indignation. "So I'm humouring him and letting him point out spots I 'missed'."

"You're a mongrel," Flaveo said as he walked over to the fire and started breakfast under Caerella's watchful gaze. "Do we have eggs?" Vera nodded and pointed near the fire. Clarus had gone out to find some in the morning.

Rubicus and Flaveo had taken it upon themselves to teach him how to survive in the wild. Just in case. "Good." He retrieved some dried meat, and soon the air started to smell like, well, *food.* It was making Vera's mouth water. Caerella sat down near Vera.

"Good morning, girl," she said. "You're recovering well?" Vera nodded, and raised her eyebrows. "Good. As am I." She flexed her shoulder with a frown. "I'll fight left-handed a day or so." She looked over at Clarus, who was still going through his routines, his shirt now drenched with sweat. "I may ask him to spar. He seems capable enough, your Prince."

Vera's face went red again, which was proving to be a bit of a pattern when it came to Clarus. She reached out to Aesling. *"Can't you do anything about the blushing? I feel blood rushing to my face at the drop of a hat!"*

"I've always been able to," Aesling said matter-of-factly, *"but, well, that wouldn't be my place, would it? Besides, it's far more fun this way."*

"Flaveo is right. You're a demon." Vera turned her attention back to Caerella. "He's not my prince," she mumbled. "He's just..." She started to crumble under the gaze of the older woman, and her slowly elevating eyebrows. "He's..." Caerella leaned forward, listening in rapt attention. "H—" She stopped. Caerella's face had split into the most unsettling, horrifying smile she'd ever seen. Caerella didn't *smile.* She glowered. She kept her face neutral. If she didn't glare and frown so much, she would've been a contender for the name of Stoneface herself.

"If he hurts you, I'm pulling his spine out through his nostrils," Caerella said sweetly, then got up and walked over to Clarus, holding a small axe, holding it up. The two exchanged words before starting a friendly sparring session.

"Is she—" Aesling asked.

"Deadly serious," Vera said, and swallowed. "And I doubt I'd be able to stop her, too."

"On the one hand," Aesling said, *"I want to fight her with every fibre of my being for daring to threaten* my *Clarus. On the other hand, you are* her *Vera, and I can't help but respect her for that. I like her."*

"Me too," Vera said and walked over to Flaveo, who held out two tins of food. She took them both and brought one over to Rubicus, who put the armour down he was working on to take the food from her with a grateful 'hrmpf'. She sat down next to him, and started to eat in silence. There were many things that could be held against Flaveo, but he knew his way around quail's eggs.

"I'm sorry," Rubicus said, quietly. He ate slowly, and his eyes were fixed ahead. If she didn't know better, Vera could have sworn he hadn't spoken at all. "I thought you weren't you. Too good to be true."

"I know," Vera said. She looked over again as Rubicus rubbed his face. She pretended not to see the tear that still clung to his beard. "It's okay." She paused. "We're okay?"

"We're okay," he said.

"We're okay." Vera smiled a little, and ate her eggs.

Chapter Twenty

About Time

They rode slowly, at first. They had to. In the saddle, her wounds healed slower, she noticed, and while Caerella was the kind to stay quiet about pain, she was also pragmatic enough to call for a break to avoid her arm and shoulder healing badly and inhibiting her in a fight. So they took plenty of breaks as they travelled South. It was also still getting warmer as they rode towards the warmer lands at the centre of the Kingdom.

While they did, the ice between them thawed too, completely defenceless in the face of Clarus' optimism. He was able to provoke Flaveo into heated debate, challenging him to a battle of wits that was as fun to listen to as it was sometimes exhausting to follow. It was clear that the Mercenary was trying to measure his years of 'real-world experience' up to the Prince's 'fancy education', and the two of them seemed to have a pretty good time bouncing off of each other.

Rubicus, meanwhile, was also starting to get back to his old self as well. He was fast with jokes, and didn't hold back any when it came to barbs or verbal backstabbery, and more than once his loud laughter echoed across a campfire. Clarus even got Caerella to smile.

Vera, in the meantime, would have been happy to observe them. It was strange — how much these four people meant to her. Had come to mean to her now that she was herself. She would have been more than satisfied with just... riding alongside them. Hearing banter like old times. Hearing Clarus' clear laugh and seeing his insufferably dashing smile.

But they didn't let her. They kept dragging her into all of it. The first time Flaveo had shot a verbal arrow at her, she hadn't been prepared. She'd still been defensive. But after a few seconds, it had become clear that the 'attack' had been a playful jab, the way he'd always done with Rubicus. So she'd retaliated.

After half an hour, she almost fell off her horse laughing when Rubicus made a face behind Caerella's back, which she'd of course somehow *seen*. In the evenings, Ruben still asked that she clean some weapons, but he did his own share now, too. Flaveo requested her help with cooking. Caerella pushed her training forwards. But none of them demanded anything, anymore. Something had changed.

Of course, there was also Clarus. In the evening, he had a tendency to stare South, in the direction of the Capital. Coalis. Out there was the Cavean, and they were catching up. When she joined him, he quickly turned his attention to her, but it was very clear that his mind was on the monster they were following, and what it might do to his people, his Kingdom.

"We'll stop him," Vera said as she joined him again. It was the third night in a row. They suspected they'd either catch up to him the next day, or at the very least reach one of the larger townships on the edge of the Capital. Whichever came first. "We'll catch him and we'll stop him." Clarus nodded. He'd already taken his armour off for the evening — they rode prepared — but he was still wearing his cloak, and he pulled it a bit tighter around himself.

"I know," Clarus said. His eyes reflected the setting sun, but not his enthusiasm. He didn't seem to entirely believe it. He put an arm on her shoulder and pointed. She tried not to shiver at his touch. Aesling giggled. "Do you see that spot on the horizon?" he asked.

Vera squinted, and she could feel Aesling helping her focus. "Yes," she said. "Is that the Capital?" The Prince nodded.

"A day's ride, and we'll see the walls of my home." He frowned for a second and then looked down at her. "Vera, I'm afraid I'll have to beg you for forgiveness. I'd prostrate myself, but I fear Flaveo would mock me until my dying breath." He put his hand on his hip and laughed. Vera just barely managed to avoid pouting when he took it off of her shoulder.

"F— For what?" Vera asked in confusion.

"We've travelled together all this time," he said, "and I've never even asked you where you are from." Clarus considered her for a moment. "If I had to hazard a guess, you're from up North? You seemed to know your way around there."

Vera nodded. "Yes. My hometown was destroyed by Caligon's forces, so Rubicus took me in. I've been travelling with them since."

"I'm sorry for that, Vera," Clarus said. "I did what I could, back then. Would've done more, but my father tried to keep me out of harm's way. I convinced him that the fort at the Northern Border would be a safe station for me. He didn't know the Cavean would strike there, though I had my suspicions, and he didn't find out until I'd already taken a battalion up there with me." His face fell. "Although I suppose he must've thought my attempt something of a... mixed victory. I wish I'd had the chance to tell him it was my choice."

Vera took a step closer to him. "I'm sorry, Clarus," she said, not knowing what else to say. It wasn't like she had known King Lucius well enough to say anything about his happiness, and she didn't really have an opinion on how the Kingdom had been run. From her perspective, the Kingdom just sort of happened. People worked the fields, tax collectors went around to get the money to rebuild a road *here* and supply the army *there*, and mercenaries cleaned up problems nobody else wanted to deal with. She'd always been vaguely aware that Kings were necessary in all that, but she had never given that much thought. Clarus smiled again, and this time, his eyes did too.

"Thank you, Vera," he said. "I'll miss him. And I'll mourn him properly, too." He looked ahead again. "Once the Cavean's been destroyed. I'll have time to grieve." His smile stayed on his face, but became a little more strained. "Although I fear it won't be much." Vera took another step closer to him. She wished she could comfort him. "You know," Clarus scoffed, "I suppose I'll be crowned King, if we manage to defeat the Cavean once and for all."

"If?" Vera said with a frown. "Clarus, we'll defeat him."

"Oh, I've no doubt about that," he said almost nonchalantly. "The question is whether I'll walk away from it. The first time I hibernated for a full decade, if you'll recall."

"*I won't let that happen,*" Vera and Aesling said simultaneously, and their voices speaking as one reverberated through the evening air. Prince Clarus jumped a little when he heard the unnatural sound, and his eyebrows shot up.

"Aesling?" he asked.

"Yes, love," Aesling said. "I apologise for that. It seems Vera and myself both feel quite strongly on the subject." Vera, who had stepped aside to allow Aesling behind the wheel, just nodded. "You are walking away from this fight *alive*, my Prince," Aesling continued. "Vera and I have decided. I don't think you even get a say in this. You are too good and too important." Aesling looked inward for a moment. Vera could feel the playful judgement. "And far too pretty." Clarus laughed and wrapped an arm around her. Aesling's arm slipped around the Prince's waist effortlessly. So effortlessly Vera couldn't *not* be aware of it.

"Thank you, my love. I'll do my best then. But if it's what's best for the Kingdom..."

"There'll always be another way, my sweet," Aesling said. Then, turning to Vera. *"Do you mind if I —"*

"No!" Vera squeaked. *"I mean, no, I don't mind."* There was a brief pause.

"Actually," Aesling said, *"you do the honours."*

"What?" Vera said out loud and looked at Clarus. She was acutely aware of the fact that her arm was still around him. "Sorry, it seems I'm here. Again."

"There's no need to apologise, Vera," the Prince said. "I quite love the fact that you are." He gave her a cheeky smirk. "Were you going to say something? Or was that Aesling?"

"Um," Vera said. "N-Not really. Just that I'm here, and that I agree with her."

"Oh?" Clarus looked at her more intently. "Which part, specifically?"

"I hate you so much," Vera said to Aesling, who only cackled in response. "All parts," she just barely managed. Clarus looked insufferably smug, so she raised her chin defiantly to look up at him. "I think Aesling and I are united front when it comes to you, Clarus."

He leaned in a little bit closer, and Vera already felt her cheeks start to glow. One of these days, she knew, she'd be useful as a lantern. "So you think I'm pretty?"

"Not the words I'd've used," she squeezed out with only the most titanic of efforts. He took a step, and was now right in front of her. The last of the setting sunlight drew out his profile, and his windswept hair framed his face perfectly.

"What words would you have?" he asked. The smile faded, his eyes were alert. He was doing the worst possible thing he could have done to her in that moment. He was listening, and he was paying attention. Her arm was still on his hip. His hand was on her shoulder, touching gently. He was close, so close.

"I —" she started, and then stammered a few more times and then stopped. She frowned, cocked her head, and looked him in his perfect eyes. "No," she said.

"No?"

"No," she confirmed. "I'm not playing the innocent, defenceless maiden." Before Clarus could ask her what she meant — and she could change her mind or lose her cool — she grabbed him by the back of the head and pulled him in for a kiss.

When she was younger, she'd imagined kissing. She'd wondered what it would be like. The way people talked about it in tales, it was a magical event that was supposed to blow one's mind, make their heart explode with feelings and butterflies erupt in their stomachs. A good kiss, as the bards told it, set the soul on fire.

The bards, she realised, were right. As his lips touched hers, she could feel his heart hammer in his chest, against the staccato rhythm of her own. His hands landed on her waist, and he pulled her closer. His lips were soft, his breathing hard, and his movements careful and gentle. It was perfect. He smelled like horse and sword-oil and her hair hadn't seen a comb in two days, and it was perfect.

She ran her hands through his hair as she kissed him right on that frustrating face of his, over and over again, until they were both out of breath, the sun had set, and the stars shone brightly overhead. When they finally pulled away, she felt a giggle rise up in her throat, and she couldn't hold it back.

"Are you all right?" Clarus asked softly.

"Yes," she said. "Yes, I am." She bit her lip and turned away. Even in the dark, she felt distinctly like her blush would be visible. *"Was that... good?"*

"Child," Aesling said, *"even I am impressed by that one."*

Clarus put a hand on her cheek and tilted her head up, then planted one, much softer kiss on her lips. "I'm glad," he said. "You deserve the world, Vera. You and Aesling both. If only I had more than one Kingdom to give." Vera would've giggled if she wasn't reeling from the last kiss. With superhuman effort, she tore herself away.

"W— I should get some rest, prince Clarus," she said, and resisted the urge to touch her lips. They tingled slightly. "Good night!" As she hurried away, she could hear him chuckling softly behind her. Walking past the campfire, she heard Carella mutter quietly.

"About time," Caerella said. Grinning from ear to ear, Vera was practically skipping by the time she got to her tent.

Chapter Twenty-One

At The Gates

"She's been carrying a torch for you for a long time, Ruben," Flaveo said. Rubicus and him were leading their little convoy, Vera and Clarus rode behind them, with Caerella bringing up the rear. "The least you can do is visit the woman."

"I'm aware of that, Flaveo!" Rubicus laughed. "And she's a kind woman. But I've no intention of settling down any time soon. Not in Coalis, leastways!" He and Flaveo had been bantering all morning, and it had been a pleasant melody to accompany their ride, and a welcome distraction from the fact that the city was getting closer.

"Ruben, from what I was told, Vera and the Prince found you holding on for dear life, barely holding it together against, what, three of the blasted things?" Flaveo messed with a flask for a moment before taking a swig.

"Four, if you must know. And that's *after* being skewered. I'm not done for quite yet, old friend." Vera leaned forward in the saddle and glared at the back of his head. She hadn't really considered it much, but he really had almost died. Well, they both had, of course, but she had a Nymph living in her head now.

"And you're welcome," Aesling said, looking at the man too. *"He isn't getting younger."*

"Maybe you *should* consider retiring, Ruben," Flaveo said with a sly grin. "You're only going to get slower. Why not take a nap? The rest of us will save the Kingdom. When the Prince gives me a manor I'll save you a room, aye?" The hooves of their mounts kicked up gravel as they made down the King's Way.

"Eat me, Flaveo. Besides, you're older than I am!" His laugh echoed across the road.

Flaveo didn't miss a beat. "Faster, too. Some people just age better than others. Let me know if your back starts acting up. You can take a long nap after we've killed the Cavean, old boy." He chuckled, until Caerella rode up to them.

"Quiet, you two," she said, and they stopped. All three of them stopped, and Vera and Clarus also held their horses. They looked around. The city gates were not far now, only a few minutes away. "Listen."

After a few seconds of trying to hear *anything*, Vera realised she was holding her breath. Flaveo looked around. "I don't hear any— Oh." He made a sheepish face. "Yeah."

Caerella was right. This was the King's Road. This close to the city gates, there should have been traffic. Noise. Carts bringing food in, and people going out. It was the middle of the day, as well. The silence was deafening. They all looked at each other.

"What do we do?" Clarus asked, although Vera could tell he was already steering his horse forward. Unless one of them quickly came up with something, Clarus was likely to break off. Vera looked to the city gates. The Capital had been built to withstand a siege, once upon a time, its walls high and thick, built in concentric circles. Over time, however, its population had grown and spilled out of its gates, houses had sprung up around its gates, and streets had formed. All of them were quiet, the city gates open.

"This is bad," Flaveo mumbled. "If it's already inside the city, who knows what damage it's doing?" Clarus looked at him for a moment, then shook his head.

"No," he said. "In the event of an assault, all of the inner city's ringed gates can be closed to keep the population safe." Vera saw the doubt on his face, plain as day, his jaw clenching and unclenching as he stared ahead.

"That would trap everyone inside as well," Flaveo said. "But it does explain why there's no-one outside."

"Why would the walls be closed if only the Cavean and a few of its demons had marched on the Capital?" Caerella said as she dismounted. "Either it was killed, and folk are having a quiet feast inside, or that infernal creature commands a larger army, now, than we feared."

Rubicus shook his head as he stepped off his horse. "No point in arguing out here," he said, and retrieved one, two, three swords from his saddle. A claymore, for cleaving, easily the largest weapon he owned and easily dropped, and then smaller ones to fall back on.

Vera couldn't help but agree. "What of the horses?" she asked as all of them checked their gear. "Will we just leave them here?" Caerella shook her head.

"Hitching them would be a cruelty. I will not assume we make it back alive." She shot everyone else a glare, daring them to speak up. Not even Clarus was that idealistic. "Best to take what we need, and send them on their way." Putting actions to her words, she removed her steed's saddle and bridle. "This is no place for you," she whispered in its ear, and then smacked it on the rump.

They found a small building, furthest from the gate, that had been unlocked. It was empty, like its inhabitants had left in a hurry. Clarus stopped briefly by the claw-mark that had been carved into the door post, but they moved on, storing their packs inside. Anything they didn't take with them, they'd be able to retrieve after. If there was an after. They gathered by the front door, and looked at the city walls again.

"Hear anything?" Rubicus asked. Caerella shook her head.

"No," she said, "though the city walls likely muffle sound. We won't know more 'till we go inside." Her thumb ran across the haft of her axe, loosely slung over her shoulder. "Prince Clarus, with your permission?" He nodded, and she turned forward. "Ruben, Prince Clarus, you two will tip the spear. Once at the gates, I want you two to inform the rest of us of anyone you encounter."

Rubicus nodded, and then looked at Clarus. "Try to keep up, Prince." He winked. Clarus laughed, and a bit of the tension in the room dissipated.

"I will try, Rubicus," he said. "Do try to leave some for me."

Caerella, not humouring them, looked at Vera. "You will be behind them. You're able to support them both, and you're capable with sword and short bow. Keep them both in sight, and call for help if you must."

Vera nodded. "Understood," she said. She knew she wasn't being condescended to. Rubicus and Clarus were both extremely capable swordsmen, and even with her enhanced reflexes, she felt she wasn't likely to match either of them in an extended fight, even if she was able to hold her own for a bit. And backing either of them up was going to be a responsibility all on its own.

"Flaveo. You'll be behind them. Have you been able to whip up any more magics?"

As an answer, he produced several flasks. "A handful, with what I had remaining. They'll all be a bit weak, but I wasn't going to risk combining them." He smirked. "The reaction would have been spectacular, but premature."

"Good," Caerella said, then looked out again. "I'll be a bit behind. Clearing stragglers. If you don't see me, do not worry. If I've trouble, you'll know." She took a deep breath, and exhaled slowly through her nose. "Finally, if any of you encounter the Cavean, do not engage it on your own." She glared at Clarus. "Especially you. You're the only one who has been able to seal that thing before, so it's important you stay alive."

"As you say," Clarus said, bowing his head. "Are we all ready, then?"

Everyone nodded in agreement, but the tension that had gripped them had returned. Vera felt anxiety gripping her, running through her veins. Not even Aesling's presence did much to alleviate it. If something went wrong, any of them stood to lose their lives. She wasn't worried for herself, after all.

"It will be alright, Vera," Aesling said. *"In a worst-case scenario, you'll be between all of them. All you must do is rush forward, and I'll heal what injuries they have. I will not let them die under my touch."* Vera thanked her quietly before suddenly feeling Clarus tap her elbow. She turned to him, and he pulled her aside for a moment.

"Vera," he said quietly, "Ash. If something were to happen..."

"None of that, my love," Aesling said. *"You are walking away from this alive, as I said. You'll face that creature and live. I promise."*

"And if I can be so bold," Vera added. "You aren't allowed to die, Clarus, because I'm not done doing this yet."

"Doing wh—" he said, then Vera grabbed his face and kissed him, much to his surprise and Aesling's delight. She took a moment, letting the feeling of his lips on hers drown out the fear and stress she was feeling. His arms slowly wrapped around her and pulled her in tight. She allowed

Aesling to slip forward, and he grinned into the kiss when he felt the difference in how she held herself. Vera tried not to be overwhelmed at how much more... forward Aesling was.

Finally, they pulled away, and even Prince Clarus was out of breath. "Very... very well, it seems I have no choice in the matter but to live through whatever comes next. But I would still ask that you hear what I've to say." Vera and Aesling both gave him the kind of stare that indicated them having little patience, but let him speak anyway. "If something *does* happen, that renders me incapable of, say, speech, for a few days, then let me tell you, right here and now, how important you are."

"Tell me tonight," Vera said, shaking her head. "No dramatic farewells, Clarus."

"Very well. But grant me *one* thing, then."

"Wh—" Vera said, and then he returned the kiss, with a vengeance. Vera felt herself melting in his arms. She reached out to Aesling for help, but found no help there. "You monster," she whispered when she pulled away.

"Truly devious," he answered, before the two of them rejoined the others. Rubicus and Flaveo gave them a pointed stare, but Clarus gave them an innocent smile and Vera avoided their gaze altogether.

"Let's go," Caerella said, and they stepped out of the building. Brandishing their weapons, they all moved into the formation they'd discussed. Vera kept an eye on Clarus and Rubicus, both of them keeping their weapons high as they approached the gates, only a hundred feet away.

There was a noise, and they stopped. It had been a roar, filled with rage. Vera knew that sound. There was only one thing in this world that made that noise. The vision of the shade coming through the gates was expected, but the hairs on her neck stood up all the same. The creature seemed to be sniffing the air, before turning to them, snarling, roaring again, and then charging. The two men facing it took their stances, and the demon was almost on them, they stepped aside slashed, simultaneously. The monster crumpled into a heap right in front of Vera, who gave it a final coup-de-grace.

They all smiled and nodded at each other. Vera was about to say something, when they heard a roar, and another monster stepped through the gate. Then another. And another. Then a shade appeared on top of the wall, followed by several more.

"Uh," Flaveo said behind her, "perhaps we should regroup. I think there's almost ten."

"More," Vera said, pointing out movement on top of the wall. "Dozens, maybe." More and more seemed to be gathering in the corners of her eyes, snarling. It was hard to keep them all in her line of sight. Further away, some started to jump down the walls. There might have been some hiding in the buildings by the road, as well.

"Hundreds," Caerella said as she stepped up next to them, with her back to the gate. "Maybe more. And we're surrounded."

As one, shades peeled away from the walls, from the shadows, and started to close in around them like a river of rage, claws and teeth. Then they charged.

Chapter Twenty-Two

The Colours of Magic

"I think," Rubicus roared in between blows of his claymore, "we should reconsider our plan!" He swiftly turned from one assailant to the other, cleaving them in half before they could land their attacks on him. Though they were surrounded, the Demons came at them in clumps of two, three or four at a time. But more and more of them joined their ranks, some of them climbing on top of each other to scream at the assembled group. Other than the walls towering over them, slowly their environment was completely obscured by the wall of colourless hatred that surrounded them.

Clarus danced from one attacker to the next, his movements fluid. Vera could tell he was concentrating hard to conserve strength. Every step was calculated and careful, every strike swift and decisive. Flaveo had switched to his bow and took out the ones that tried charging him or Vera. Caerella stood off a little ways on her own, swinging her battle-axe in wide arcs, moving her body with the motions like a dancer, chopping and cutting limbs and heads like she was trimming a houseplant.

"Nonsense, Ruben," Flaveo quipped. "It'll be fine as long as your rheumatism doesn't act up! Any joint pain yet?" Vera could hear the concern in his voice, and she knew where it was coming from. If the Demons attacked them all at once, they'd be torn limb from limb in seconds. So why didn't they?

"I'll show you joint pain!" Rubicus laughed as he cut one of the monsters from stem to stern and the pieces fell to the floor with a wet gurgle. "How are you holding up, Vera?"

"I'm fine!" she answered just as one of the creatures attacked her. Recalling the attack made by the then-possessed Caerella, she deflected the clawed strike and stepped aside, striking upwards. The creature fell to the ground, and she quickly finished it. "Why are they playing with us?"

Clarus danced aside and decapitated two monsters as they charged at him, then stepped backwards to Rubicus' side, wiping some of the sweat from his brow. "I fear," he said, "they may be trying to wear us down." Vera shot him a glance, but couldn't afford to let her eyes linger, tempting though that might have been. "I've seen it before. To the Cavean, every death is an opportunity, but it is the living that make up its most powerful servants."

"Well," Caerella said casually, "I'll slaughter its entire army before I allow myself to be captured that way again!" Putting word to deed, she hacked away at three Demons that charged simultaneously. "It can try as long as it wants!"

"Then where is it?" Rubicus bellowed. "We all have a bone to pick with the bastard," he said, "and I swear on my life there will be a bloody *reckoning!*" He only barely sidestepped a charging Demon, his claymore stuck in its chest. He drew one of his short swords and quickly finished the creature off. Vera could tell there was no time to lean down and pick it back up. Not for him, anyway.

Though the bodies of the monsters disappeared after seconds, leaving only a shadowy imprint on the ground, even the act of ducking was something the large mercenary was not being given the space for, as several more of the monsters charged at him. Vera quickly closed the distance between them with a pouncing roll, and grabbed the weapon by the haft. Even with Aesling's improvement of her physique, trying to pick the weapon up one-handed almost dislocated her wrist. Nonetheless, she managed, and as she raised herself back up, she brought the weapon back up with her. "You dropped this," she said with a wink.

He just flashed his big grin. Vera suddenly became aware of several of the monsters rushing in to attack her, and for a brief second, she remembered what it had been like for the creatures to run her through. The *cold* of it. Then, Rubicus grabbed the claymore's haft, and nodded. "Duck," he said, before swinging the weapon in a wide arc. Three bodies fell to the floor. He wanted to say something, but Clarus got in there first.

"Rubicus!" he shouted, then pointed. "Flaveo!" Rubicus and Vera looked over at the man. He was frantically firing one arrow after the other, but he wasn't fast enough. Isolated as he was, he simply couldn't draw and fire with enough speed to stop the tide of advancing monsters. The three of them rushed over to his side just as one of the Demons swiped a taloned claw at him.

Vera took it off at the wrist, Rubicus cut off the rest of the arm, and Clarus' sword pierced the creature through the head. "Well," Flaveo said, brushing himself off, "aren't you all concerned for my safety."

"I ought to wallop you," Rubicus said, then turned around. The four of them now all stood back to back, inside of a slowly enclosing circle of violence. Caerella was slowly making her way to them. Though Vera wasn't *really* worried about her — she was a terrifying whirlwind of death on her off-days — it was only a matter of time before their movements would slowly start to become sluggish, before weariness set in their bones and the energy of battle started to subside.

"Maybe later," Flaveo said as he fired off two more arrows. "I think we may be here a while." As if to illustrate his point, a scream rippled across the monsters, coming from the direction of the walls, and the attacks ceased for a moment. "Though maybe not."

Caerella quickly joined them during their moment of respite. Vera took a deep breath. She was only now noticing how out of breath she was. While she was fighting, it was easy to lose herself in it, but now that she had a moment to think, her arms felt heavier, and her mouth and nose were filled with the smell of sweat and dust. It was suffocating.

"What's happening?" she asked, just as the sea of Demons split. There it was. The Cavean. It strolled between the Demons as casually as going for a walk in the gardens, its colourless, eyeless skull-mask scanning left to right, grinning at them with infinite malice.

"Welcome home, Princeling," it said. "Come to serve your people, no doubt." It raised both its arms at the mass of monsters around them. "Here they are."

"I'm slaying you, Demon," Clarus said coldly. "And saving everyone from your evil."

"Very well," it said, the hollow sockets of its eyes resting on the five of them. Vera felt cold just being under its gaze. Aesling inside of her shivered, though the creature didn't seem to recognize either of them. "I will stop."

"What?" Clarus said.

"I will cease. Everyone still within the city walls will live," it said, slowly pacing in a circle around them. It drained the colour out of the world, every time it set foot on the ground. "In return, all I wish you to do… is kneel."

"You're mad," Clarus said with a snarl, "if you think I'd *ever* kneel to you!"

"My, my," the Cavean said, "So you value your *own* freedom, more so than the lives of your subjects?" It laughed, a sound like stone scraping against stone that made Vera's teeth hurt. "I think dethroning you might do the people of your kingdom a *favour* if you're so… selfish." It gave Clarus a pointed stare, and Vera could tell the Cavean's words had shaken him for a moment.

In the campfire stories she'd heard growing up, heroes always knew what to say and when to say it. They had sounded… heroic. Effortlessly so. Vera, however, was shaking in her boots. "There is no reason for us to believe anything you say," Vera said. She had to keep her voice from wavering and stammering. "A-and if we kill you, we save everyone anyway."

"My, the stripling speaks." It paused in front of her, just out of reach of her blade. "If you slay your Prince now, I give you fair passage to the edge of the kingdom and beyond."

"Not on your life," Vera said, and lunged forward, faster than it probably expected her to be able to, and sliced her sword upwards at the bony thing that was its face. It shattered in half, and the Cavean screeched.

"You!" it screamed as it jumped backwards, the mask cracked but not broken, all the shadowy Demons around him echoing its rage. "How *dare* you!"

"Step closer," Vera said, emboldened, "and I'll show you how." The Cavean glared at her for a few seconds, and then straightened itself again to its statuesque height.

"Kill them. Kill them all. I can find others." Then it turned and walked away through the sea of monsters. Flaveo fired an arrow at it, but it sailed right through him and struck a Demon in the eye. "Goodbye, Princeling," the Cavean called out across the sea of noise, "you failed your people beautifully!"

"He's just saying that to get to you," Vera whispered to him, and though she saw him nod, his jaw was tight. The Cavean had gotten to him. Had he made a mistake, not trading his life for his people? Vera could see the doubt in his mind. Then she saw that doubt make place for determination. Clarus, beautiful, wonderful Clarus, smiled.

"He will not," Clarus said, and stepped forward, his sword a silver blur, just as the army of Demons descended on them. And then there was no more thinking. There was only fighting. One after the other, the Demons charged. The only luck the five of them had was that the creatures got in each other's way while charging, giving Vera just enough time to slice, cut and stab, as quickly as possible.

This was different than it had been before. Before, it had been exhausting because there was always another attack. But now, they were in the thick of it. They were being overwhelmed with sheer numbers.

And yet, they held. Caerella danced like a leaf on the wind, her axe swinging in wide, beautiful arcs. Flaveo chuckled as his knives flew and pierced skull after skull. Clarus laughed, his sword like a painter's brush as he struck, again and again. Rubicus roared with mirth as his claymore cut line after line to pieces, and when that was struck from his hand, he wielded both shorter swords, one in each hand, and continued on.

Sometimes, one of them would get hit, a scratch here, a cut there, and then Vera would take a step back and rest her hand on their arm, and the wound would close in front of their eyes.

It wasn't enough. There seemed to be no end to them. They cut, hew and slew, and the creatures kept coming. Vera's arms were getting heavy. In time, Caerella's movements became stilted. She missed a step here, tripped there. Flaveo grew quiet as his quiver emptied. Rubicus grew quiet. Clarus stopped laughing.

None of them said anything. There was only the sound of battle, and it became everything and nothing. Just noise. It was almost like being under water. The whole world was slowing down. Teeth clamping down on the blade of her sword as it pierced through a monster's skull. It was all noise.

Just noise and the smell of blood and dust and... something else. Something unnatural. Something chemical. Something unnatural. Something familiar.

"I'll make a path," Flaveo said. "Get ready to make a run for it."

Vera looked at him just as he tossed the flask aside and he wiped his mouth. She wanted to ask him what he meant, but she couldn't find the breath or the words. She couldn't find the time.

He raised his arm, a knife outstretched, away from the walls. The tip of it glowed, and Vera threw herself aside just in time for the wall of fire to burn itself in a path, through the creatures, through the monsters. There was a path.

"Go," Flaveo said, and he smirked at them. Caerella glared. Rubicus raged. Clarus just nodded. Vera screamed as she saw him down another one of the bottles of magic. And another. And another. All of them, one after the other. By the time he'd uncorked the last one, light was bleeding through his skin.

Vera felt her cheeks sting with hot tears as Clarus and Rubicus dragged her away. Flaveo bled light from his eyes, and Vera heard him laugh one more time as his limbs became pillars of fire, burning through swaths of the Demons descending on him. Vera couldn't even think as she began to run, her heart pounding in her head.

Behind her, Flaveo became a roaring inferno, everything he had ever been now a pillar of triumphant heat, blasting heavenward.

Chapter Twenty-Three

Dusk and Dust

"He's gone." Vera sat against the wall with her arms around her knees. She probably looked sadder than she was. She wanted to be sad. She wanted to cry. It would be easier to cry, in a way. Instead, she felt numb. It felt unreal. It felt like something that hadn't happened.

Everything had happened so fast. Fire. Running. Flaveo bursting open, so filled with power it had seared her skin dozens of feet away, and taking away hundreds of demons with him, as well as a chunk of the outer city and even putting a dent in the city wall.

And then there had been nothing. Silence, deafening. Rubicus speaking without words. Movement from the walls made it clear Flaveo's sacrifice had not killed every shade. He'd bought them the space to run, and the time to do it. So they had.

Now she was trying to make the reality of the situation sink in. Flaveo was dead. Vera *knew* that. Consciously. But she didn't feel it yet, and that was almost more upsetting. "He's gone," she said to herself again. They sat in the house, the one furthest from the gates. No fire, that might have attracted attention. No light in the dark. Not too much talking, just in case. Night hung like a suffocating blanket on them all.

"I'm sorry," Aesling said. *"I understand he was important to you."*

Vera nodded. "A bit like an uncle," she said quietly.

"I — I don't know what that means." Aesling sounded almost guilty. *"Father's brother? Is that relationship significant?"*

"He's family," Vera clarified, maybe with a bit more bite than Aesling deserved. "Sorry."

"I think, given the current situation, you're owed a bit of grace in social situations."

"What do you mean?"

"No need to apologise."

"Thank you."

"If it helps," Rubicus said from the other side of the room, where he'd been slowly cleaning his armour, "he never figured he'd make it to the age he did."

"It doesn't," Vera said quietly.

"It will," the large man said quietly. The loss likely hit him harder than it did Vera. The two of them had known each other for decades, drawing swords together all that time. She didn't know that much about their life before she'd been taken in by them, but she'd heard the stories. The adventures.

Caerella sat next to Rubicus, getting some rest. She was up next on guard duty, after Clarus. Wordlessly, she put her head on her friend's shoulder. In any other situation, the display of affection would have seemed out of place, strange and out of character. She locked eyes with Vera for a moment and blinked slowly, like a cat might. *"Are you okay?"* her eyes seemed to ask.

Vera shrugged, thought for a moment, then shook her head and smiled. Of course she wasn't okay. None of them were. Not being okay *was the point.* Caerella blinked again. A quiet understanding.

"What now?" Vera mumbled quietly. She realised she'd spoken loud enough for the others to hear her when they looked at her expectantly. "We failed. We came to the Cavean and…" Well. That sentence didn't need finishing, did it?

Flaveo was dead.

"We try again," Caerella said. "Of course we try again, Vera." She looked at Rubicus. "Perhaps you and Rubicus can distract them and draw them out, while I get Clarus up and over the wall. I'm sure I can bring him in close enough to deal that final blow."

"I think I could scale the wall on my own," Clarus said quietly as he walked into the room. "Especially after what your man did to it." He sat down close to Vera, but not too close. She appreciated him giving her space. "I don't think any of my forebears ever imagined someone doing something like that."

"Yeah," Rubicus said. "Flaveo was like that."

"He was a brave man," Clarus said, bowing his head. "I am glad I had the chance to meet him." He shot Vera a slight smile. She gave him one back, and then scooted a little bit closer to him. There wasn't much in the room. The house had been abandoned in a hurry, but the owners had clearly been of simple means. It was cold and getting colder. He took the hint, and relocated, sitting next to her, and wrapped an arm around her. "I truly am sorry for your loss."

"It's okay," Vera lied. "Or it's going to be, at the least."

"It will be," Clarus said resolutely. "And his sacrifice won't be in vain, either." He spoke a little louder now, loud enough for the others to hear. "The Cavean's forces will have been severely thinned out. Perhaps carving our way to it is no option, but stealth may be our ally now. It will not have the eyes and ears everywhere it did."

To Vera's surprise, Caerella nodded. "Agreed. It is highly possible we die tomorrow. The wounds healed by Vera and her... Aesling—" She still sounded hesitant when she acknowledged Vera's companion. "— They healed well, but not perfectly. They pull at my muscles."

"I'm sorry," Aesling said quietly.

"She apologises," Vera translated. "She, no, *both* of us did what we could."

"I do not doubt that," Caerella said. "If there was no limit, the Cavean would not have stood a chance. This isn't an indictment, Aesling, Vera. An observation. When I fight tomorrow, I will likely not be my best." She shrugged. "I may die."

"Aye," Rubicus said. "That's the truth of it."

"How can you be so calm about that?" Vera asked in disbelief. "Both of you? Don't you care?"

"Of course I care," Caerella said. "If we do not help Clarus take that creature down, it will consume the Capital, then the rest of the country. Everything and everyone I have cared about would die." She stood up. "That can not happen."

Clarus gave her another nod. "Whether you would do so for your country or for the people in it, you are fighting for the lives of the people in my kingdom. Thank you." Caerella nodded back at him. Rubicus saluted him with two fingers.

"You had better do something sensible with it, then, if me and mine are to die for it," Caerella said, gesturing at Rubicus.

"I'll avoid that if I can," Clarus said frankly, and then smirked. "If not for you, then for Vera. She's already lost one family member today." Caerella smiled, quite genuinely.

"I believe we understand each other, Prince Clarus," she said, and then turned on her heel. "It's my turn on watch, if I recall correctly. Get some rest, Ruben. The night is long."

Rubicus just grumbled in response, crossing his arms, but he closed his eyes all the same. Vera knew she ought to do the same. She had to get some rest before dawn. But well...

Clarus was here. Next to her. His arm still around her shoulders. Earlier, she felt like she had trouble feeling like anything, numb more than anything. Now she was full of feelings, and all of them were loud and conflicting. A part of her dreaded the possibility that Caerella was right. That tomorrow, they might not be alive at all. It had all seemed so hopeful, before. Before Flaveo.

But then there was the voice in the back of her head. If this was her last night with Clarus... She had to make it last, didn't she? Make the most of it? She looked up at him, his handsome features only accentuated by the blonde stubble that lined his jaw.

"Can we speak?" she asked. "Alone, preferably?" He looked at her for a moment, his eyes steely even in the dark.

"Of course," he said, then pushed himself upright. Vera expected him to have his usual flair and grace, but he stumbled slightly before offering his hand. His face didn't show it, but the exhaustion was there, in the stiffness of his shoulders. In his eyes.

Vera gladly took the hand, and found that despite everything, his strength was still his. She almost fell into his arms, the ease with which he pulled her up making her blush and Aesling positively giddy.

"Do you wish me to... retire?" Aesling asked. *"I understand if you'd like a private moment. Clarus and I have had a long time to know one another."*

Vera shook her head. "I want both of you to be there," she said quietly as she led Clarus to the only other room in the house, which appeared to be both a living space and a bedroom. She deliberately did not look at the bed, knowing the heat in her cheeks would spread across her face and all the way up her ears like a wildfire.

Clarus leaned against the table, happy to let her make the first move. *"That bastard,"* Aesling quipped. *"How dare he."*

Vera walked up closer to him, not sure how to begin the conversation now that she was in front of him. What was she supposed to say? "Clarus," she said.

"Good start."

"I know you wished to have this conversation yesterday..." she said, "but if something *were* to happen tomorrow—"

He shook his head. "No," he said. "No dramatic farewells, after all." He smiled. "Though I did promise to tell you how important you are."

"Wait," Vera said, feeling the conversation slip between her fingers. Clarus closed the distance between them, stopping in front of her. She wanted him to put his arms around her, but she also knew he wouldn't. Not just like that, at least. So she took the last step. Simply resting against him. Her head against his chest. His hands rested on her back.

"You have no idea how important you are, Vera," he said. "Yes, your body is host to my beloved Aesling, but that isn't why." She felt him smile. "Well, not just."

"Good."

"You're brave and beautiful, and that too contributes to how important you are, in ways you can't imagine." Clarus softly kissed the top of her head. "Without you, I doubt myself, Rubicus, Caerella." He paused. "Flaveo. I doubt any of us would have made it as far."

"I barely did anything," she mewled. "I did not come up with any plans, and I am not as good with a blade as you or Rubicus, and—"

"And yet you are here. You harbour a spirit unknown to yourself, while going through changes that would have most in this kingdom reduced to nothing, preparing to fight a monstrosity that has made every fight in your life pale in comparison." He kissed her on top of her head again. "I understand that, where we are, in this moment, strength is not a choice but a necessity."

"But—"

"And it is not where you are strong but where you are *not* that takes my breath away. You helped me find my way when I felt lost. Stood by both Rubicus and Flaveo when they did not stand by you. You are vulnerable, uniquely so, and yet you are here. At the gates, by my side. That's... There are no words for that, Vera."

"I... thank you... I didn't really have a choice..."

"You did. That, I think, is my point."

"Thank you," she mumbled, resting her head against his chest. This conversation hadn't gone like she'd expected it to, and now she was crying.

"Now what did you want to tell *me?*" he asked a little sheepishly.

"I don't want tomorrow to be here," Vera said. "It will come, I accept that, but not yet." She sighed. "And I don't want you to go. I don't want to go, myself. This..." she tapped his chest. "I want this."

"As do I, Vera." His hand rubbed soft circles between her shoulder blades, relaxing her.

"This is lovely."

"Ash enjoys it too," she said with a little smile. "Both of us... enjoy your arms around us."

"Well, I'm happy to oblige. There's nothing on this earth — or beyond it — more important than the two of you."

Vera took a deep breath. Her heart skipped a beat in anticipation, then hammering in her chest, like a drumbeat.

"I love you, Clarus." There was no sound in the room for a second, only her breathing and the deafening roar of her heartbeat in her ears.

"I love you too," he said. "Of course I do." He gently lifted her jaw, making her face him, and kissed her.

Chapter Twenty-Four

Fool By Morning

Vera stirred in her sleep. Dreams came hard, and heavy. At first, they were dreams of loss, and that made sense, in a way. Powerlessness. Pain. Watching it happen, over and over again. Trying to do something different, and none of it mattering. Flaveo dying. There was a part of her — maybe it was Aesling — that seemed to be aware of all of it. That this was grief. That this was normal.

That didn't make it easy. Watching Flaveo erupt like a candle, sparks striking his skin like a match until he *was* fire and lightning and white, bright power. Over and over and over again. His smirk as he looked at them one last time, his fate already sealed.

It was happening again. She fought off the Demons, even harder this time. Every time, every time she hoped that if she fought harder, if she was just a little faster, just a little stronger, she would be able to stop him. To save him. But she heard his voice again. Telling her to run. She refused. Shouted that she wouldn't let him, but then Rubicus and Clarus dragged her away as she saw him drink his doom, vials shattering in gravel and sand.

Then fire.

The next dream was different. It was quiet. Calm. It was *Dark*. Hollow. Worse. She was in an empty field, at night. There was nothing in any direction. No grass grew.

The world if the Cavean wasn't stopped, of course. A pillar of flame was better than this. Everything was cold. The world was cold. And in the distance, there was that laugh, that laugh that made her remember that time she'd ventured into a cave and something had stirred in the darkness, something slick and wet shifting against stone, stones bouncing off the cavern floor in infinite echoes. It was a humourless sound.

It was everywhere. The laughter of the Cavean, its horrible, malicious glee, rang through her head until it tore her heart from her chest and she could only try to run with legs that refused to go, claw at the air powerlessly with with arms that had no strength.

"Vera."

She cried as she opened her eyes and realised she was awake. It was still dark. But not *as* dark. Not *as* cold. Not as hollow. It was the healthy, normal darkness of healthy, normal night. In the back of her mind, Flaveo was still dead, but it was... well, it wasn't okay. It wasn't going to be okay for a very long time. But it was... accepted. A thing that had happened. A truth about the world. Not a horror to be fought.

She sat upright. *"You were having a nightmare,"* Aesling said. *"Several, in fact."*

"I was," Vera said. "I'm sorry if that was upsetting for you. I don't want you to have to deal with that every time I close my eyes." She wondered what it'd be like if Aesling ever had nightmares. Would they show themselves in her head? Like nightmares? Or would she experience them too? Or would Aesling suffer in silence?

"I don't dream," Aesling said. *"I sleep deeply, as the trees do. But do not worry. Your nightmares are not... intrusive. But I thought it best to let you suffer them anyway, if only to grant you the rest you needed. Was that all right?"*

Despite her general confidence, and the sense of protectiveness she exuded, Aesling seemed insecure, unsure.

"Yes. It was." Vera swung her legs off the side of the bed and stretched. "Don't fret, Aesling, if I didn't trust you with my well-being, I'd have picked an earlier time to say something. Thank you."

Aesling chuckled, and was about to say something — Vera could *feel* the intent coming off of her — but then stopped. *"Vera, look."* Vera looked around the room. It was dark, but her eyes were quickly adjusted to the gloom. She assumed it was one of Aesling's little gifts. Nothing stirred. Nothing that she could tell would have put the Nymph on edge.

"What is it? I don't see anything," Vera said. "Is there a threat I'm not seeing?"

"No," Aesling said, *"it's Clarus."*

"I don't see him," Vera said, and then suddenly realised what that meant. They'd laid down together. She stood up and got dressed as quickly as possible, shoving her feet into her boots and barely lacing them. Stepping out of the room, she looked around. Caerella was asleep against the far wall, her head resting on her bedroll. There was no-one else in the room. "Caerella," Vera said. As she expected, the woman's eyes opened immediately. She barely moved.

"Rubicus is standing guard," Caerella said as if by explanation. She looked at Vera. "Clarus isn't with you." Vera shook her head, so Caerella went from sitting to standing, seemingly without going through the steps people usually took in between. "Vera, I need you to answer a question, and I'll need you to be honest with me."

"Anything," Vera said, biting her tongue. She got the feeling this question wasn't going to be a pleasant one. She didn't look forward to it.

"How smart is this prince of yours?" Caerella said as she began strapping her battle-axe to her back. "If I look outside the door, what are the chances that Clarus is out there, keeping Rubicus company?"

Vera had to think about that for longer than she cared to admit. Clarus was a clever man. He had a quick wit and a sharp mind to go with it. He was also, when it came to heroics, as subtle and considered as a rockslide. "Low, Caerella. The chances are low."

"I thought so. Grab your gear." She shot Vera a glance. "And lace those boots, or you'll break your ankle." Guiltily, Vera bent down and did as she was told while the woman stepped out. She heard Rubicus swear loudly, immediately afterwards shushed by Caerella. A second later, the large mercenary barrelled into the room, his jaw squared and thunder and lightning coming off of his brow.

"Your man is trouble," he said as he grabbed his pack and threw it onto his back in a single move. "Let's go save his sorry ass." Despite herself, despite her worry and fear, despite *everything,* Vera couldn't help but crack a smile.

They needed Clarus, of course. To save their land. Their people. Maybe even the world. But even then, neither of them had hesitated for even a moment. Clarus was in trouble. Clarus was going to be rescued. There was no deliberation. Just a series of factual statements. She grabbed her own pack, and the four of them, counting Aesling, stepped out of the building, and suddenly Vera realised she didn't know where Clarus had gone. He probably hadn't used the front gate. She looked over there. It was barely standing, and even from where she stood, she could see the stirring of shades in the shadows in the rubble.

"Focus," Aesling said. *"You do know where you went. I have sharpened your senses. Focus them. See. Smell."* Vera closed her eyes and opened them again. The night's darkness seemed to give way to… depth. Depth in shadow. Like there were more hues of shadow she could discern between. Details she hadn't noticed before. Okay, she reasoned, he likely used the back door of the building. Then what?

Walking around the house, she found a set of footprints in the dirt, and then knelt down. She smelled his scent, ever so slightly. She looked up. "I think I know where he went." Caerella raised her eyebrows.

"Lead the way."

Vera followed her nose, and the trail, as best she could. Clarus had gone a little ways off the road, dodging between the buildings to avoid being seen by any stray Demons, but closer, ever closer to the wall. Once there, the damage done by Flaveo's fire really became clear. Even here, hundreds of yards away from the epicentre, the stone slabs had shifted and tilted, leaving enough space between them for someone with determination and some serious grip strength to climb their way up to the top.

Clarus had made his way to a tall building, a watchtower or firehouse. It leaned against the city wall. Vera looked up. "I think he used the building to get up on the wall."

"That's what I would've done," Caerella said. "Dumb, but not stupid." With that enlightening statement, the three of them began the climb. First up the ladder to the roof of the building, and then the much more arduous task of working their way to the top of the city battlements. The outer walls of the city were high, but not as high as the inner rings.

They took a moment at the top of the wall to catch their breath while Vera made sure they were still on his trail. His scent was faint, but it was still here. And then she saw it. Some sand disturbed there, more recently than anything around it. Her senses were razor sharp now, and she was grateful Aesling didn't do this all the time. She could already feel the headache coming on, the constant hyperstimulation of her vision, her hearing, was starting to make itself felt.

"Come on," she whispered. "He can't be far." It was true. Below them, inside the walls, in the city streets, she saw shades moving, but not many. Flaveo's sacrifice had not been in vain. There weren't that many left. Too many to take on, maybe. And if the Cavean was unleashed on the inner city, it would quickly rebuild its army. But for now, they moved unseen. And the Cavean couldn't be far.

They followed the movement of the Demons, as a point of reference. It took her a moment to notice it, a moment of deliberately unfocusing her eyes, to notice it. The Demons moved… not exactly as one. It was more like wind through a field of grass. Some moved first and then others, further down the street, and then those even further moved. Then the first stopped, and then the next and so on. Always with the slightest of delays.

She pointed at a point a bit further. A large meeting hall, close to the inner-city gates. All movement of the Demons started there, and then ebbed outwards. "There," she said.

"I see it," Caerella said. "Ruben?"

"Aye," he said. "Not far. Think it's there? Think it's got your prince?"

"No," Caerella said, "if it had the Prince, it'd be outside the gates, taunting the defenders with his corpse. And if they were fighting, the Demons would be rushing in."

They snuck closer, while Vera scanned the streets. Clarus wasn't on the wall up ahead anymore, that much was certain. But if he wasn't there, where was he? She stopped at a rampart. There was a rope tied around one of the merlons. "He went down here," she said, and looked down. It disappeared into the street below. No Clarus.

"I've found your prince," Caerella said with a voice weary from a life of hardship, decades of fighting and travelling, and at the moment, Prince Clarus. She pointed. Vera followed the direction.

She saw the large gathering hall. She saw Prince Clarus, sneaking on the rooftop. She saw Prince Clarus, drawing his sword. Then, Prince Clarus, in all of his beauty and grace, uttered a battle cry and crashed through the roof.

"I love that man," Aesling said. *"Go save his life."*

Vera, Caerella and Rubicus all looked at each other. Without another word, Vera grabbed the rope, and threw herself off the wall, on her way to keep the man they both loved so much from heroically dying at the hands of the Cavean.

Her boots hit the ground with a thud she felt all the way up her spine, and she broke into a sprint. The snarling of Demons already bounced off the walls of the street around them, and they were starting to close in. She wasn't going to get there in time, she knew, but that fact wasn't going to keep her from trying.

Chapter Twenty-Five

A Turn For The Worse

It had been a day. One day to recover, when she'd fought for her life. And now, again, she was in the thick of it. Contrary to some, Vera had never enjoyed fighting. Sure, the rush of adrenaline was as overpowering for her as it was for anyone, but she'd never felt "the joy of a good battle" like Rubicus had described it.

But fighting for someone, even if it was someone who had gotten himself into trouble, made it easier somehow. She wasn't trying to stop an unstoppable wave of hatred and teeth, she was pushing forward. They weren't with their backs up against a wall. They were on the offensive, and they were going to rescue Clarus. *She* was going to rescue Clarus, if it was the last thing she did.

"It won't be." Aesling was with her every step of the way. When she wasn't increasing her strength and speed, she was drawing Vera's attention to what she *wasn't* noticing. A grunt from Rubicus as his leg acted up. A cut or a nick on Caerella's arm she'd try to pretend she didn't have. In a single leap, Vera would close that distance and heal them if necessary.

The three of them, in the middle of the road, were being attacked, but not swarmed. Demons poured in from all sides, but not nearly to the degree that they had been in front of the gate. Hope mixed with dread in her stomach. On the one hand... the Cavean's army could be beaten. On the other... What if she was too late? What if Clarus was already bleeding out inside the hall on the other side of the street they were trying to cross?

"Not worth thinking about," Aesling said. *"We'll save him."*

"We will," Vera said, gripping her short sword with renewed purpose, and led the three of them continuously forward, when something struck her. "Where," she said, between strikes and dodges, "is the *army?!"*

Rubicus dented a Demon's face with the edge of his shield, and then cut it off with a single strike. "We're fighting them, I reckon! The war's been over for ten years, the Cavean showed up at the gates without fanfare... Nobody was ready!"

"But the rest of the army, they outnumber this lot a thousand to one!" Vera said through gritted teeth.

"If it gets inside those gates," Caerella added, "no army will stop it."

"And there's not a man that can stand up against that thing and live!" Rubicus bellowed as he cut a Demon stem to stern. "Trust me, I'm a fair better fighter than most and I wouldn't want to fight it!"

"Well, there's one who's bested it, and he's in there," Caerella pointed out.

"All the more reason to save his ass!" Rubicus laughed. Vera couldn't help but crack a smile. Despite the events of the previous day, Rubicus was giving it his all again, and Caerella was calm as ever. Under the surface, Vera saw the cracks, but they were... normal. Normal, regular, expected pain. Manageable.

"Lead the way, Ruben," Vera said, and found that she had enough space for a little bow. She had to quickly abandon the little gesture to dodge an attack, and countered it with a strike to the spine the way Caerella had taught her.

Then their bulwark, Rubicus, pushing forward with his shield, barrelled past her and crashed into another one of the creatures. She decapitated it almost casually as she walked past it, and realised how easy it was coming to her. Not long ago, she'd been almost paralyzed in fear when she'd first come into contact with the creatures, and now they were just that. Creatures. Mindless in their rage and lust for carnage, and therefore a threat only for as long as she didn't keep her wits and her head about her.

Caerella closed ranks behind her, as the three of them advanced on the building. The Demons didn't let up. While their band killed many of the things, now ashen silhouettes in the street that would stain the ground for years, there was seemingly no end to them.

"Any sight of him yet?" Caerella asked. Vera looked over her shoulder. The woman was doing all of her fighting while walking backwards, her axe a whirlwind of steel. It was like she was swinging a baton at a fair.

"None that I can see," Rubicus said. They'd reached the other side of the street. Now-inside the city walls, the streets were well-worn but well-built, with raised pavements and stepping stones. The large hall that Clarus had barged into was some kind of gathering hall, Vera reckoned, and the large doors had been closed.

She tried not to think of the people that had been inside when the Cavean had entered it, closing the doors behind it. The creature was certainly cruel enough for something like that. Instead, she tried to think of Clarus, bravely fighting and defeating the monster, saving his kingdom or, barring that, holding his own until his allies arrived.

"Hold on," Rubicus said. "I think I see something." Vera peered past him at the building, and she understood why he was being vague. There was a sort of flashing behind the windows, but it was hard to tell what was actually happening in there. Whatever it was, it was likely magic, and therefore bad news.

She looked at Rubicus, and then Caerella. They both nodded at her. "Go." Vera nodded back, then broke into a sprint without saying anything more. Nothing more *needed* to be said. Behind her, she heard Rubicus bellow a war cry and the whistling of Caerella's axe. She knew they'd hold the creatures off while she went to rescue Clarus. She wasn't going to risk him. Her Clarus. Aesling and hers both.

"Our fool," Aesling said.

"Our fool," Vera said with a smirk as she reached the door just in time for them to swing open and the hard oak slammed her in the face. Without really being aware of how she got there, she found herself looking up at the clouds.

"Get up!" Aesling said, and Vera, realising, she'd fallen over in a daze, quickly rolled over. On top of Clarus. *"Clarus?!"*

"Clarus?!" She pushed herself up and blinked at him. He blinked back.

"Vera!" Clarus said. He had several cuts and bruises, but was otherwise alive and filled to the brim with his impossible, infinitely endearing enthusiasm. "Careful!" He threw her off of him, and then rolled the other way. A second later, a sword, larger than that of any man she'd ever seen, crashed into the ground splitting stone. Shadows curled around the blade, and she knew the thing that wielded it.

She jumped upright, vaguely aware that Clarus was doing the same off to her side. She stood opposite the Cavean again. The creature felt even taller now, its death-mask a cruel facsimile of death itself. It stared at her, and for some reason she felt more malice and hatred come off of it than she ever had before.

"Well, Princeling," the Cavean said, with a voice like dying metal and rotting wood, "it seems you will watch your beloved die in front of you anyway." It turned to face him. "Or would you rather I devour your soul in front of her, instead?" With a dry rasping sound that Vera realised to her horror was a chuckle, it strode towards Clarus, raising the sword again. It was as tall as she was, a thin sheet of metal that wouldn't have to be sharp to cleave someone in two. The Cavean wielded it in one hand, and brought it down with a strength ten men couldn't muster. Clarus dodged it with an almost casual ease.

"I don't think either of those will happen, foul creature," Clarus said as he sidestepped another blow. He made the fight look easy, until Vera realised that he was out of breath. He wasn't dodging because the Cavean's blows were that easy to avoid, but because blocking its blows was likely beyond impossible. Nonetheless, Clarus wore his trademark grin like a badge, gleaming in the morning sun.

The Cavean advanced at him. "Foul creature? Is that the best you can do? You lack the cruelty to match me, Princeling." It swung the sword, cutting a groove a foot deep into the earth, leaving shadows in the air. Vera kept low, trying not to draw attention to herself as she flanked their enemy.

"It's what you are," Clarus said as he swung his sword in gentle figure-eights in front of him, baiting the Cavean to swing at him. "Foul. A failure. You failed your emperor, you failed your foul, infernal armies and you failed your mission," he continued. "You were stopped by a boy not even halfway through his third decade. You are nothing, Cavean. A mistake." Vera could barely believe this was the same Clarus she'd grown to know. His jaw clenched. His eyes cold. The Cavean said nothing, but simply observed him. "I'm *capable* of being cruel, Cavean. I simply choose not to be. You are not worth me lowering myself to that level."

The Cavean's response was just to swing its sword again, a strike that would have taken Clarus off at the torso if he hadn't dodged underneath the blackened blade. Vera saw the mistake before he did, the creature following up the swipe with a backhanded strike. The sound of its gauntlet of shadow and steel hitting Clarus square in the jaw as he was thrown backward rang across the street. Even Rubicus and Caerella, in the distance, turned to look for a moment.

Vera screamed and rolled past the Cavean to run to Clarus' side. Thankfully, he'd managed to roll with the punch, though he'd been thrown quite a ways away. He was bleeding quite heavily from his head, and he felt his jaw. Vera heard it pop in and out of its socket and she grimaced. "You're okay," she said quickly as she put a hand on him. His wounds started to heal, and she saw relief in his eyes. Relief, quickly replaced by horror as he looked past her. She saw the hand reflected in her love's eyes before she felt it, grabbing the back of her collar and throwing her back against the wall. It knocked the wind out of her, all her senses screaming only pain in unison.

"Vera!" Clarus shouted as she fell to her knees. Aesling was already knitting her bones back together, but it was hard to breathe nonetheless. She heard her prince scream with rage as he charged at the Cavean. When she looked up, she saw to her surprise that he was driving it backward. The infernal general moved its sword with more speed and precision than any person could with a sword that size, but it didn't seem to be enough. Clarus' sword was a silver blur, and he pushed forward.

To all their surprise, the Cavean stood, quite literally, with its back to the wooden wall of the gathering hall. Clarus wasn't letting up, seizing the upper hand as he had it, using the advantage of his speed and finesse to its fullest.

And then the Cavean made one more desperate swipe, which Clarus avoided with an angry ease, bringing his sword down with all his strength and rage, onto the Cavean's wrists, following up with a strike aimed directly at the creature's heart.

Time stopped as the sword dug deep, then came to a sudden halt, piercing the Cavean's armour. Vera heard her own breathing first, her heart pounding in her ears. Then a sound, more horrible than any she had ever heard in her life. Like a millstone grinding her mind to dust, the Cavean's laugh burrowed itself into her heart. The thing took Clarus by the throat. Its other hand, equally unharmed, grabbed the Prince's wrist.

"You fought well, Princeling," the Cavean said. "Now, you'll die in front of her."

Chapter Twenty-Six

The Inevitable

Her body moved before her mind had even made a conscious decision. With all of its strength, its malice, the Cavean would likely think of dozens of ways to make Clarus die gruesomely in front of her.

It wasn't going to. That wasn't a desire, or a plan. It was a statement of fact. Her bones and muscles screeching, barely holding together, it was like moving through water. It all slowed to a crawl as her boots thudded the earth like a war drum. She was vaguely aware that Aesling was spurring her on, just like there was an awareness at the corner of her mind that she was shouting.

There was nothing in the world but the Cavean and Clarus and Vera. The creature towered over them both, and seemed to grow even taller in its victory. She was barely half as tall as it was, it seemed. Maybe it was her imagination, and maybe it didn't matter at all. Her sword had been thrown aside, but that didn't matter. There was only that forward momentum. The Cavean slowly turned its head to face her, and Clarus followed its gaze. He screamed something and raised his hand.

Maybe it was her imagination, but she imagined she saw the Cavean's death mask grin as the creature slowly pulled Clarus' sword from his chest and brought it to bear. It was going to make her watch as her love was skewered. Well, that's what it thought it was going to do.

Ash stopped trying to heal her now. That wasn't important anymore. Instead, she did everything she could to speed Vera up. Make her even faster. Her muscles were on fire, and she felt like she was going to explode. But she was faster than it was, and that was all that mattered.

With all the inevitable relentless force of a glacier, she descended on the two of them. And then time seemed to resume. Her hand found the Cavean's wrist, and she yanked as hard as she could while she rolled underneath it. She thought her shoulder was going to dislocate, but she felt it move. In the same move, she slammed her heel into the Cavean's knee. She hit the ground face-first, dust and sand clogging up her nose and her eyes, and none of that mattered, either. Because her ears were clear. And what she heard was the most beautiful sound in the world. It was divine. It was the sound of Clarus' triumphant laugh as he wrested himself free of the Cavean's grasp and hit the ground with a roll.

She forced herself up on heavy arms — it was getting harder, even Aesling was having trouble keeping up — and unsheathed her dagger. At this point, it wasn't likely to make a difference, but its heft, the weight in her hand, was a reassurance. More importantly, she had a sneaking suspicion that would require a blade to verify.

"Vera!" Clarus yelled as he jumped over to where her sword had fallen, then made his way to her. "Are you all right?!" She raised the hand with her dagger in response and nodded, still too out of breath to reply verbally. The Cavean bent over almost casually and picked up its oversized sword. It still had the Prince's in its off hand.

"You," it said, looking at Vera, "are determined, are you not, to become a footnote in history? When they tell of the death of Clarus and his Kingdom, they will mention the waif who delayed his death by seconds. You must be proud."

"I know I am," Clarus said, flashing his teeth in a grin that had never been more infuriating. If he wasn't so far away — and there hadn't been a deathly general trying to kill them — she could have kissed him. "Come on, foul one. Or would you kill us with barbs as weak as your strikes?"

"Very well," the Cavean said. "I will permit you to die together." The speed with which it swung the massive blade was staggering. Vera only barely managed to avoid the arc. It would have split her head in two, and she saw that Clarus had also dodged at the last moment. But the Cavean kept coming, two blades slicing through the air with lethal force and determination.

Vera, too, had to constantly dodge and sidestep the largest of the two blades, though Clarus did what he could to keep that one from hitting her. For her part, she tried to parry the other sword when she could, to keep it from slicing her prince to pieces. But that was a losing game. She looked up at Clarus.

"Trust me," she said. It wasn't really a question. He looked down at her, his blonde hair sticking to his sweat and dust-covered forehead, and grinned.

"Always," he said, and Vera dove past the blades into a roll. Clarus laughed again, seemingly bolstered by her confidence. Good, because she didn't actually have it. But she had an idea and sometimes ideas were enough. And his enthusiasm was both infectious and, to the Cavean at least, infuriating.

Despite its quiet composure, it was coming for Clarus with wild abandon. The Prince had trouble dodging the attacks, but something was different. Despite the Cavean's speed and strength, it was getting predictable. The finesse with which it had wielded its massive blade was gone.

"What are you thinking, Vera?" Aesling said. *"I can feel your triumph, but in its rage it will only kill Clarus faster, and us with it."* Vera circled around behind the Cavean, dodging its swipes when it remembered she was there. She occasionally feinted, so it didn't think she was planning something.

"Clarus' sword went right through it," Vera mumbled as she tossed the dagger from hand to hand, trying to keep her wrists supple the way Flaveo had taught her.

"Yes," Aesling said, exasperated. *"It ignores steel like a tree would a housefly."*

"No, it doesn't," Vera said. Aesling stopped cleaning the dust out of Vera's lungs and the pain out of her knees and back, and gave her a confused stare, insofar as that was possible in her own head. It was easy to imagine Aesling standing next to her and giving her a disapproving stare.

"Yes, it does. Didn't you just say you saw Clarus' sword going through it like it wasn't even there?" Aesling sounded annoyed now. It was funny, Vera thought, how much room for emotion there was when in a fight for their lives. She wasn't the person she'd once been.

"Yes. Clarus' sword went right through it. But you fought it once before, right? How did that end?"

"I barely remember, but back then, something was different. Clarus slew the creature, sealed it away inside himself and forced us all to sleep along with him. Until you woke him."

Vera circled around again. Clarus was on the defensive, but he was holding his own. The Cavean was far less coordinated now, through rage, confusion or perhaps its own form of exhaustion. And Clarus was making use of that, expending minimal effort to redirect its blades. There wasn't much she had to do to keep the creature between them.

"Something was different," Vera said. "You're right." She flipped the dagger in her hand a few times and felt its weight. She took a deep breath, and then another. *Everything* hurt. Her whole body had been pushed to its limit. "Hey!" she shouted. "You! The bastard!" The Cavean turned her face to her. It seemed almost astounded that she'd address it so casually. Even Clarus was nonplussed, letting his sword hang by his side for a moment.

The Cavean raised itself to its full height and advanced. Its stature blotted out the sun, and she really, *really* hoped she was right. "Do you wish to die first, child? I can obli—"

"You were right, Aesling," Vera said loudly, talking the Cavean into a stunned silence. "Something *was* different ten years ago!" She spun the knife in her hand and took a low stance, knowing it was likely going to attack her again, and there wasn't going to be much she'd be able to do to defend herself. The Cavean raised the giant sword again. She was going to get exactly one chance at this. "You were!" Her arm flashed, just like he'd taught her. The sword came down.

The dagger flashed through the air in a perfectly straight line. Flaveo would have been proud. Its thin blade embedded itself in the Cavean's mask, right in the forehead, with a hollow *crack*. Its weapon crashed to the ground, missing its mark. It screamed. It roared. Its mask cracked. Just like it had the day before. Just like it *hadn't* when Clarus had struck it. There was a line, like a lightning bolt, that ran down between the hollow sockets, and shadows themselves seemed to be seeping out from it like thick, viscous tar.

She ran forward. Stunned by a knife still wreathed in Aesling's magic, the Cavean would nonetheless soon recover. There was no time to explain to any of them. Clarus had never sealed the Cavean away. There was no divine birthright of kings that granted such power. But the trees? Nature? They knew what to do with a shade like this. The forests were full of shadows.

"Vera!" Aesling said with a mix of horror and triumph. *"What are y—"* But there was no *time* for questions, questions couldn't be risked. Words couldn't be risked. She put one foot on the giant blade, and jumped.

She soared. The Cavean looked up at her, its hollow eyes empty as ever. She had hoped for maybe a hint of fear, but there wasn't a thing that could escape the infinite nothing behind the mask. Not even fear. Not that that mattered.

Slamming into the thing's chest knees first, Vera grabbed the hilt of the dagger with one hand, and pushed the pommel with the palm of her other, as hard as she could, driving and twisting the dagger deeper into the inky blackness.

Her impact against the thing's torso had pushed it off-balance. But now, the cracks in its mask widening and the black ichor burning into her hands, it was starting to topple backwards. She screamed right in the thing's face, the thing that had killed so many, that had taken Clarus' father and almost him with it. The creature that had killed Flaveo. The Cavean. The Hollow One, all-consuming.

She pushed.

It fell and she did not let up for a moment, holding on to the dagger as much to drive it forward as she was using it to keep from falling off of it. She slammed the heel of her hand, over and over again, into the pommel, until the Cavean's mask shattered. But that wasn't enough. Screaming, Vera shoved the dagger, hilt and all, deep into the Cavean's mask, until her hands were coated in the burning black shadows of its form.

"Now!" she screamed. "Aesling! Now!!" She shoved both her hands into the creature's skull, and felt the Melia's magic course through her body and into the thing's skull.

"If we seal it back into its slumber," Aesling said, already understanding what was happening and helping as best she could, *"it will take us with it. Please, look at Clarus one more time. I want the last thing we see to b—"*

"No," Vera said, gritting her teeth so hard she thought they were going to explode. Magic poured into the Cavean and she could feel it. The line between herself and Aesling was blurring. She wasn't *just* a vessel for the Nymph's magic. "That's not what... we're..." There was the sound of tearing souls and rending flesh and roaring hatred.

Then Vera and Aesling stood in the glade. Their glade. They looked at each other. "Ah," Aesling said. "I believe I understand now."

"You cannot kill me," the Cavean said, not nearly as large or intimidating now, standing between the trees. "I am immortal."

"Oh," Vera said. "Then this is going to be extremely unpleasant for you."

Chapter Twenty-Seven

Horror Vacui

"We finally meet face to face, monster," Aesling said with not a hint of the mirth or pleasantness usually found in her voice. "Much as I dislike fire, burning you out of this world will provide me with satisfaction I can't put to words."

"I don't even know who you are," the Cavean said. It was complete again. The destroyed mask was whole within this realm. Hollow eyes glared unblinking from under a tattered black hood. "I have burned many forests and groves, you will be simply another in my path, Nymph." It took a step forward, raising its hand. Out of the shadows, its wretched blade began to form.

"No," Aesling said. "You will not. You are *nothing.* You pride yourself in it. A hollow, a vacuum in this world that sucks in all light and leaves nothing in its wake." Her words seemed to make the Cavean chuckle, but she wasn't done. "You are *abhorrent,* creature." She raised a hand. The trees moved around the Cavean, the canopy opening up to let through the light of an imaginary sun. The sword vanished like a snuffed-out candleflame. "Nature," the forest guardian said, "abhors a vacuum."

"Your threats are empty," the Cavean said, its voice like a rumble through metal, but Vera heard an uncertainty in its voice. "I will *destroy—*"

"*NOTHING!*" Vera bellowed as she stepped forward. "You will destroy *nothing*, you despicable, fleshless *thing!* You are a bad dream, a spectre from a time we have moved on from!" With that, she closed the distance between them, and stood before it.

Before, in the world of the real, it had towered over her, not quite twice her size. It had been a terrifying, imposing thing. She didn't know if she was taller or it was shorter, in here. It didn't matter. She stood face to face with the Cavean, the creature that had upended her world, killed so many, both ten years ago and now. She faced it, and smiled.

"You end here."

"You *cannot kill—*" the Cavean began, and was interrupted when Vera decked it in the face with a full-bodied haymaker that would've made Rubicus proud. The Cavean went flying backwards and landed among the dead leaves and fresh vegetation with a wet thud.

"You said that already," Vera said, rubbing her hand. Even though as she understood it this space was a construct of Aesling's, that had still hurt. Worth every cracked knuckle. "This is not your world, Cavean." She spat out its name like bile. "This is mine. Ours."

Aesling stepped up next to her. "In here, there is nothing to keep you from our wrath."

"You can not keep me, wenchling," the Cavean spat as it rose to its feet again. "I will escape this feeble place, burn the mind out of you, and I will wear your face when I kill that pathetic prince."

"No," Aesling and Vera said at the same time, then looked at each other. Aesling bowed, and Vera continued. "No," Vera said. "You will not. And that was the wrong thing to say." She stepped forward again. The Cavean reached for her but she swatted its hand away. It was strong, still, but in here she was too. She was as strong and much, much faster. She grabbed it by where the collar should be.

Holding it in one hand, it was strange to see it be as formless up close as it had been from far away. She'd always imagined it as a being cloaked in shadows, disguising its true nature, but there was… nothing. Hollow armour wrapped in black cloth. Nothing beneath. Her hand had closed around shadows where its throat should be, but there was resistance nonetheless.

"I had originally planned to seal you away like you had been ten years ago. Sacrifice myself and Aesling in a slumber and lock you in here with us. Clarus would have either done the noble thing and sealed us away, or maybe some zealous Godsman would have slain us in that sleep," Vera hissed. "And that would have been the end of you, and of us. It would have been a good end."

The Cavean, grabbing her arm, tried to wrestle itself free. It was failing, losing strength by the minute. "I will escape," it said. "Your Prince will not be able to live without you and will raise you from your slumber. I will—"

"You will do *nothing,*" Vera interrupted. "But you're right. The plan was flawed. It didn't contain you last time. So that is not what will happen." She grabbed the mask and threw it to the ground. As she suspected, there was nothing underneath. Just shadows and malignant nothing. Still, she wanted to look at it, naked and vulnerable.

"You can not destroy me either, child. So which shall it be? Doom or oblivion?" It laughed, laughter turning to a confused snarl as vines started to wrap around it. Aesling appeared at Vera's side.

"Neither, hollow one," Aesling said as she walked around it. "You will be awake. Chained. Guarded." Vera ripped off the hood, and the shadows where its head had been quickly grew faint, now that they had nothing to hide within. Aesling stood behind it, and she and Vera shared a brief glance.

"By us," Vera continued. "Nobody will know you are here. You will fade into history like a bad dream. Nobody will remember you as anything but a footnote of a war long won." Aesling's vines stripped the creature of its blackened, shadow-rotten armour. Each piece fell to the ground like tired hammers striking an anvil, sealing the Cavean's fate. What lay underneath was not even a creature. Just the suggestion of form.

Aesling leaned forward and hissed next to its head. "You will not be honoured. You will not taste success, or freedom, or victory, ever again." The Cavean didn't even react.

"You will not die," Vera continued, "just as you said. But you will not live, either. Not for your old master, not for yourself, not for carnage or death or the end of our world. You will exist. Within us. Powerless to do anything but rage."

It took barely any pressure from Vera to force the thing to its knees. Its growling voice was reduced to the hum of hollow whispers, like someone scratching at a window. Aesling's grove grew around it. Vines, though hissing at the touch with the thing, strengthened their grip and pulled it down against the roots of a large oak. "And the trees," Aesling said, "care not for your rage. Your words will not be heard."

Finally, the Cavean spoke again. Moss slowly began to cover it, roots grew over it. Even the bark of the trees bent to deny it freedom. Its voice was a low whisper, a gust on the wind. Even laid low, it still had the strength for a curse. "I will seep into the soil," it said. "I will drink from the wells beneath the trees. I will corrupt your grove and come for you when you are laid low. As I am never free of you, you will never be free of me. Your nightmares and fears will be *mine*, until the day you succumb."

Vera kneeled down next to it, and looked at the thing. Usually, pity came easy to her. Not here. Not now. Some things were beyond pity. Understanding, maybe. But not pity. "You," she said, "are nothing special now. I have lived with monsters like you my whole life. You are a voice in a muted choir." She stood up and turned away. Aesling didn't waste another word on the thing. Behind them, the Cavean spat more hissed threats and curses their way, but they were lost on the wind.

Standing in the middle of their grove again, Vera and Aesling sat against a tree. The sun shone on their faces.

"Did we do right?" Vera asked. "Maybe we should have sealed it like you did once before." She looked at Aesling. Despite her confidence in the face of it, now that there was distance between her and the fight, it was hard not to think about things that could have been done differently.

"I believe so," Aesling said. "It wasn't wrong. If we'd repeated the actions from last time, we would've repeated the same mistakes. And the cycle could have repeated, easily. I love Clarus more than anything, but he would have never stopped searching for a way to wake us. And who knows what he would've found on his search."

"You're right," Vera said as she closed her eyes, letting the sun fall on her face. Through her eyelids, the red warmth filled her vision, and she smiled at it. She felt she hadn't had a chance to really relax. "Still, it was probably not lying either when it spoke of infecting the soil. Will you be able to keep it at bay?"

"I will," Aesling said. "It isn't one for empty threats, but neither am I. There is no curse it can levy that I can not match. There is no shadow older than the stone or tree that cast it. And if it does try something?" She nudged Vera with her elbow. "We'll defeat it. Together. Again." Vera grinned.

"Yes, we will."

"What now?" Aesling said. "Are you ready to return?" Vera opened her eyes.

"Not yet," she said. "I would like to stay in here a little bit longer. I have the feeling that these next few days... It'll not be quiet."

"There will be celebrating and grieving to be done," Aesling agreed. "I do not envy you, Vera. I live here." She waved at her grove. "I witness your world, but you are the one who walks it every moment of every day." She smirked. "With the occasional exception," she said, clearly thinking back to her moments with Clarus.

"I can retreat here when I have to," Vera said, "and I may just do that in the coming days. It'll be a lot, and I will value your companionship and your advice as much as I have your saving my life these past days and weeks." Aesling shrugged casually, but Vera wasn't having it. "No," she said. "I feel as if I've not properly thanked you for what you've done. You have kept myself and my allies alive. You saved Caerella from what was done to her. You made me into the woman I am now, and I would have nev—"

"You may have," Aesling said. "Stranger things have happened. I only cleared the way for you." She smiled. "But you are welcome for saving your life. That was my pleasure."

"Fine," Vera said. "But I owe you a great debt, Aesling. I don't know if I'll ever be able to repay you adequately." The Nymph scoffed.

"Nonsense," she said. "I get to see my Clarus, hold him, kiss him, and I do so with your blessing." She looked over at Vera, who nodded, a quiet confirmation that this wasn't changing any time soon. "Without you, that would not be my reality. As far as I'm concerned, you don't owe me a damned thing."

Vera chuckled softly. "Very well, have it your way, Aesling." She stood up and stretched, then held out her hand to Aesling, clasping each other's wrist as she pulled the Nymph to her feet. "You have been a good friend to me. Allow me gratitude for that, at least."

"As long as you allow me gratitude of my own," Aesling winked. "Now, let us wake up, or Clarus will go grey with worry."

"You're right, of course," Vera said with a laugh. "Let's."

She opened her eyes. She had expected to be laying down next to the corpse of the Cavean, or whatever body it would have left. Instead, she was looking right in Clarus' eyes, wet with tears.

"Vera! Aesling!" he said, his voice breaking. "Are you all right?" Vera raised an arm and realised how weak the fight had left her body. Even Aesling'd had trouble keeping up with the damage done to it.

She smiled weakly. "I am sorry for worrying you, my Prince," she said. "I'm here."

"I thought I'd lost you."

"Never," Vera said. "Although I may want to rest a while."

"Then rest you will," Clarus said with determination, like he was planning to fight an army to get her to a bed. He lifted her with ease, one arm under her back, the other under her knees. Vera giggled in surprise and wrapped her arms around his neck. "I will carry you as long as you need me to."

"I love you," Vera and Aesling said, their voices out of her mouth together. Clarus looked at them in surprise, and then smiled.

"I love you too," he said. "Now, let us get your friends, and tell them the news. The Cavean is dead."

"Something tells me they know already," Vera said, looking over at Rubicus and Caerella, who stood as sole pillars in the middle of a street. The Demons surrounding them had sizzled into blackened scorch marks. Rubicus' bellowing laughter could be heard all the way over, much to Caerella's feigned annoyance.

Chapter Twenty-Eight

Congratulations

This wasn't Vera's first time in Coalis. It was, however, her first time being carried by a Prince through the streets of the Capital. It was strange seeing them so empty. The first time she'd walked through here had been accompanying Rubicus and Flaveo. They'd put her up on the horse, so she could see above the crowds. She'd barely been responsive, but even back then there'd been the sense that there had been more people there than she'd ever seen together in her life, even if she was later told it had been a market day. It was strange seeing these streets so empty, now.

As Clarus got to the gates, however, she heard voices. Good ones, full of life and excitement and very human fearful hope. Then there was more shouting as people high up on the walls seemed to realise there were people in the streets, rather than Demons.

The outer walls of the Capital were the thickest, to withstand invasion, but the inner walls were higher. From where Vera was clinging to Clarus and consciousness, they seemed impossibly tall. She was pretty sure Aesling was helping her stay awake.

The gates, titanic, imposing, slowly opened. Ordinarily, they'd never close, and the metal and wood groaned in protest as the old hinges were put through their paces. Whoever had built them so long ago had built them with foresight, however, because they swung open steadily, without hitching.

On the other side was a wall of scared soldiers, spears raised. Behind them, on rooftops and barricades, wherever they might've fit, were people far too young to hold a weapon, awkwardly training bows at the gate. It felt like the whole city had been prepared to make a stand.

At the front stood an old man in full plate-mail, his sword and armour polished and gleaming almost as brightly as his moustache in the mid-day sun, looking suitably confused as he raised his weapon. Then, thinking better of it, he sheathed his weapon and approached them. "Allow me to do the talking," Clarus said quietly. "Commander Tolemo is... old guard. I can't believe he's still alive, really." Vera nodded. She was happy not to have to carry a conversation in her current state.

"This is a trick..." he said, with no conviction at all. Clarus smiled and shook his head.

"Tolemo, I can swear on whatever you like that it isn't."

The man frowned, his moustache quivering. "We lost you, my Prince. It's been..." Behind him, Vera saw several people peering up and over each other to get a look, maybe catch a word of what was being said.

"Too long," Clarus said, then looked behind. "Its doing, I'm afraid."

"Well, looks like you came back in the nick of time to save us single-handedly," Tolemo said, looking around. "I can't believe y—" Clarus interrupted him with a raised hand.

"Not my doing." He lowered Vera until she was standing, slightly unsteadily on her feet. Tolemo looked at her as if he only just now noticed the fact that Clarus had been carrying her the entire time. "She's the one who killed the creature. Saved the Kingdom. And myself, I might add." Vera gave a weak wave.

"Hi," she said as Caerella and Rubicus joined them. "They helped," Vera added.

"Oh... Oh m— I mean... Well... Congratulations are in order... I mean..." Tolemo's face seemed to be going through a lot of different emotions at once, seemingly trying to process the new information. "Well... a statue... and, and a medal are surely in ord—"

"I intend to marry her," Clarus said matter-of-factly. Tolemo's moustache bristled, and his eyes seemed like they'd pop out of their eyes. "However, we're both very tired, and we'd like to get inside the city. The Demons are gone. Their master is dead."

"After a fashion," Ash said internally. Her voice was muted, like she was face-down on a pillow. Vera envied but didn't blame her. She felt like she could sleep for a week.

"We must alert the King..." Tolemo started, and Clarus' face fell. "The King had travelled up north in secret..." Slowly, the pieces seemed to fall into place for Tolemo.

"There's a corpse-witch outside the Winter Palace," Clarus said. "My Father is in her care. I would travel up there to collect him myself, but I'm afraid I'm barely standing as it is." Despite the weight of the days leading up to their final confrontation seeping into his voice, his grin was bright as ever. "I think I'd like to sit down."

"I... Yes, of course... Prince Clarus." He looked back at the troops, then back at Clarus. "Allow me?"

"All yours, good man," Clarus said. He looked at Vera with a smile as Tolemo turned around. The Commander unsheathed his sword again and held it up. "Victory!" The roar from the crowd was deafening. Spears hit the ground, and Vera saw that most of the soldiers were wearing older armour, ill-fitting or hastily worn. There had been a lot of spirits at the front gate, after all... But none of that mattered now. The air was thick with joy.

If Vera hadn't had a headache before, she would've had one now. But it didn't really bother her. People swarmed them, but Tolemo, clearly a bit more savvy than Vera would've given him credit for, still had his sword out, and no matter how jubilant, people did tend to keep their distance from sharp steel. Rubicus' imposing presence probably helped too. Tolemo quickly ushered them forward through the gathering crowd, when an older man's voice broke through the noise.

"Prince Clarus?" he said, and for a second, everyone grew quiet. Whispers spread outwards, until it was like they were standing in an autumn cyclone, dry leaves whirling around them. And then, of course, as dry leaves so easily do, the whole thing erupted like wildfire. The cheers of victory were replaced with additional jubilation. The Prince had returned to save the kingdom!

Clarus' attempt to stifle the rumour fell on surprisingly deaf ears. He smiled apologetically at Vera. She returned the affection happily though. She wasn't exactly looking to become famous anyway.

Clarus looked up. Somewhere in the distance, above the sea of people and houses, was the Palace. Vera presumed, anyway. She'd never seen it up close. It was going to be a long walk, and she was already starting to buckle again. That's when Rubicus' voice broke through the din.

"Alright, you sods!" he bellowed. "Out of the way! You two!" He pointed at two militiamen who had been cheering on a cart. "*Get down from there!*" They did as they were told, their legs obeying the command before their brains had really processed who had actually told them. Rubicus had that effect on people. Even Tolemo looked up at the man for a second, probably getting ready to salute out of sheer force of habit.

"Army man?" Tolemo asked.

"Not for a long while," Rubicus said with a grin, then turned back to the men. "Get those horses moving! Or do you think your Prince ought to walk the whole way?!" Once again, they sprang into action. Despite how silly the whole thing was, Vera was happy for Rubicus' intervention, and Clarus was happy to help her onto the cart once it had turned around. Rubicus climbed up onto the box, the cart lurching a bit when he pulled his full weight onto it, balanced only slightly by Caerella.

Slowly but surely, the chaos was beginning to fold itself into something resembling structure. Tolemo seemed to have managed to get some men on horseback to flank the cart. It wasn't a very fancy cart. It was made of wood and it creaked and smelled of cabbage. Vera and Clarus sat next to each other, their legs dangling off the back, waving at the people excitedly following them.

There were *so* many people. "Should you say something?" Vera asked him. He shook his head.

"Not until we get back to the palace. For now, all anyone needs to know is that the threat's gone. The war's over before it had a chance to really begin again. And people will be able to go outside and reclaim their homes. Also," he added, with a little smirk, "I just want to catch my breath, if it's all the same."

"That's entirely fine, love," Vera said, reached over, and then pulled her hand back. The last thing she wanted was to put him in an embarrassing situation. The Prince had returned — though he'd be King now, she realised — and this was supposed to be his moment, after all.

He seemed to have figured her out, wrapped an arm around her shoulder, pulling her close to him, and kissed the side of her head. "If I'm going to marry you, my beloveds, I think my subjects are going to have to put up with a public display of affection."

Already, the crowds following were whooping and hollering at them. Several younger women looked absolutely furious at Vera. Any other day, her cheeks would've burned and there'd have been a pit in her stomach. Right now she was too tired, though. The rush of battle still pumped gently through her veins.

What she did wonder was how she looked. For the first time in her life, Vera was actively self-conscious about her appearance. She hadn't cared for ten years. But now, she wanted to at least splash some water on her face, to make herself presentable. Clarus, next to her, was covered in dust and grime, his armour bloodied and scratched, his hair tangled and matted. But his smile was as powerful and radiant as ever. Nobody could look at him and not see him for who he was. How would she look next to him?

Her thoughts were interrupted when the carriage came to a stop. Vera looked behind her. "Oh," she said. There was a whole palace there. It had clearly been built a long time ago, with practicality in mind first. It was, in short, a fortress. But over the years, someone had decided that if the fortress was to be a palace, it'd have banners, minarets and some gold trimmings. But even with all the things that had been added over the years, the palace towered. Hard.

Clarus, with a resigned sigh only Vera could hear, stood up onto the cart. When he raised his arms, the crowd cheered. People had come out of their barricaded houses and had flooded into the square in front of the castle. And now, all eyes were on Clarus.

"People," he said, his voice clear without him having to shout. There was a chorus of cheers. "*My* People!" A bigger cheer, and some who hadn't realised who Clarus was were being informed by the people standing next to them. "You've likely heard it by now. The monster that was outside these walls has been defeated!" That one seemed to have hit the spot. The roar of triumph rolled outwards of the square, and through the streets, although it paused occasionally for the hard of hearing or those too far away to hear him. He smiled down at her, and she smiled back. He looked so... perfect, covered in dirt and standing on a cart in the middle of a busy square.

"And he's ours," Aesling said with a grin Vera felt in her soul.

"Lives were lost," Clarus said. "Many lives. Of friends. Of your countrymen. Of family." He paused. "My family. My Father... King Lucius did not survive. Tomorrow will be a day of mourning, of course. But we can not dwell on what we lost," he continued. "We have to rebuild. Celebrate the lives of those we lost. Those who laid down their lives so that we might live." Clarus looked down at Vera, who remembered Flaveo with tears in her eyes. "And yes," he added at the end with a wink and a smile at the crowd. "I'm back."

After that, it was hard to hear anything over the crowd at all anymore.

Chapter Twenty-Nine

Acting The Part

"Stop fidgeting."

"I can't, it's these bloodrotten, dungfecked buttons."

"Ruben," Caerella said, "if you don't stand still, I'm going to shove this here candelabra all the way up y—"

"Shh," Rubicus said, with a grin on his face, "you're missing the ceremony."

Vera was having a really, really hard time keeping a straight face. In front of her, one of the most important events in her life, in Clarus' life, and in the life of most of those gathered was taking place. The crowning of a new king was the kind of thing people didn't easily forget, but the ceremonial burning of the old crown and the forging of a new one by King-To-Be was a long process, with lots of pauses for chanting in languages nobody had spoken in centuries. And *next* to her were Rubicus and Caerella completely failing to take any of it seriously.

"Do we have to wait for the metal to cool or is he going to put it on his head like that?" Rubicus asked. "Even after dunking it in water like that, that's got to sting, right?"

"That's not water," Caerella said, "it's some kind of resin."

Rubicus and Vera both slowly turned to look at her while still trying to keep up the impression that they were guests of honour who were honoured to be there. "How do *you* know *that*?" Rubicus whispered.

Caerella's face was a mask of steel. "I asked." In the centre of the throne room, on an elevated platform, Still-Prince Clarus was reciting some old and awkward text, recanting the responsibilities of Princehood and pledging himself to those of Kingship.

"*Why*?"

"So that I could answer stupid questions, Ruben," Caerella said with a sly smile.

"You *bi*—" Rubicus started, when Vera stepped on his toe and he clenched his jaw. The twinge at the corner of his mouth betrayed the effort that went into not laughing out loud.

"Behave, both of you," Vera whispered. "This is important."

"Is it?" Rubicus whispered. "I can't tell, the Godsman just keeps waving that incense and chanting." He did straighten up again a bit, then scratched at the front of the jacket. It was honestly surprising they'd found a uniform in his size, and he looked suitably out of place. "How much longer do we have to stand here, anyway?"

"Until Clarus is crowned king, Rubicus," Caerella hissed back playfully. "I thought that was obvious." She pursed her lips. For the ceremony, an official had attempted to get her to wear a dress. He'd walked backwards out of the room under her withering glare, much to Vera and Rubicus' delight. And then she'd shown up in a modest-but-nonetheless-elegant dress anyway, and her friends, Clarus included, hadn't known where to look. Her muscular shoulders and arms were covered in a network of scars from a lifetime of battles, and the metal bands she wore on her upper arms did nothing to hide them.

By contrast, Vera had opted for a long-sleeve dress. Well, that wasn't entirely true. Clarus had offered her the dress and she'd fallen over herself to accept it. It was beautiful, white lace on black silk, it made Vera look more elegant than she'd ever felt in her life. Of course she'd cried when she'd seen herself in the mirror, and Aesling had been more than happy to let her bask in it. The dress had belonged to Clarus' grandmother, apparently, easily signalling to everyone present exactly who she was supposed to be. Whispers had bounced off the walls of the throne room from the second the doors had opened.

"They're likely done soon," Vera said, "so at least try to look like you've been paying attention." On the dais in the middle of the room, Clarus handed over the newly forged crown, kneeled, and the Godsman placed it on his head with a bunch more old poetry. The piece itself was cast mostly out of a mould, but its centrepiece was unique to each ruler. Of course, the sigil that adorned the crown on Clarus' forehead was a tree.

He looked over at Vera, who gave a small wave, and was then reminded by an annoyed Godsman that he was now king and that he should stand up instead of looking at the gathered guests, no matter how important they might personally be to King Clarus. There were a few sniggers from the audience, and Vera felt eyes on her. She blushed slightly, knowing what was being implied.

As soon as Clarus stood upright, however, everyone fell silent. He looked around the room, his almost-white hair framing his face under white-gold crown. The weight of the title seemed to immediately make itself known. When he raised his head, it was with the knowledge that he was Prince Clarus no more. He was a king now, and Vera had never seen anyone in her life who wore that mantle as naturally as Clarus did in that moment. Those gathered seemed to all hold their breath as he looked at the crowd. He looked *regal,* and Vera knew how everyone in the audience felt. Every single one of them felt like he was looking at them, specifically, and like they were the most important person in the world. And then, of course, he smiled. The applause was immediate and enthusiastic.

And when Clarus finally rested his eyes on Vera, she felt herself melt inside. She even managed to ignore Rubicus' boisterous laugh when he caught her blushing like a twelve-year-old girl, or the noise he made when Caerella elbowed him in the ribs.

Shortly after, everyone was ushered outside. As tradition dictated, coronation was followed by either the official resignation or the burial — Kings have a limited shelf-life — of the previous regent. Nothing, Clarus had explained to Vera, put your regency into perspective as laying your predecessor to rest.

A large circle was formed out in front of the Palace, around two stone sarcophagi. King Lucius' face had been carved into the largest one, resting for the rest of eternity. King Clarus walked up next to it and put his hand on the carving of his father's.

"My father," he said, "was… a great man. In his prime, he stood against a foe of such overwhelming might that a lesser king would have buckled. But he stood. No matter what happened in the past ten years, that is how I knew him, and it's how I will always know him. A man who stared the death of every single one of his subjects in the face and politely, yet firmly, declined." He looked at everyone gathered. "That seems like an example worth aspiring to, don't you think." There were nods of confirmation, and a few smiled as they remembered King Lucius the way Clarus described him.

Vera just nodded along. Most of the affairs of kings had been so far removed from her life, they might as well not have happened. The way she'd seen it, the actual people who had held off the Emperor's armies had been individual men and women on the front lines, laying down their lives. But if Clarus was to be believed, his father did sound... kingly.

"I loved my father, and I wished I had been there to say my goodbyes. But I would not have been able to bury him if it wasn't for the help of just a few individuals." Suddenly, Vera realised who the other sarcophagus was for. "If there's one thing I would do differently than my father, it's that I am not... as much a stickler for tradition." A murmur went through the crowd, and a few frowns failed to hide themselves. "This sarcophagus will be buried alongside those of my family, as protectors of the royal family deserve."

He looked at Vera. She looked at him. Clarus had promised her that Flaveo would be honoured in some form or another, but she'd expected some kind of footnote in a history book and maybe a payout to Rubicus and Caerella. She hadn't seen this coming, and it was... welcome.

"I did not know Flaveo very well," Clarus said. "I had only a few days to become acquainted. As far as I can tell, he was a man of a great many talents. He was loved, as befits great men. And he saved my life. He saved the life of every person in this city, and for that, he will be remembered." He looked over at Rubicus, who was no longer laughing, and nodded. Rubicus took a step forward, hesitated, and then Caerella put a gentle hand on his arm. That seemed to give him the courage he needed.

"Flaveo was my brother. He was a right bastard at times." There were shocked gasps going through the crowd, but Rubicus pushed on. "If you've any brothers of your own, you know how good it is to have a right bastard on your side sometimes." Some of the older generals chuckled. "He was a great man, like Pr— King Clarus said," Rubicus continued. Large tears started to roll down his cheeks, and his voice started to crack, but he kept going. "But he was, he was also a good one. And— And, I think that matters more, I think."

Vera hadn't even realised she was crying until he nodded, frowned to himself, and then stepped back, wiping his face. The people gathered hadn't known Flaveo, of course. But Vera hoped that maybe Rubicus' testimony would have given them some idea that Flaveo had been exactly the kind of person that was worth remembering. She put a hand on Rubicus' back. "That was beautiful," she said. "He would have hated it."

That got a chuckle out of the large man, and even Caerella cracked a smile. The remainder of the ceremony consisted of everyone paying their respects to the two stone coffins. Most stopped at the first to lay their old King to rest, and then, often a lot shorter, at the second one to thank him for saving the life of their new King. They clearly didn't understand.

Then Vera was up. She stopped by King Lucius first. The carver who had created the stone death mask had done an amazing job. She'd only seen the man across a room, of course, but the amount of detail was remarkable. And she could see Clarus' features in the King's. He'd been a handsome man, once upon a time, until the years had worn him away. But here, immortalised, he was forever as Clarus remembered him. "Thank you," she mumbled. She didn't know what else to say.

"It's okay," Aesling said. *"Pain simply needs to be felt, sometimes."*

The other one, the one without a face, with only a name carved into it, caused her some pause though. She stopped in front of Flaveo's coffin. He'd been like an uncle to her most of her life. And then he'd barely accepted her for who she was. Well, until Caerella had threatened to turn him inside out. And Vera didn't know if he'd actually changed his mind, or if he'd only done so out of respect for the other woman. To say she was conflicted was an understatement. But at the end… he'd looked at her, right? She put her hand on the stone. She knew he wasn't in there — there hadn't been enough left of him to bury — Maybe she was that obvious, or maybe she wasn't the only one thinking it, but Caerella put her hand on Vera's shoulder.

"He did," Caerella said. Vera looked up at her. "Love you," the woman said. "He might have been an idiot about it, but he did." She pulled Vera a little closer, and Vera pretended not to see the tears in Caerella's eyes. She moved over as Rubicus cast his shadow on the sarcophagus.

"Bastard," was all he said, but he smiled anyway, and Vera did too. Between the two of them, they had known each other long enough that words weren't always necessary anymore. Flaveo being dead hadn't changed that in the slightest.

Chapter Thirty

One More Goodbye

She didn't have a lot of time left for things like this, Vera knew. In a week, she'd be a queen. *The* Queen. How did she even *get* here?

"Falling in love with Clarus probably had something to do with it," Aesling offered. And she wasn't wrong, but it was still strange to think about. It was now over three months since they'd found his motionless body up on that tower in the mountains, but it somehow felt both like yesterday and a lifetime ago simultaneously.

She had been nobody at all. And soon, most people in the Kingdom would know her name, and she'd have to read *so* many books, and she'd have to learn to write without moving her lips, and—

"You may want to pay attention, Vera," Aesling said playfully, just as the sword clattered against the bricks next to her head. She dodged down and to the right, into a roll. Getting to her feet quickly, she tried to clear her head.

"Almost had you there," Rubicus said with an amused glare, and he spun the short sword in a small circle. "C'mon, at least give me a *challenge.*"

"I've got things on my *mind*, Ruben!" Vera shot back as she lowered her stance. Against Rubicus, she had to use her speed more than anything. He was larger, stronger, and his reach was almost double hers. "I'm going to be Queen next week! *And,*" she added while she circled him slowly, "I'm wearing a dress."

"I'm sure anyone you fight will be happy to wait until you're all done processing and getting changed," Rubicus said, and then lunged, raising his weapon, then pausing for a second, before slamming the weapon down swiftly where Vera had been a second ago. "Better," he said. "But not good enough. You can't afford to muck about."

Vera took a deep breath and weighed the wooden sword, trying to read his movements and intentions. Usually, the eyes were a dead giveaway, but lately she'd been fighting... things without eyes. So she'd gotten into the habit of reading her opponent's motions. And Rubicus was very hard to read when he wanted to be. "I mean, you're not giving me a reason to do my best, are you?" she tried. With a bit of luck, he'd try to do something to prove her wrong. Baiting an opponent was always an option.

"No need to show off, girl," Rubicus chuckled, "your audience is already captivated." It was true. The courtyard they were in wasn't especially large, but the colonnades were slowly filling up. Vera had hoped that early morning palace life would have given them some privacy, but apparently it wasn't to be. News of the Queen-to-be — was she technically a princess? She'd have to ask Clarus — sword fighting in the Eastern Memorial Courtyard had made its way through the Palace faster than any invading army ever could.

Vera looked at the gathered faces and thought she saw Clarus for a moment. That was her mistake, of course, and Rubicus made his move. She saw him step forward and turn his shoulder to her, using his sizable bulk to obscure his weapon for just a second before swinging. She saw it coming, though, and moved her sword just right to deflect the blow and hopefully get a parry in. The strike never came.

Rubicus' feint had worked like a charm, and she felt like an idiot as his shoulder hit her in the sternum.

Vera had fought Demons and walked away. She had fought an undead thing, a Lich, general of the armies of a foul emperor, not just to a standstill, but *won*. But Rubicus putting his entire weight behind a shoulder check really knocked the wind out of her.

She was thrown back, and a gasp of shock went through the audience as Vera was thrown backwards. For a brief moment, she wanted to just take the hit and catch her breath on the ground. But then again, it would probably reflect badly on Rubicus if he just knocked Clarus' consort to the ground like she was a teenager playing pretend and he was... well, a weathered veteran. She'd decided for herself not to rely too much on Aesling during the fight, but now, maybe an intervention was in order.

"On it," Aesling said, and Vera felt her body spin in mid-air, tipping her foot against the ground just once to land gracefully on the edge of the courtyard. Aesling grinned. *"Not even a challenge,"* she said internally, and then slipped back, letting Vera step back into the driver's seat. "Is that the best you've got, old timer?" Vera said smugly.

There was a small applause from the audience. She imagined she probably looked like the hero who saved their city right now, but she knew she couldn't afford to let up now. If there's one thing Rubicus punished quickly, it was hubris. Right on cue, he rushed forward and immediately led the charge with a series of quick blows, but not particularly hard ones. The sound of wood on wood filled the small space.

"Cheating, you two? Really?" Rubicus said in between his attacks, just loud enough for her to hear it. Vera felt a little bad. With Aesling's helps she could probably overpower him, but he'd been adamant that she should still be able to fight without the Nymph's help.

"Just putting on a good show for the audience," Vera replied. Rubicus stopped for a second, stepped back, and then started laughing, throwing his head back. When he looked back down at her, his grin bisected his greying beard.

"That's my girl," he said, before launching into a roaring charge that sent several of the ladies-in-waiting scampering. But Vera noticed the wink he'd given just before. And he was coming in low, his stance wider than usual. It reminded her of the way the Demons attacked. Taking the hint, she dodged under his wide swing, and tapped the back of his leg with her sword, and he immediately dropped to one knee.

She raised her sword for a theatrical coup de grace, but he spun around just as she landed her blow. Both their swords stopped a hair's length from each other's necks. Both panting, they stood there for a moment, before both laughing.

Vera offered her hand. Rubicus' coal shovel happily took it and let her help him up. "Well fought, your highness," the big man said, and immediately the crowd whooped and hollered in a very ignoble way. "Next time," he said more quietly, "you're not walking away until one of us has a black eye, you understand."

"Perfectly," Vera grinned. "But I'm not going to go easy on you."

"Better not," Rubicus said as he slapped her on the back, hard enough to make stars appear in the corners of her vision for a second. "Come on, your highness, let us go wave Caerella off." Vera nodded. She wasn't looking forward to that, really, but it wasn't goodbye. Not really, anyway. Caerella and Rubicus would be back.

"I wish you'd stay a while longer," Vera said. "It's going to be awful quiet here." They walked next to each other through the beautiful halls of the Palace. Someone was probably going to complain later because of her and Rubicus dragging dirt inside.

"Eh, we'll be back in a few months," her old friend shrugged. "Six at most. But I can't sit here and be pretty all day. That's your job now." He nudged her, almost knocking her into an alcove. "And we've got to do something with all the gold that King of yours showered us with."

"You could do that *here*," Vera argued, knowing it was a lost cause.

"There's a rumour of a great warrior out there, and I'm going to either recruit the little bastard or beat him into the ground to teach him a lesson about hubris," Rubicus said matter-of-factly. "And Caerella needs to scout some places."

"Still…" Vera said, not really having anything more to add than that. "I'll miss you."

"Good," Rubicus said. "I'd be furious if you didn't." They stopped in front of the guest door. "You'll do fine, Vera. Besides, you'll be so busy, it'll be over before you know it. You'll have to be queen, I'm sure Clarus will keep you plenty busy running things because he'll be too busy getting himself into trouble."

"You're one to talk," Vera said, smacking his shoulder. "You're, what? Pushing ninety?"

"I'm going to pretend I didn't hear that," Rubicus said as he knocked on the door. After a few seconds, Caerella opened the door. She was wearing her travelling clothes. "Housekeeping," Rubicus said with a big grin. Caerella rolled her eyes, but smiled when she held the door open anyway. Vera stopped in front of her. The other woman nodded, and then they had their arms wrapped around each other.

"You better come back soon," Vera mumbled into Caerella's shoulder. She got a gentle squeeze as a response before they stepped away. "I mean it."

"Well, technically you *can* order us to stay," Caerella said, and then looked over at Rubicus, who sat down on the bed. It creaked under his weight. "You know how well that would go." She smiled, genuinely. "I'm just scouting new locations, Vera. Jokes aside, Ruben is getting wise enough to decide he'd rather die lying down, but neither of us are ready to stop just yet. And we do need a few more people in our merry band."

"Yeah," Vera said. "I mean, I could go with you..."

Caerella put her hands on Vera's shoulders. "No," she said. "You couldn't."

"I'm just..." Vera said, walking through the room listlessly. "I'm not ready for the two of you to leave, Caera." That got her a raised eyebrow. Vera dramatically waved her arms. "It feels like only yesterday when the two of you were mere babes, and already you're taking your first steps into a wider world—"

She stopped when she was hit in the face with a pillow. "That's enough out of you," Rubicus laughed. "We'll be fine, Vera. And so will you. You're a grown woman, you're clever, and you're never alone." She looked her deep in the eyes. "Take care of her."

"I will," Aesling said. "While I am here, I would like to wish both of you the best of luck. Thank you, for being there for Vera when she needed you."

"You as well, Aesling," Caerella said. "From both of us, even if Rubicus is too much of a giant baby to admit that he's afraid of you."

"Am not," Rubicus grumbled. "Thank you, Aesling," he added. "See? I'm fine."

"Clearly," Caerella said. "Anyway, the two of you... take care of each other, and of that fool King of yours."

"Oi," Vera said, "he's... okay he *is* a fool, I can't really deny that. But he's a clever one!"

"Most clever ones are fools," Caerella said. "Consider that my last lesson before I head off." She walked over to the bed, kicked Rubicus' legs to make him lift them, and then pulled her bag out from under them. "We'll be back before long, Vera. You're Queen now, which means..." She stopped.

"Means what?" Vera asked. Rubicus propped himself up on his elbows.

"I honestly don't know," Caerella said, and then laughed. "I don't have any advice for you, Vera. I think, out of the two of us, you'll have the more difficult job." She threw the bag over her shoulder, and then put a hand on Vera's. "You'll do great, Vera. Make us proud."

"Promise," Vera said. "Now go, before I order you arrested for a few days."

"Yes, your highness," Caerella said with a perfect curtsy, and left.

Chapter Thirty-One

Feared and Beloved

The world, Vera realised, looked different from high up. The city, the Capital, spread out below her. The concentric circles of its walls, and the houses built between them according to a pattern that made less sense with every passing year. With the sun down, she could see lanterns moving through the streets. It was like watching candles float down a stream.

"Not bad," Aesling said. *"You know. For humans."* Vera smirked. *"I'll grant you that the view from up here is… pleasant."* The 'up here' Aesling was referring to was the King's quarters' balcony. They were wearing a gorgeous green dress that had been specifically chosen because it went with their eyes so well, flowing gently in the evening breeze.

"I assume it's to remind the King every morning who his subjects are," Vera mused.

"More likely," Clarus said, "it's so that could look *down* at his domain or some such." He wrapped his arms around her from behind and kissed the back of her neck. "The Kings who built the Palace, and the city around it, were conquerors first and foremost."

"Is that why everyone just calls it 'The Capital'?" Vera joked. She knew almost nobody called it Coalis. Clarus rested his chin on her head as they looked out together.

"Most likely. I know that's why they named their kingdom 'The Kingdom.' They were great warriors, if their histories are to be believed, but great poets they were not."

"Nobody named it afterwards?" Vera looked behind her with a sceptical smile, which Clarus promptly planted a kiss on. "How dare you," she giggled.

"Just like that," Clarus said. "Anyway, plenty have tried. It was 'Fortitudo' for a generation or two, but it didn't stick. 'Nativitatis' didn't even survive for two years. Someone tried to name it the Kingdom of Lucis after himself, but he was beheaded after six days." He smiled sheepishly. "The Country's history is a bit of a mess."

"I'll say," Aesling laughed.

"Lucis?" Vera asked. "Like Lucius? Like your father?"

"Yes," Clarus said. "My father was actually Lucius the Twelfth. I am, I'm happy to say, Clarus, First of my name." He looked back at the city. "Maybe you can name it?"

"The Vera Queendom," she said with a dramatic sigh. "I don't hate the sound of that."

"Feared around the world," Clarus said, "she ruled with a stern yet gentle hand."

"Feared and Beloved," Vera corrected him. "She brought about an era of peace and prosperity." She turned around and wrapped her arms around his neck. He smiled faintly like lilacs, his shirt of a material softer than any she'd ever felt, let alone before she'd been moved into the Palace. "I think I have no idea what I'm doing, and I'll be more than happy being 'Vera the Quiet, Queen Consort to Clarus the Bright,' if it's all the same."

"I don't believe for a second that *you*," Clarus said with a little kiss on her nose, "will fade into anything as obscure as that." He raised an eyebrow. "That goes for both of you. Although after the attack, it's probably best the general public isn't aware of Aesling just yet."

"We did the same when I was with Clarus," Aesling explained after taking over the reins for a moment. "The scrutiny would have been unbearable, so we decided to hide my existence. From everyone."

"Including my father," Clarus said. "He wouldn't have understood."

"I don't like the idea of hiding you," Vera said, slipping back forward. "But I see the wisdom in it."

"Regardless, I've never met any two women, any two *people*, as capable as you two are. Together? I wouldn't be surprised if you *didn't* take the world by storm." He smirked. "Although I'd like to enjoy peacetime for a while."

"I wasn't planning on starting any wars," Vera laughed. "But I'll keep it under advisement regardless, your highness."

"You had better not call me that after tomorrow," Clarus said.

"I'm nervous," Vera said. Clarus kissed her softly, and then gently held her against him.

"There's no need, love. First of all, the ceremony is *very* difficult to ruin, I promise you. My great-great-great-grandmother set a precedent, and with it a very low bar to clear."

"What did she d—"

"She burned the palace down," Clarus said matter-of-factly. "She dropped a candle on her dress and, while running outside to the pond, she lit up the banners and several guests."

"Oh *Saints,* I shouldn't laugh at that," Vera said, absolutely laughing at that.

"And beyond that, there's not a soul in this city that does not think you're worthy of the throne," Clarus continued. "I think some of them consider you more qualified than myself. You *did* slay the Cavean, after all." Vera just grumbled, unwilling to admit defeat. "And *finally,* if someone decides to oppose your coronation and our marriage, I'll be happy to duel them."

"You are, and will ever be, my hero, Clarus," Vera said. She was only kidding a little bit. "I just hope I'll do well."

"I know you will," Clarus said. "You've been deserving of the title of Queen since the moment we met. All we've left to do is formalise that fact."

"If you say so," Vera said. "Are you sure there isn't more I should do? The official words are... sparse." She'd been rehearsing the coronation ceremony with the majordomo. Despite the actual ritual apparently taking over three hours, she had only a few sentences she was expected to repeat.

"I am sure," Clarus said. "The words were shortened after my great-great-grandmother forgot her lines."

"Don't tell me she also set the Palace on fire," Vera joked.

"No, she stabbed the Godsman," Clarus said. The noise Vera made was distinctly unladylike. The two of them spent a few minutes chuckling at things they shouldn't, before relaxing into each other's arms again. "Anyway," Clarus continued, "you've nothing to worry about."

"If you say so, love."

"I would ask that you do not stab any officials or burn down the Palace, though."

Vera nodded sagely. "It'd be frowned upon."

"Exactly."

"*But* in keeping with tradition."

"True."

"I'll try to restrain myself. I'll ask Aesling for help."

"I appreciate it," Clarus said, and he finally stepped away, leaning on the balcony railing and looking out at the city, the moon bright in the night sky. "It's strange," he said.

"It feels like I've been fighting for so long, this peace feels… unreal."

"I'm sorry," Vera said. For Clarus, the war had never ended, after all. His slumber had gone by in the blink of an eye. His magical sleep, though it had capped off the war for the rest of the Kingdom, had been a gambit. He'd closed his eyes to violence, and he'd woken up to it. "But you can rest, love. Please do."

"Sadly," Clarus said, "I can't." Vera raised a curious eyebrow. "Sadly, there are one or two more things that need my input for tomorrow that I've been putting off."

"Well then go *do* them," Vera said, scolding him with a playful swat on the shoulder.

"I would have expected you to try and keep me here!" Clarus laughed.

"Well, for one, this way you'll be back in your room, and our arms, sooner."

"Royal We?"

"Practical We," Aesling said with a wink.

"And *secondly*," Vera continued, "it's not every day I become Queen. If there's something that still needs to be done, I'd rather it be done sooner rather than later."

"As you wish, my Princess," Clarus said with a deep bow. "I will attend my duties, then find my way back to you, as I ever will."

"You'd better," Vera said, and then grabbed him by the front of his shirt and pulled him in for a kiss that briefly, but brightly, set the night aflame, and then she let him go. "I love you."

"I adore you, Vera, Aesling," Clarus said. "If every star in the night sky came down right now and burned a hole through the earth itself, it would be like a candle compared to even a fraction of my burning love for you."

"You," Vera and Aesling said together, "are ridiculous. We adore you. Now *go!*" They laughed. Clarus' perfect grin drew their gaze with him all the way out the door, until it closed behind him.

"What a fool," Ash said. *"Our perfect fool."*

"Ours," Vera said, sighing wistfully as she leaned against the bannister. "How'd we get so lucky?"

"All thanks to you," Aesling said. *"For which I'll never stop being grateful."*

"You've already done more for me than I could ever repay you for," Vera said, "so don't you start." She smiled into the evening air. Spring had warmed the stones, and it was taking a wonderful moment to lose its heat.

"How touching." The voice set Vera's teeth on edge. She frowned and closed her eyes. She was not going to permit tonight — or tomorrow, for that matter — to be ruined by something like that.

"Quiet, you," Aesling said to the Cavean, but Vera nonetheless allowed herself to slip into Aesling's grove. They stood next to each other in the clearing, the Cavean on its knees in the shadow between the trees, a desiccated form, barely recognizable as something even resembling a human. *"It's been attempting to free itself all night."*

"I know," Vera said, "I can feel it, gnawing at the back of my mind. Did it make any progress?" Aesling shook her head as she kneeled in front of the faceless thing.

"No," she said. "My bonds are too strong. But I can not shut it up, no matter what I do."

"You can not cage me forever," the Cavean said. "I contain the power of infinities."

"Yeah, you seem plenty contained," Vera said. "At the end of the day, you were never more powerful than us."

"Wrong," it snarled. "I will survive you both, and I'll wear your face as I burn this wo—"

"I told you to be quiet," Aesling interrupted.

"One day," the Cavean said, ignoring her. "You may keep your guard up forever, but one day, you'll realise the power contained in my very being..."

"And you will break out, yes, yes," Vera said.

"No. You will be desperate and alone and afraid. And then you'll have no choice but to come to me."

"Over my dead body," Vera snarled.

"It may very well come to that," it said, and Vera could swear it was grinning, despite not having a mouth to grin with. "You have had a taste of power, Vera, but this woodland sprite's magic *will* fail you, in time. And when it does, I will be here. Waiting. And th—"

"I think I can silence it for a while," Aesling said, talking over it, "but not indefinitely." She stood up and joined Vera again. "At the very least I can shut it up for the ceremony tomorrow."

"Thank you, Ash," Vera said. "I'm sorry you can't officially marry him."

"Don't worry, this is much better than simply existing in his head," Aesling grinned.

"Does he know?" Vera and Aesling turned back to the Cavean.

"Does Clarus know *what?*" Vera asked, her voice sharp.

"That the one who killed his father lives inside of the body of his Queen to be." The usual gravel in the Cavean's voice had given way to something more viscous, like tar. "Does he know, Vera, that I will always be with you? That every time he holds y—" Vines and moss grew over the Cavean, its voice muffled. The growth was already blackening as its monstrous presence eroded Aesling's magic.

"Get some rest, Vera," Aesling said. "And don't listen to it. All it wants is to upset you."

"Yeah," Vera said. "Yes. You're right." She looked at the Cavean, no longer visible as it was covered in plants. She stepped out of the grove and back into the real world.

The evening breeze had become cold, and she wrapped her arms around herself. When she went back inside, the cold came in and stayed with her, all the way until Clarus found his way back to her. By the time they fell asleep, the Cavean's words were barely a bad memory. By morning, she'd forgotten about them.

She was going to be a Queen, after all.

Not The End.
Not by a long shot.

About the Author

Ela Bambust is, ostensibly, an author. What this actually means is that she spends a lot of time drinking coffee and stressing about the relationship status of fictional characters, and bothering her cat, before launching herself at an old and battered keyboard for several hours like a bumblebee at a window. Somehow, words come out the other end, and the result appears to be something approaching literature.

In two years, she wrote twenty novels and novellas, and has shown no signs of stopping, much to the horror of English and literature teachers everywhere.

On Verdant Wings

A Terrible Idea

When later ranking the worst ideas he'd ever had, jumping backwards off the roof would barely make the top five, maybe three. At the time, though, it felt like the smartest thing he'd ever done. Flipping off the two large and *very* angry men as they skidded to a halt at the edge of the rooftop, Roja grinned to himself.

He was going to be rich, he thought as the whole world was reduced to a single moment. Weightlessly floating through the air, the fiery red hair he was named after catching the evening sunlight in his face, he was going to remember this moment for a long time. For better or for worse. Rich.

Well, not literally rich. He didn't really know what wealth was, coming from nothing and then somehow finding himself even poorer when both his parents were killed five years ago. But rich for *him.*

There was an "oomph" from underneath him, exactly as he'd planned it. Planned, and perfectly executed by his co-conspirator. "Wh— *Roja?!*" the Godsmaid gasped as she tried to pick herself up. Legima was a nice enough woman, thirty and therefore too old to even be considered the same species, and she'd been moved to that exact spot to break Roja's fall by his partner in crime. He didn't waste a second, rolling over and pushing himself up off the gravel. There was no time for dusting off, no matter how his back screamed at him.

"You got it?!"

Roja grinned a toothy and likely slightly bloody smile — he'd smacked into a door on his way out — at Maria, and tossed her the bundle. She caught it deftly and broke into a sprint, Roja right behind her and Legima's shouting hot on his own heels. They ducked into a side street, and began the track back to their own district.

Slipping through the gate that separated Coalis' inner city from the outer was relatively easy. The guards weren't paying all that much attention, and mostly trying to keep people *out.* They did need a distraction though, and it came right on time. A small rock hit one of them right between the eyes, and they immediately chased down the culprit, a blur from a nearby rooftop. Maria and Roja made use of the noise, and moved onto the next spot on the route.

Jumping through a doorway into a courtyard, Roja knocked on the wood for good luck. He knew where he was going. This had been a multi-stage operation, and now they needed to make their way through the escape-plan. The next member of their entourage joined them, jumping down from the roof sling in hand. He did *not* look happy.

"This was a bad idea," Selico said as he stuffed the sling into his pocket and ran to keep up with them. "Do you have it?" Maria tossed him the package and he took a quick peek at the contents before closing it again. It'd be a shame to have gone through all this trouble only for them to lose it now.

"You *bet* we do," Roja grinned. "Don't look so glum, Seli." In his defence, Seli *always* looked glum. He ate his food looking miserable, and he enjoyed hanging out with friends looking like he didn't. His friends knew him well enough to know he was just really, really bad at expressing himself.

"I'll look happy when we get home safe," Selico replied, lying as he tossed the package back to the boy. Roja just gave him a blisteringly cheeky grin he knew would annoy the older boy, and pushed himself to run harder. They just had to get into their dormitories, hide the stash, and then he could just pretend his run-in with Legima had been a misunderstanding, and deny everything else.

They skidded around a corner, kicking up dust and stones, only to come face to face with two diacons, men studying to become Godsmen in their own right, though right now they were studying Roja and Maria's faces for what they were sure was either mischief or crime.

Of course, they were guilty of both.

"Scatter!" Roja was already moving while making the call, throwing himself between the two diacons. They both tried to grab him at the same time, got in each other's way and gave the boy *just* enough time to slip out of their grasp and run on, Maria and Selico running around them.

Okay, that hadn't been according to plan. But since he didn't recognize the men, odds were they hadn't recognized him either. After all, the orphanage was a big place, and the city even bigger. He could've been any old street rat. With bright red hair. Surely.

They were basically home free now. He tossed himself through a window that had been broken a while ago — it had been an *accident*, but nobody would listen! Maria helped him up, while Selico went around the long way. If the three of them were seen together, people would definitely be suspicious.

Roja and Maria dusted themselves off. They were in an empty storage room, one where the autumn harvest was usually stored. That was months away, so they wouldn't be accused of anything if they were seen coming out. Maria opened the door a little, still catching her breath.

"Clear," she said. Roja took a step forward, and smacked into her hand. "Wait," she said too late. He rubbed his twice-sore nose again, though it didn't seem to be broken. Well, it wouldn't be the first time. Him and Maria had both gotten into enough tussles for aesthetics to not be their primary concern. "Okay, *now* it's clear," Maria said with a grin and a wink, and stepped into the hallway, a cautious Roja behind her.

If he carried the package like he looked annoyed to be carrying it, nobody was likely to stop him for it. He'd learned early on that nobody bothered you that way, and he'd gotten away with a lot of smuggled food. The haul was a lot more valuable this time around, though.

The peristyle surrounded a small courtyard, the columns' once-ornate carvings eroded over generations. There was a small class being held for some of the younger kids. Things hadn't always been this way. Class? For orphans? It was almost absurd to think about. Coming to the first door, Maria knocked. A young, sleepy-looking face opened it, brightening up when it saw them.

"Do you have it?" the kid asked, practically salivating.

"Keep your voice down," Roja said. "And yes, I do." He retrieved the book from the parcel, and slipped it through the door. "If anyone finds this, you've never heard of me."

"Roja, we live in the same building," they said.

"Okay, fine, yes. But you didn't get it from me." The kid grinned, nodded, and closed the door. Good. That was one. Casually but carefully doing their rounds, Maria and Roja went from door to door. The posh and the rich from the inner cities had more books than they knew what to do with, and it was more than the kids here would ever get to see, no matter how many lessons they got from well-meaning noblewomen and strict Godsmaids.

The last stop. Roja gave the secret knock, and Selico opened the door quickly. They slipped inside and slumped down against the door, releasing all of the built-up tension in excited giggling. Selico glared at them, but finally cracked a smile too.

"Go on," he said. "Open it."

The package on his lap, Roja dug into its depths. There was one book remaining. When they'd gone up to the inner city for the first time, they'd found there were several houses *full* of books. A lot of those were books about natural sciences and history, but there had been stories as well. Heroes and monsters and magic and faraway lands.

Of course, some kids had *wanted* the history books, and Roja had been happy to oblige them, too. He'd made sure to do his research — that was to say, badger every adult he could — before he'd started even planning his grand heist. But it had come to fruition, and they'd gotten away scot-free. And the three of them, of course, had made absolutely sure the haul included something for them, too.

The book was ornate, and very new. The hinges were still slightly slick with oil, and the carvings on the front looked as sinister as they were fascinating. The cover depicted a dragon in flight, except that the artist had managed to imbue the wood with so much life it looked like it could almost pull itself free from the page.

Dragons weren't real, of course, but legends were legends and kids were kids. And if and when Roja and Maria and Selico had gotten their fill of whatever was in this book, they knew they'd be able to sell it for a pretty price that could buy them... Well, Roja wasn't quite sure about that. He didn't know how much this book would actually sell for, and what things were actually valued at. He ran his hand over the meticulously designed cover, and read the title, with a bit of effort.

"*De Ratione Magicae*," he mumbled. "A pra-practical guide on the nature and nuh-nurture of magic, magical beings, entities and other p-pen-pneo—"

"Phenomena," Selico said. "Fancy way of just saying 'stuff'," he added. The three of them chuckled as Roja opened the book. There was a hole in it. For a brief moment, Roja worried he'd ruined the book in the fall, but quickly realised it was a part of the design. In the middle of every page was a hole that ran through the entire book. In *that* was a little green gem. The text wrapped around it, and on several pages, small notes had been made around it, and diagrams used it as a centre.

"Woah," Maria said, "you reckon that's real?"

"Why wouldn't it be, right?" Roja said. "Why? You wanna wear it as a necklace?"

"Shut up," Maria said. *"You* wear it."

"You shut up," Roja grinned and flipped through the pages. There were drawings of foreign plants and whole talks about monsters and magic. He bit his lip in his excitement. It would take him *months* to make it through all of this, and he couldn't wait. Then he got to the centre page.

It was wrong. Specifically, the drawing on it was wrong. It was a drawing of a creature that haunted his nightmares. Everyone knew it by now, of course. The attack had shaken the Capital to its very core. The death toll had been... too high. But there it was. A figure, cloaked in shadow. Hollow, even on the page, a mask that resembled a grinning skull. His blood froze in his veins and he quickly turned the page, but it felt almost wrong to touch the paper now.

"Hold on," Maria said, her voice a little unsteady too. "What's this one?" She stopped on a page that had a drawing of the gem. "What does... Do... Do *shoitheach* mean?"

"Probably a dirty word," Roja joked. Maria elbowed him in the ribs. "Ow! I don't know!"

"I'll ask Adhamh next time he comes through," Selico said. "It sounds like something he'd know." Roja nodded, but Maria was already going down the page.

"It's like someone's diary or something," she said, and read out loud. "'I truly believe I've found what was supposed to be the vessel for a spirit, once upon a time. If it is, then this spirit is long gone.'"

"All right, all right," Roja mumbled. "You don't have to show off."

"You're just mad because you skipped reading classes," Selico said. Roja stuck out his tongue. Maria ignored them both and pushed on.

"'The magecraft who sold it to me,'" Maria continued, her voice a little droning, "'swears high and low by the incantation to release its energy, but it has so far proven to be inert. It is too simple to be true, regardless. *Sgaol mi*—'"

Maria hadn't finished speaking the syllable when Roja's sight blurred slightly, little stars sparkling at the edge of his vision while a headache burrowed his way behind his eyes. "Ow," he shouted, and then looked at the others, also rubbing their heads. They'd all cried out in pain at the same time.

"What was th—" Selico said just as the door was pushed open. Legima and two diacons stared down at them. They stared back up. Before anyone else had a chance to move, Selico's sling was already out, and a small pebble hit one of the diacons square on the nose. "Run!"

Maria and Roja dove between the men's legs, not thinking about the repercussions. Right now, they needed to get away, and hide this book, no matter how hard it was to focus with their headache.

Back through the peristyle, their only obstacle was a young-ish woman, probably another Godsmaid in training, although she wasn't wearing the traditional headdress. Not that she was a problem. Roja dove left as Maria jumped right, around the woman.

Well, they would have. Both of them found themselves lifted off the ground, one in each of the woman's hands as she held them by their tunics. That wasn't right. He was practically fifteen, there was no way a woman her size would've been able to pick him up like that.

"Hello?" the woman said. Just then Legima and the diacons came up behind them, and Roja closed his eyes. They were going to lose the book for sure.

"Your Majesty!" Legima said as the woman put Roja and Maria down, although she kept a firm grip on their collars. "I… I apologise profusely…"

Roja looked up at the woman in shock. "Your eyes," she said. "Yes, I see it too." Who was she talking to? She didn't seem regal at *all! This* was the Mad Queen Vera?

Ela Bambust

Five years after the events of Through Verdant Mirrors, Coalis, Vera and their kingdom have changed significantly. New faces – and some old ones – find themselves in new adventures in a world that is rapidly becoming more magical, whether they want to or not. When Queen Vera and her new wards travel north, to the nation of Raasland across the mountains, they will face challenges none of them are prepared for, both within and without. There might be romance. There will be dragons. Hold on to your britches, magic is about to become a lot wilder.

Keep an eye out for *On Verdant Wings* in the second half of 2023!